ARABIAN DECEPTION

A NOVEL

JAMES LAWRENCE

Arabian Deception is a work of fiction. Apart from the well-known actual people, events, and locales that figure in the narrative, all names, characters, places, and incidents are the products of the author's imagination or are used fictitiously. Any resemblance to current events, locales, or living persons is entirely coincidental.

ISBN-13:978-1720492504
ISBN-10:1720492506

Dedication

This book is dedicated to my wife and family.
Without their support and assistance,
it would not have been possible to complete this book.

About the Author

James Lawrence has been a soldier, small business owner, military advisor, and international arms dealer. He is the author of seven novels in the Pat Walsh series: *Arabian Deception, Arabian Vengeance, Arabian Fury, Arabian Collusion, Rising Sea, The Somali Affair* and *The Q Dilemma.*

Chapter 1

Washington, D.C.

A hard gust of cold wind stung my face and caused me to shudder. I must've been a sight as I walked across the Pentagon parking lot from my beat-up Ford Windstar in a half shuffle to keep from slipping on the ice. I made a mental note to buy a set of regulation gloves and an overcoat on payday.

It was ninety-two degrees when I left Baghdad last week, and it was going to take some time to adjust to winter in D.C. I was on day six of a one-year stint at the Pentagon. An assignment sold to me by the guy who cut my orders as a favor from a grateful nation. My transfer is a prepo assignment, I was being pre-positioned to attend the National War College at Fort McNair in D.C. the following year. The Army didn't want to put my family through the hassle of moving two years in a row. It was a thoughtful gesture and I appreciated it.

I managed to find my office without having to ask for directions. Navigating the labyrinth of the world's largest office building is no small feat. I share an office with two other lieutenant colonels and a major. Officially, we all have grand titles, but from what I've seen so far, we're all nothing more than slide monkeys for the Chief. The Chief being the Army Chief of Staff.

Our four desks are crammed together, bullpen style. Were it not for our computer monitors, we'd be forced to stare at one another all day. I was last to the office and could feel the attention from the other guys as I took off my uniform jacket and hung it on the stand behind my seat.

The Chief's inner circle is a group of hand-selected officers who he's worked with in his previous commands. The Chief's a tanker, an armor officer, which means those commands were all armor and cavalry units. As an infantry officer with a special operations background, I'm the man out, I've never met the Chief.

I slid into my workstation.

"What do you need me to do?" I asked Lieutenant Colonel Chris Mattingly, the senior member of our team.

"Review this presentation. You're going to brief it sometime today, whenever the boss gets in to see the SecDef," Chris said.

"I'm going to brief the Secretary?"

"Yeah, the Chief will back you up and I'll be there as the slide flipper. Is that a problem?"

"No, not really."

"You look nervous, what's the highest level you've ever briefed?" asked Chris.

"POTUS," I said.

"Which one?"

"All of them, since Clinton."

"Really?"

"We got a lot of supervision in my last unit," I said.

"This should be a walk in the park for you. Familiarize yourself with the slides and be ready to go when called," Chris said.

For the first time, I noticed the red eyes and wrinkled shirts on Chris and the rest of the team. "Have you guys been up all night putting this together?" I asked holding up the presentation in my hand.

"Yeah," Chris said.

"You should've told me. I would've stayed."

"It's okay, we needed you to be fresh this morning," said Chris.

During our first meeting, Chris had made it clear that my only role on the team was to be the talking head and I guess he really meant it. According to Chris, the reason I was diverted from the special ops cell in G3 to the Chief's inner sanctum was to be the designated briefer to the Secretary of Defense.

"SecDef is infatuated with special operations. He gets all weak kneed and wet when he hears about SEALS, Rangers and Green Berets. Your job around here is to be the SecDef whisperer. Use those idiot sticks on your collar to put some reference power behind the Chief's messaging," is how he explained my job. It wasn't the most inspirational first day on the job speech I'd ever heard.

I spent the next two hours rehearsing my lines, which were dictated below every slide in the notes section along with the occasional reminder not to ad lib.

"You're on. The Chief's waiting for us," said Chris.

I put my jacket back on and Chris grabbed a laptop and walked with me into the Army Chief of Staff's waiting room. Chris breezed by the secretary with a nod and led me into the office.

The general is a small but imposing figure. We'd never met, but I'd read a lot about him. He lost half of his foot in Vietnam and was widely regarded as a deep thinker and a futurist. We shook hands.

"Are you getting settled?" he asked.

"Yes, sir. The family is moved in."

"Where are you living?"

"Woodbridge."

"How's the commute?"

"It's a couple of hours depending on the traffic."

"D.C. traffic is enough to make someone miss Iraq."

"It's good to be back," I said.

"What are your thoughts on the briefing?"

"Makes sense to me," I said.

He smiled. "Let's get moving."

We filed out of the office by seniority, the Chief in the lead, Chris in the middle and me in the trail. We wound through a maze of hallways and then took a private corridor into the SecDef's office suite. The conference room furnishings consisted only of a single rectangular table with six seats around it. Chris connected the laptop to the AV system. Minutes later, the SecDef and two of his assistants came in. Chris and I popped to attention. The SecDef didn't greet either of us. He took a seat at the head of the table and acknowledged the Chief with a nod. Two assistants in civilian clothes sat on his right. Neither introduced themselves. The Chief and Chris sat on the opposite side of the table from the civilians. I stood at the end of the table in front of the screen and waited for my cue to start.

The SecDef stared at me for what felt like an eternity. It was an uncomfortable silence, and I looked to the Chief for a signal to start.

"Sir, today we'd like to brief you on some analysis we've done for your consideration regarding future troop levels in Iraq," the Chief interjected.

"Has Dick seen this?" asked the SecDef, referring to the Chairman of the Joint Chiefs of Staff.

"No, sir," replied the Chief.

The SecDef made a disapproving grimace and then went back to staring me down. He was an older gentleman, with silver-gray hair and steel-rimmed glasses. He and I were ten feet apart, and I could feel his eyes inspecting the details of my uniform.

"How long have you been in the service, Colonel?" he asked.

"Twenty years."

His eyes went from my uniform to those of Chris and the Chief.

"Why do these two officers have eight rows of ribbons and a pile of shiny badges, and you only have one row and two badges?"

"I like to keep the things to a minimum, sir."

"Why?"

"I don't wear participation awards. Too much fruit salad makes me feel like a South American dictator," I replied.

The SecDef chuckled. "Tell me about the ones that made the cut," he said pointing at my chest.

I pointed to the first ribbon with my left index finger. "I got an enemy marksmanship award in Mogadishu and again in Iraq," I said pointing to the purple heart with an oak leaf cluster on it. "This is a Bronze Star with V device and four oak leaf clusters, Silver Star with one oak leaf cluster and this is the Distinguished Service Cross," I said pointing to the last ribbon.

The SecDef went back to staring at me for another minute and then he took out a mechanical pencil from his shirt pocket and made some notes on the notepad in front of him. Finally, he looked up.

"Begin," he said.

"Sir, this briefing is classified top secret. The subject is the proposed force levels for Operation Enduring Freedom..." For the next forty-five minutes, I went through the slides and briefed the Army Chief of Staff's recommendation for increasing the force levels in Iraq. The SecDef and his staffers didn't ask any questions, but occasionally the Chief would cut in and provide additional information and insights. The logic behind his argument was straightforward. Basically, it was a historical comparison of US peacekeeping missions and the ratios between US troops and the occupied populations. The argument was that the people of Iraq were no less hostile than the people of Kosovo and that if they used the same ratios that were required to pacify the population of Kosovo, in Iraq, it would require a minimum of four hundred thousand additional troops.

"Sir, this completes the briefing, subject to your questions," I said as I reached for the bottle of water on the table in front of me.

The SecDef's face looked like he just bit into a lemon. "You do realize that this subject has already been reviewed and a decision has been made by the National Command Authority," the SecDef said to the Chief.

"Yes, sir, I do, However, I feel compelled to provide you this information. I don't think the historical context has ever been fully considered," replied the Chief.

The SecDef started tapping his heavy mechanical pencil against the table. Then he turned to me. As if noticing the name tag on my uniform for the first time, he said, "What about you, Walsh? What do you think?"

"Sir, I was in the invasion and I've done five short tours and a long one that just ended last week. At first, we were welcomed as liberators, but lately, the situation is much more hostile. The population's turning against us. I think we either have to go big or get out. We have enough boots on the ground to give our enemy enough targets to choose from, but we don't have the forces needed to suppress the threat sufficiently to prevent attacks," I said.

"Suppress the threat—what does that even mean?" The SecDef snarled.

"It means a show of force big enough to dissuade the enemy from attacking. Except for crazy suicidal people, who are rare, most people, when they know they're guaranteed to die if they rise up, as a general rule, they don't rise up. Showing overwhelming force reduces attacks. It has a suppressing effect," I said.

"What did you do in Iraq?" asked the SecDef.

"I commanded a JSOTF responsible for the prosecution of high-value targets," I said.

"And how's that going?"

"We've taken out almost the entire deck of cards from Saddam Hussein, the Ace of Spades, all the way down to the Two of Clubs, and yet the security situation is deteriorating."

The SecDef returned his attention to the Chief. He started out politely in a Yankee patrician dialect, the kind of diction I imagine you pick up at one of those elite boarding schools in New England. In a scholarly and at times slightly condescending tone, he rebutted point by point every argument made in the briefing. He took special pains to ridicule my comment on "suppressing the threat" by explaining that you didn't need a massive amount of people in the modern era to accomplish that task. He explained that all you needed was the effective employment of technology and Special Forces.

A couple of times the Chief tried to respond, but the SecDef cut him off each time with a hand gesture. I started to tune out when I realized that it wasn't a conversation, it was a reprimand. At the end, the SecDef launched into a tangent on "known knowns," "known unknowns," and "unknown unknowns," followed by an explanation of military tactics that was completely foreign to anything I'd ever been taught, so I just stood at a rigid position of parade rest and watched as the SecDef became more and more abusive to my new boss. After a twenty-minute berating, the SecDef and his two minions abruptly got up and left, leaving the three of us dumbfounded at the table.

The Chief's face was ashen. He's Asian American, and the difference from his normal coloring was stark. Chris loudly packed up his laptop, his jaws clenched and his eyes bulging with fury.

"You know the only military experience that guy has is two years as a pilot in the Navy in the 1950s," said Chris.

"I don't want to hear any of that. We need to get back. I have other things on my schedule," the Chief replied.

Chapter 2

Washington, D.C.

The routine over the next two months was pretty much the same. The pace of the "Slide Monkeys" as I'd begun to refer to my cell mates stayed at a high tempo. We did briefings for the Chairman of the Joint Chiefs and the SecDef and various congressional oversight committees. I only did the talking when the audience was the SecDef. The topics were budget requests and modernization programs, and all were well received.

It wasn't the best assignment in the world, but it wasn't that bad either. I was marking time until the War College and at least I was home at night and weekends. The deployments had taken a toll on my family and for the first time in a long while my wife seemed happy and kids were doing great.

I came into work one Monday and was ushered into the Chief's office along with the rest of the team. The boss had to testify in front of the Senate Armed Services Committee that Thursday and we had the week to prepare the backup material. Our task was to build briefing packages and responses for any question he could possibly get asked. Most of the answers came out of the files. As the head of the team, Chris's job was to work with the military congressional liaison and get as much advance notice as possible on what the senators were going to ask.

It was an intensely busy week. The day of the hearing, I was surprised to learn that I was the only member of the team accompanying the Chief to the Capitol Building. We started out together in the Chief's black Suburban. I was in the back with the boss. His aide de camp, a lieutenant colonel, rode up front in the passenger seat.

"Do you have everything?" he asked me.

"Yes, sir," I replied.

"What about the briefing on OEF force levels I gave to the SecDef?"

"I don't have that. It wasn't identified as needed," I said.

"Go back and get it. Take another car, and I'll meet you on the Hill."

I went back into the building and printed out hardcopies of the brief and collected a USB with the file on it. It had originally been a top-secret briefing, but I noticed it'd been recently declassified.

Three months on the job and I'd only been to the Capitol a few times, it took me a while to find the right room. When I arrived at the hearing room, the Chief was already seated at a table, facing the assembly of senators who were still filing in. I dropped the material off on the table in front of him and took a seat behind him.

The first three hours of the hearing went as expected. The issues were training, readiness, budgets and modernization programs. The Chief had a good relationship with the elected officials of both parties. It was a forgettable afternoon until the end, when a senator from Georgia yielded his time to the ranking minority member of the Committee, the senior senator from Arizona.

The senator didn't look up from the paper as he read his question from a prepared text in a monotone.

"The ambush of American forces last week in Sadr City resulted in seventeen wounded and five killed. General, do we have adequate forces on the ground in Iraq to accomplish our mission?"

I watched the Chief give the USB to a congressional aide. Once the presentation was on the big-screen televisions behind him, he launched into the same briefing we'd given to the SecDef three months earlier. The same briefing the SecDef had rejected while making it clear that the subject was closed. I was watching the Chief commit insubordination, not to mention career suicide and here I was right along with him for the ride.

When I came to work the next morning, the first thing I did after I turned on my computer was to open up the day's version of the *Early Bird*. In the early internet days, the *Early Bird* was a collection of military-related newspaper articles that were assembled every morning by the Army Public Relations Staff and then disseminated electronically to senior Army leaders around the world. The first article on the list was from the *New York Times*. It was titled: *Pentagon Contradicts General on Iraq Occupation Force Size.*

I read the article twice looking for a ray of sunshine, but from every angle, it was a disaster. The Chief told the SASC that the SecDef and the POTUS were making a mistake. The *NYT* even got a comment from the office of the SecDef, stating that the Chief was wrong. The President and most of Congress was backing the SecDef while only a few other members of the Senate and House Armed Services Committees were backing the Chief. The Chief was outgunned and outnumbered.

The SecDef had to know that the hearing yesterday was a setup. The senator from Arizona and the Chief had clearly conspired to introduce the topic. I'd been duped into getting caught up in the middle of a battle between two giants, the SecDef and the Chief. There was no way it was going to end well. I could feel the blood rushing to my face as I read the damage report. I looked over my monitor and across the desks to Chris, who was drinking coffee from a mug and staring at his computer.

"Did you know anything about the Chief's plan yesterday to conduct gross insubordination in front of Congress, the press and the American C-SPAN watching population?" I said in a loud voice.

He put his coffee down, pushed his seat back and to the side, so he could look at me without obstruction. I could see the veins in his neck pulse. "I don't like your tone. You better check it before I check it for you."

"Would you two give us a moment?" I said to the other guys in the room. I waited until they left.

"For what it's worth, the Chief is probably right. But this is the Army, and in the Army, we follow orders. You've involved me in a palace coup and didn't even have the decency to let me know you were doing it," I said.

"Someone had to go with the General and since you didn't know about it, you at least have deniability. Don't take it personally, you're just the grunt we brought in to be a talking head. Everybody knows that and nobody is going to hold you accountable for what the Chief said and did," Chris said.

"Who do you think you are? That's not your call to make," I said.

"Listen, Pat, you're way out of your depth on this. Just keep your head down and it'll blow over."

Chris was right about that much. I was out of my depth when it came to Machiavellian treachery. I could see on Chris's face an animosity that I hadn't noticed before. I don't know what he had against me, but it was clear he had it out for me. He set me up and now he seemed upset I'd dared to question him about it.

Chris and I wore the same uniform, but we were from different worlds. I didn't grow up in the suburbs and I didn't go to West Point like the Chief and the rest of the guys in the office. Unlike officers like Chris, when I started out, I never had any ambitions of making the military a career. My expectations were pretty low and I'd exceeded them many years earlier. I grew up in a housing project in Southie and went to a commuter college in Boston. I accidentally discovered the special operations route because I had skills and I kept getting asked to try out for different organizations. I was always willing to endure the selection processes, because I liked the challenge and I enjoyed the camaraderie of the other likeminded individuals in the units.

"Do you really think you could stab me in the back and that I'd just accept it?" I said.

Chris's fat face flushed red with anger. He sprung up out of his chair and stepped around his desk to get closer to me. At six-one, two hundred and thirty pounds, the former college offensive lineman must've thought of himself as an intimidating figure.

I was still seated, with his pointed right index finger wagging inches from my face. "Somebody had to go with the Chief, and you were the best choice. Like you said, we take orders in the Army, and yeah, I do expect you to keep your mouth shut about it," Chris yelled down at me.

I slapped his hand away from my face with my right hand. As I was discovering, Chris was a hot head. His response to my slap was a full escalation. He led with a roundhouse left that I blocked with my right elbow. Still seated, I used the momentum of his punch to spin him away and give me time to stand.

He charged forward and when he got in close enough, he threw a right haymaker that had everything he had behind it. The punch never reached me. I snapped a lightning fast left jab that stood him up straight and exploded his nose like a tomato hitting the sidewalk. Against someone with skills, I would've ended the fight as quickly as possible, but Chris wasn't a fighter and I wanted him to understand that. Dazed from the punch, he threw a half speed right hook that I slipped under as I rolled my hips into him. In a split second, my left hand held his right arm and my right hand was on his belt buckle. I lifted him up over my head and military pressed him straight up until his butt was touching the ceiling tiles. I paused for a moment to give him time to realize just how badly overmatched he truly was. Then I pile drove him face first into the floor. He regained consciousness with my right foot pressing down on his throat.

"Now it's my turn to talk. I don't know who you think you are but let me explain to you what you are not. A fighter, seriously, don't ever pick a fight against another adult, I'm embarrassed for you right now. Another thing you're not is the person with the right to make decisions that jeopardize my career and my ability to support my family. You'd better hope you're right and that I have nothing to worry about, because if you're not, the next time I see you, I won't be so gentle and kind. Once you clean yourself up, the first thing you're going to do is get me transferred out of this office, you don't want to ever see me again."

I took my foot off Chris's throat, grabbed my jacket and stormed out of the office. The two other guys in the hallway glared at me as I left but didn't say a word. I walked past them and went home.

That afternoon, there was a press release identifying the next Army Chief of Staff. The SecDef didn't have the authority to fire the Chief, so he did the next best thing which was to make him a lame duck. The Chief's replacement was named before he'd even finished half of his four-year term, which was a first, and a supreme insult.

I was transferred that same afternoon. Working in the operations center was infinitely more interesting than being a slide monkey. After two months, my anxiety over any repercussions from my time in the Chief's office had receded. I thought I was in the clear until out of the blue, one night after work, I opened a letter that came in the mail from the Army Human Resources Command. It was an official letter like the ones I was accustomed to getting. They usually were sent to provide a heads-up for promotion boards, or they were official notifications on selections and assignments. This message began with, "I regret to inform you."

My class slot for the National War College had been cancelled, no reason given. The next morning, I called my branch manager, an officer I'd served with previously. He wasn't a close friend, but we knew each other.

"Pete, what's going on? Why are my orders revoked?" I asked.

"The order came from the top," Pete said.

My hands were shaking with fury. "From who?"

"Department of Defense."

"Is there an appeals process, or do I have to recompete on another board?" I asked.

"There's no appeal and there's no other board," Pete said.

"What does this mean?"

"It means you've gone as far as you can go."

It took a few seconds for me to process that information.

"If I'm capped at colonel, that's fine with me. Just send me back to the unit. The Army of the Potomac is a toxic place. I don't belong here."

"Without the War College, you can't go anywhere, Pat. You've already punched every ticket there is for an O-5. You need the War College so you can take an O-6 command. Without it, you're stuck where you are."

"Seriously, that's it? I have to stay where I'm at for the next ten years?"

"No, you can move to another duty station in another two to three years, but what I'm trying to say is they won't be Pat Walsh jobs. Without the War College, you're off the command track. You'll still get promoted to Colonel, but no more operational assignments, just staff work with the major commands."

"Come on, Pete. Are you seriously trying to tell me you don't have a single black book or shotgun assignment that you're trying to fill?"

Pete paused for a few seconds. I could sense he wanted to tell me more but couldn't. Finally, he said, "I told you everything I can. I'm sorry, Pat. You don't deserve this."

I hung up the phone in stunned silence. There was no way I could ride a desk and stare at a computer monitor for the next ten years. I considered calling a few of the general officers I'd worked for over the years, who I knew would go to bat for me. In the end, though, I decided it would be futile. No one in uniform had the power to take on the SecDef, and only a fool would try. It took a day of brooding silence before I accepted my fate.

When I told my wife that I was dropping my retirement papers, she was thrilled. It was the happiest I'd seen her in a decade. Our oldest was about to enter high school, and it was a perfect time to put down some roots and offer the kids some stability. I'd been running so hard on the Army treadmill that I'd badly neglected my family. As I processed the reality of retiring, I began to see the end of my military career as an opportunity to be a better father and husband. My new focus became figuring out what I was going to do next for work.

When word of my retirement got out, I received a lot of calls from people who'd already left the Special Operations community and gone into the contracting business. The wars in Afghanistan and Iraq were making a lot of guys rich. Some of the job offers I received paid two and three times what I was currently making, but my wife and I agreed that my days of deploying were over.

I was attending a mandatory transition class at Fort Belvoir when I was introduced to a vice president at Toll Brothers. The VP asked for my résumé, and a few days later I went to Raleigh and interviewed for a job as a project manager in residential construction.

I left D.C. early in the morning and drove four hours to interview at 9 a.m. John Kleinschmidt met me in his office. He was wearing blue jeans, a polo shirt and work boots. When the interview was over, he took me to a huge subdivision they were developing, and we walked through one of the construction sites. Next, we stopped for a late lunch at a Jason's Deli in a nearby strip mall.

"If you want the job, it's yours," John said to me.

"I'll go home and talk it over with my wife. When do you need an answer?"

"We'll get you a written offer by the end of this week, and we'll need an answer by Monday. Do you have any concerns?" he asked.

"How do you see my future?" I asked.

"The market is the best it's ever been. We completed three hundred and forty homes last year, and we expect to complete five hundred and thirty this year. We have plans for two more major subdivisions that will provide year-over-year growth of more than thirty percent for the next five years. You'll start as a project manager with an assistant PM who knows what he's doing, but once you understand how to build, we'll move you into an area manager slot and eventually, if you do well, into a district manager role. Once you make area manager, the money gets very good."

The drive home was a long one. I was happy for it, because it gave me time to think and I had a lot to think about. It was 2005 and the housing boom was in full force. I really liked John Kleinschmidt and Toll Brothers. The money sounded okay, but what I really liked was working outside and building something. What I didn't like was joining another big organization. The more I thought about it, the more it made sense to just build houses on my own instead of for someone else.

Kleinschmidt seemed like a great guy, but after my experience in the Pentagon, I had enough of big organizations and office politics. By the time I pulled into the driveway of my split-level in Woodbridge, Virginia, I'd concocted a plan to borrow against everything I owned and go into the home-building business in Raleigh, North Carolina. It was exciting stuff. No more politics, no more polyester green suits, no more two-hour commutes. I was going to drive a pickup truck, wear jeans, listen to country music, work outside and report to nobody but myself.

Chapter 3

Cary, North Carolina

I pulled up to the double-wide trailer that served as the Trident office. It was seven in the morning, and there were already two cars in the lot. A red Infinity Q36 belonging to Jessica, my office manager, and a black Ford F-150 owned by Stan Winthrop, our site manager. Stan had joined Trident after I'd finished my second house. It was a memorable event, because it was the first house I ever made a profit on.

The first had been a disaster. Even though I stayed up nights memorizing the building codes, it seemed at every inspection along the way, I had to pay someone to fix something. The competition back then for subcontractors was fierce and I was the new guy that none of the accomplished subs wanted to work with. The lessons were costly, but I never made the same mistake twice.

Stan came to Trident after his wife wiped him out in a divorce. He's an authentic North Carolina country boy, and he'd forgotten more about building than I would ever know. Stan's a wiry middle-aged guy with long blond hair and a thick beard. He usually has a cheek bulging with Redman when he makes his rounds to inspect the work done by the subcontractors. He and I became fast friends, and the company has really taken off. In only a few years, we'd reached the point where Trident was developing its own thirty-unit subdivision.

Jessica joined soon after Stan. She manages the finances and the logistics of the company. Jessica is a young Korean American girl and a recent graduate of UNC-Chapel Hill. Her dad is a retired special operator who'd been my SOT instructor at Fort Bragg many years earlier. An original Song Tay Raider and Desert One veteran, her dad was not known for his social skills. When he called out of the blue one day and told me his baby was looking for a job, I hired her sight unseen. Her dad was a legend.

The three of us are an unlikely team, but we work well together. The subdivision was ahead of schedule. The roads were finished, the power and the sewerage lines were done, and we already had six homes under contract and under construction.

"Pat, I was just telling Jessica here I need an assistant," Stan said.

"He's just being lazy. Your boys spoiled him over the summer. Now he can't do anything for himself," Jessica replied.

My two oldest sons had both gone back to college the previous week. They'd worked the site during their summer vacation. It was the first week in September 2008 and the schools were back in session.

"What's the problem, Stan?" I asked.

"It's no problem, it's just that we have six homes being framed and three more ready to start, and I need to go through the punch list on two this afternoon. Problem is, there's only one of me, and you're too busy selling to spend any time building. I need some backup."

"He's got a point, Jessica," I said.

"I don't know if you two read the papers, but the economy is changing. Lots of stories about subprime mortgages. This is not the best time to be hiring," Jessica said.

Stan looked over at me. "Are you having trouble selling homes?"

"No, I have four already under contract. This location and our luxury niche are in big demand. I have two real estate agencies telling me I need to hurry and finish the whole subdivision because they're positive they can sell it out this year," I replied.

"So, what do you want me to do?" asked Jessica.

"Hire Stan a sidekick," I said.

The three of us then sat down and went through the daily task list. It was a morning ritual we completed each day before the crews arrived. After going over the work schedule, I went into my office and did some email and paperwork before heading out onto the worksite.

The days were predictable and enjoyable. Most day's I'd go home for lunch. The subdivision was only ten minutes from my house. The quality of living was the best I'd ever had.

A week later, I was picking up my two remaining stay-at-homes from the local Catholic high school in Raleigh when I got a panicked call from Jessica.

"What's wrong?" I said.

"The bank just called our loan," Jessica said in a breathless voice.

"What does that mean?"

"They cut off your credit line, and now they're demanding immediate repayment," she said in an exasperated voice.

"That has to be a mistake. Everything is current, I'm sure of it. I'll drop the kids off and then swing by the bank."

"Are you watching the news?"

"No, I'm driving. What's going on?"

"Lehman Brothers just went bankrupt. Something big is happening. People are panicking."

Hal Frazier, the loan manager at the Wachovia, wasn't available when I stopped in to see him that afternoon. I went back to the office and followed the news more closely. There was a financial crisis. The banks had been bundling subprime mortgages with AAA-rated mortgages and grading the bundles as AAA. Then they'd made derivative products out of those toxic bundles until they had a ton of mortgage products that were many multiples of the real number of outstanding mortgages. The credit rating agencies, like Moody's, Standard & Poor's, and Finch, all gave these bundles of mortgage products AAA ratings, even though they were mostly filled with subprime junk. This had gone on for years, until one day it all just blew up.

When I finally got in to see Hal the next day he wasn't his normal exuberant self.

"Tell me this is a mistake?" I asked.

"It's not."

"I'm current, I have a perfect credit rating and there's no provision for you to call the loan," I said.

"The terms of the loan allow us to call the loan under certain circumstances, such as when the repayment is in jeopardy or if the loan-to-asset ratio exceeds the call level. Pat, the repayment is in jeopardy, and with the market in free fall, the value of your property has been cut in half, which means the loan-to-asset ratios meet the call level."

"The only reason the repayment is in jeopardy is because you swept the two point one million in cash I had in my checking account and applied it to the balance of the loan."

"That still leaves an outstanding balance of over four million. We had to get the loan-to-asset ratio down as far and as fast as possible."

"You froze my credit line and confiscated my cash. How am I going to complete the houses I have under contract and pay you back?"

"I can't answer that. But you should know those sales contracts you have are conditional on the buyers finding mortgages, which I doubt will happen, so don't plan on getting paid even if you do finish those houses. All I can tell you is that no more credit can be extended to you or to any other builder."

"Why me? I don't sell homes to people with subprime mortgages. I don't have anything to do with the idiotic situation the bankers in New York City have gotten themselves into. I'm not asking for a bailout like every billionaire banker is doing right now, including your bank. I just want to keep my cash and be given the time to repay my loan according to the original terms. That two million is more than eighteen months of payments, for crying out loud. This whole problem will blow over in eighteen months. Give me my money back," I said.

"Sorry, Pat, I can't help you. It's not in my hands."

"I'm not asking you to help me. I'm asking you to stop screwing me," I said.

Hal just looked at me like a deer in the headlights. It was obvious that he couldn't fix the problem even if he wanted to. I walked out without saying another word.

The good news was that they didn't confiscate all my cash. I had some money stashed away in a personal account at another bank, and I had a solid stream of rental income from the apartments and properties that were already paid off.

The only problem was that my rental income was barely enough to cover the loan payment, and the remaining cash wasn't enough to cover the overhead, especially salaries.

I spent the next two months trying to keep things going while hoping for a turn around. I had to hire a lawyer to fight the bank, because even though I was still making monthly payments of fifty-seven thousand dollars, because the loan was called and I couldn't pay it off fully, I was getting zinged with a penalty each month of forty-two thousand. Stan chipped away at finishing the houses on the subdivision. Progress was difficult to make without the cash to buy materials and hire subcontractors. In December, I went to my CPA, who told me my tax bill for the year was going to be over ninety thousand. Taxes were never something that I'd factored into the equation on how long I could keep things afloat. Everything I'd built was crashing in all around me.

My lawyer, Jack Sullivan, fast-tracked our case against the bank into binding arbitration. Jack invited me to the reading of the decision made by a retired judge who was serving as the arbitrator. We met at a law office on Fayetteville Street, next to the county courthouse in downtown Raleigh. The two opposing counsels had tables facing the judge. I sat next to Jack who looked calm and confident. I'd pestered Jack the previous night with a dozen phone calls, going over every possible outcome. We had nothing left to say to each other. When I sat down, he just put his hand on my shoulder and said, "Let right prevail." It was February and even though the room was cool, the shirt under my suit was soaked.

I'd been up all night going over different courses of action based on different outcomes from the judge. If he reversed the bank's actions, returning my two million and removing the penalties from the default, I was golden, but if he held that the bank's action was permissible, I was heading into bankruptcy, and the bank was going to foreclose on every asset I had including my home.

Following the edict, I went straight home to speak with my wife. The kids were at school and I thought it would be the best time to talk. As I pulled up into the driveway all I could think about was what a great life we'd built together. I was dreading the discussion. The ride from the lawyer's office in Raleigh was twenty-five minutes and I used the time to make two phone calls: the first to my wife, to explain the arbitrators' decision; the second to my old Ranger Regiment commander to accept a job in Afghanistan.

"We have no other options. I have to take myself off the payroll and contract out to support the family," I said to a very angry woman with her arms folded across her chest seated across from me at the kitchen table.

"You need to stay right here and be a father and a husband," my wife said.

"If I stay, there will be no here. The bank is going to repossess this place. There's not enough cash coming in to cover the loan on the sub-division and our living expenses," I explained.

"You can lay off Stan and Jessica."

"We spend more than what the two of them make combined. Laying them off won't solve the problem," I said.

"We can tighten our belts."

"Two college tuitions at a hundred and twenty-five thousand dollars; high school is another twenty-four thousand. Do you want to pull the kids out of school?"

The tears began to flow. "You could figure this out if you tried. I'm not going back to that life. You miss it. I know you do," she said.

"That's not true," I said.

She stood up. "If you go to Afghanistan, don't come back!" she screamed before turning and marching out of the room.

I didn't expect her to take the news well, but I'd never expected this. I left the house, got in my pickup and went to the office. When I arrived, both Stan and Jessica were hovering around the common area outside my office. I was looking for an escape and in no mood to talk to anyone. Even so, I decided to put both of them out of their misery.

"I can tell by your face it didn't go well. Just tell me what you have in mind for a severance package," Stan said.

"There's no need for a severance package. Neither of you are going anywhere. We're going to have to take some drastic actions to keep this thing afloat," I said as both moved in closer. "We won half of our case. The loan is still active. It's not called, and it's not in default. The back penalties have all been removed. The two million is gone. It will remain against the balance."

Jessica was doing the math in her head. I could see on her face as she realized that, with nothing coming in from home sales, there was only enough revenue to cover the loan and her and Stan's salary.

"What are you planning to do, Pat?" she asked.

"I'm going to take myself off the payroll for a while. I'm going to work a job in Afghanistan. While I'm gone, I need you guys to keep the rental income going, and I need you to make as much headway as you can on this development with whatever free cash we scrape up," I said.

"When do you leave?" asked Stan.

"Next week, unless my wife kills me first," I said.

"Is she taking it bad?" asked Jessica.

"Yeah, you could say that."

I could see tears forming in Jessica's eyes. Stan was quiet, which was even more rare. I left our little meeting and went to my office to sulk. I looked out the window from my desk. It was an overcast gray winter day, which fit my mood perfectly. I wondered if I'd made the right decision.

Jessica's husband had been out of work for months. He was a car salesman, and the recession had devastated the industry. Her job was the only thing keeping them from being thrown out onto the street. Ever since his divorce, Stan lived paycheck to paycheck, and if he lost this job, his next stop was a homeless shelter, because there was nobody hiring in the building industry, which was all he knew.

I needed both of them to work the daily tasks with the rental properties to keep the bank at bay. My kids' future depended on their continuing in the same schools they were already attending, college and otherwise. Going to Afghanistan and working a contract was my only option. Why couldn't my wife understand that?

I knew she couldn't understand. We had too much bad history. My time in the military was hard on my wife. Now that I was going back, it was too much for her to handle. The ultra-secretive nature of the Tier-1 Special Mission Units is tough on the family. Except for scheduled deployments to Iraq and Afghanistan, most of the time when I deployed, I wasn't able to tell anyone where I was going and when I'd be back. Sometimes, when things went bad, she'd find out from watching the news. During the debacle in Mogadishu, she didn't know I was there until a notification team came to the house to tell her I was in a hospital in Germany, critically wounded. Even though I was taking a noncombatant job in Afghanistan, my return to the military was reopening some old psychological wounds.

Chapter 4

Afghanistan

My first visit to Afghanistan was via parachute. It was a HAHO jump into Kandahar Province days prior to the 2001 invasion. The five times after that were in a C-17 that landed at Bagram Airbase. This time, I was arriving on a Sophia Airlines commercial flight from Dubai. The no-frills 737 was full. The passengers were a mix of defense contractors and Afghans. The contractors were easy to pick out because they were all Europeans and Americans sporting the latest in tactical fashion. During my absence from the Army, military tactical gear had somehow become stylish. It even had logos. The Afghans were all testing the limits of carry-on with items they'd purchased in Dubai, and were in local dress, which consisted of dirty-looking loose-fitting cotton pants and matching shirts that went down to knee level. Since it was winter, most also wore heavy vests and turbans.

The plane flew over Kabul International Airport and then cork-screwed rapidly down to the runway to avoid ground fire from outside the airport fence. The tight turn strained the old aircraft, but it held to-gether as we bounced onto the runway and came to a jarring stop. Burned-out skeletons of helicopters and airplanes littered the grounds surrounding the tarmac as we taxied to a small dilapidated terminal.

I spent a week in Camp Eggers, located next to the ISAF headquar-ters in the protected zone that includes the US embassy, the UN Headquarters and the other major Western institutions. After my orien-tation was complete, I went out to my assignment in Camp Blackhorse in Pol-e-Charki, which was on the eastern border of Kabul Province, adjacent to the province of Laghman on the Kabul River and Jalalabad Road. I was given my own B-hut to sleep in, which was a room that was about eight by eight feet in a mobile building. The shower was in a small trailer, a short walk across the gravel-covered compound.

Camp Blackhorse is a tiny US camp next to a large Afghan National Army camp that houses an ANA Corps headquarters, a commando battalion and a basic training element. Blackhorse is home to two Special Forces A-Teams and a Marine Regional Combat Assistance Team (RCAT). My new job was to support the RCAT. I was going to train and advise the 201st ANA on operations and intelligence. The RCAT commander, a Marine colonel, had the same role, but he was also in charge of over a hundred Marines embedded within the 201st ANA battalions who were scattered all across Eastern Afghanistan. The 201st was responsible for eleven of Afghanistan's thirty-four provinces. Everything east of Kabul to the Pakistan border belonged to the 201st, which meant the RCAT Commander had small teams of his guys in some of the most dangerous places on the planet. Because of his other responsibilities, giving unheeded advice to Afghan generals fell far down on the colonel's priority list, which pretty much left the daily training and advising to me.

It only took a couple of months to get into the swing of things. My three charges were the Corps commander, Lieutenant General Wardak, his operations officer, Brigadier General Aqa, and his intelligence office, Colonel Khan. I was supposed to help them with planning future operations and the command and control of current combat operations. I also helped the ANA coordinate with the NATO forces in the 201st area of operation. The US had two Army Brigades under the leadership of the Eighty-Second Airborne commander operating in the same eleven provinces. There was also a brigade of the French Foreign Legion and a handful of smaller NATO contingents.

It wasn't a very difficult job, because when it came to combat operations, the ANA avoided them at all costs. The commander and staff listened to me just fine during planning. But, when it came time to actually execute those combat plans, something always seemed to come up. It was uncanny. General Wardak was a regular Patton during the planning stage, but every time he was ready to kick off another bold offensive to drive back the evil Taliban, those generals in the Ministry of Defense denied the mission.

General Wardak then made a big show of expressing his frustration at those timid souls back in MOD and then disappeared for a day or two.

After another rigorous day with the Afghans, I passed through security and entered tiny Camp Blackhorse. I had a set routine every day. First the gym, then a couple hours of Trident paperwork sent to me by Jessica via email, and then the highlight of the day, the dining facility. The gym was fantastic. It was always crowded late in the day, because many of the Marines and Green Berets had the same routine as I did when they weren't out on mission. The equipment was top-of-the-line. When you're fighting trillion-dollar wars, you didn't skimp on treadmills and ellipticals. My workout, according to the thirty-something Special Forces ODA "operators," was outdated. Those guys were all doing ropes, kettlebells and weird CrossFit routines. I was happy for them, because it left the free weights available for me and my fellow luddites, the Marines.

One day I left the shower trailer wrapped in a towel and walked across the gravel compound in my flip-flops to my room in the B-hut. I checked my cell phone and saw that I had a message. I don't get many phone calls. Once I leave for the day, the Afghans usually forget about me, and when the guys in the RCAT want to talk, they just come to my room. The camp is that small. It was a cheap Nokia phone with only a few contacts in it, and the call wasn't from one of them. I didn't recognize the number, so I ignored it. I sat at my small desk and went through the electronic documents sent by Jessica. Approving small invoices for apartment maintenance and the like. When I got done, curiosity got the better of me, and I decided to find out who it was.

"Hello, this is Pat returning your call."

"This is Mike Guthrie. How've you been keeping?" It took me a few seconds to process the information and remember the person on the other end of the line.

"Good, how about you? It's been a long time," I said.

"I'm on my way to Camp Blackhorse. Can you meet me at around six?"

"Sure, let's meet at the DFAC."

"Okay, I'll see you at six."

I hadn't spoken to Mike Guthrie in eighteen years. He was the last person I'd ever expected a call from. The only reason I even checked my messages was in the hope that one day, my wife would call me back.

The last time I'd seen Mike was at tryouts in West Virginia in 1991. Up until then, Mike and I had parallel careers. We met while serving as platoon leaders in the Second Ranger Battalion at Fort Lewis, Washington. We both did a stint in an operation called Blue-Light, which at the time was a classified JSOC mission in Honduras. We'd worked out of the same compound and ran small-unit combat patrols, mostly ambushes and recons against the Sandinistas along the Hondo border who were coming in from Nicaragua. It was the Cold War, and it had made sense at the time. We both returned to the battalion just in time for Just Cause, and jumped into Rio Hato during the seizure of the Commendacia. Then we attended the Infantry Officers Advanced Course at Fort Benning together.

After that we went our separate ways; Mike was assigned to the Second Armored Division at Fort Hood, Texas, and I went to the First Armored Division in Germany. We both commanded mechanized infantry companies during Desert Storm. The next time I saw Mike was at Delta Selection. Our class consisted of fifteen officers and one hundred enlisted. It's not a very social experience, so we never really had a chance to catch up. A lot of the attrition was through injuries, which was the reason I heard Mike washed out. I was the lucky officer who made the cut, along with three enlisted guys. After selection, I lost track of Mike.

The DFAC is the social hub of Camp Blackhorse. When the ODA teams and RCAT staff aren't outside the wire on missions, it can get crowded. Like the gym, everything is top-notch. The food is better than anything I've ever had anywhere else in the military. It was Air Force quality.

I recognized Mike immediately when he walked into the cafeteria seating area. He was a little heavier, with some graying. He walked with a slight limp, but otherwise, he was still the same. I stood and walked over to meet him. We shook hands and went through the serving line together.

"You picked a good night to come. It's surf and turf Thursday," I said.

"People talk about the Camp Blackhorse DFAC countrywide. I feel lucky to have gotten a reservation," replied Mike.

After we finished eating and after the crowd cleared, Mike got down to business.

"I'll bet you want to know why and maybe even how I looked you up," he said.

"Yes, that would be a good start," I said.

Mike leaned forward. "I'm with the Agency. I work out of the embassy. Every advisor gets vetted before being hired, and I get a courtesy copy of the slate. When I saw your name on the list, I talked to a guy at ISAF. He talked to someone at your company and had you placed as the advisor to the 201st Corps Commander."

"Why did you do that?" I asked.

"General Wardak is a problem. I don't know if he's corrupt, or if he's Taliban, or if he's both. I need a guy on the inside who can keep an eye on him. I think his actions are killing American soldiers, but until I can prove it, I can't do anything about it," Mike said.

"What is it exactly you want me to do?" I asked.

"I want you to spy on Wardak and his operation and report to me regularly on what you find."

"I don't have any training or experience in espionage. When I was active-duty, I was a door kicker. You know that."

"And a good one from what I remember. But not much of a politico is what I've heard."

"You heard correct. My business skills are also a bit suspect at the moment, which is why I'm here. I can't really afford to lose this job if I get caught playing super spy. There's a whole bunch of people back in the States counting on my monthly paycheck."

"The only thing I can tell you is that Wardak is a bad actor, and if my suspicions are correct, he's getting American servicemen killed."

I thought about what he'd said for a few seconds. "If I'm going to be a CIA asset, the only person I am going to report to is you. I don't want anyone from my company knowing, and even within your organization, the fewer people who know, the better. I don't want to be reading about myself on WikiLeaks."

"WikiLeaks, really?"

"Hey, I just read a story in the paper about some gender-confused private first class who spilled the names of a whole bunch of agents and assets working for you guys."

"Done," Mike said reaching over the table to shake my hand.

Chapter 5

Pol-e-Charki, Afghanistan

When I entered the 201st the next morning as a newly minted CIA asset, the experience was no different than in the past. Each morning began with a battle update brief. When he attended, I always stood next to Colonel Chu, the RCAT commander. We both stood off to the side in the bullpen area with a small receiver in our ear to hear the translation. Colonel Khan, the intelligence officer, began with a quick summary of enemy activity. He was followed by Brigadier Aqa, who provided an update on the dispositions of the various units and a brief summary of where and what had been attacked over the previous twenty-four hours. He was followed by the logistics officer. It was the same routine every day. The Corps Commander concluded the meeting as he always did, by praising the brilliant performance of his Corps and complaining about the support from the Americans. This morning's grievance was because he had not been notified of an American SOF mission conducted within his area of operations the previous night.

After the briefing, Colonel Chu and I went to Lieutenant General Wardak's office on the second floor. The camp had been built by the Russians in the 1970s, and the building reflected the Soviet utilitarian style of the time. Wardak's office was huge. The walls were covered with white fabric, the huge windows were adorned with heavy red velvet curtains, and enormous bouquets of roses covered every flat surface. His desk was an enormous slab of heavily varnished mahogany. Colonel Chu was a no-nonsense Marine officer. He was an infantry officer with Force Recon experience who wore diving and parachute badges on his camouflage uniform along with the eagle that represented his rank as a colonel. We got along very well.

We both sat across from Wardak's desk with Chu's TERP (translator/interpreter) seated behind us. Colonel Chu's deputy, Lieutenant Colonel Collins, Brigadier Aqa, the G3, and the deputy G3, Colonel Fareed, sat in chairs against the wall off to the side.

Neither Wardak nor Chu had much use for the other. Both tended to be antagonistic in their conversations. Chu made me look like a regular diplomat. They went through the perfunctory tea ritual with the obligatory small talk.

"Was there a reason you asked to meet this morning?" Chu asked.

"Americans attacked my people last night in Logar. One of my captains was killed, two others were wounded. What do you have to say about this?"

"Your captain fired at an American SOF unit that was conducting a mission to capture a high-value asset. He was killed when they returned fire," replied Chu.

"The report I received was that the Americans confused the target and attacked my forces. There was no provocation."

"Bud, bring me the laptop." Bud, Chus deputy, was a giant. He was a Navy officer and not a Marine, and he was an F-14 pilot. Naval aviators all had call signs, and since Bud had a face only a mother could love, his was Big Ugly Dude, or Bud for short. Chu turned the open laptop to Wardak and played the video. I got up and stood behind Wardak so I could see the screen.

The video had been taken from an Apache helicopter. It began with the thermal image of a Blackhawk helicopter hovering near a village. Operators were fast-roping down from the aircraft. As soon as the Blackhawk left the screen, a stream of machine-gun fire could be seen impacting near the operators. The audio was a conversation between the Apache crew and the assault team leader.

The TERP provided a translation of the communication to Wardak. The short version was:

"We're receiving fire, do you have eyes on?"

"Roger, target identified. Are we cleared to fire?"

"Affirmative, cleared hot. Fire."

The video showed the focus of the camera move from the operators to a bunker adjacent to what must have been an ANA combat outpost. Then we saw the reticle pattern and display of the gun camera, followed by the launch of a hellfire missile and the deadpan report by the aircrew: "Target destroyed."

"The real question is why your forces are engaging US forces," said Chu.

"President Obama and General McCrystal have new rules that you're not following. We are supposed to be warned of any operations in our area. We were never warned. How can you fault the captain?" replied Wardak.

"It was a Blackhawk helicopter. How could your captain not know he was shooting at Americans? When was the last time the Taliban fast-roped out of a Blackhawk?"

"I can't tell you what the captain did or did not see. The point remains that the Americans are not following the rules. Additionally, if you are going into Afghan homes, you are supposed to have Afghan forces with you. Once again, we received no such request."

"Nothing you've said is an excuse for shooting at Americans. Your captain caused his own death. We have an expression: *death comes to those who seek it.*"

"We expect compensation. I will be meeting with your commander, and I will explain to him your view toward Afghan and American cooperation. Especially the part about death coming to those who seek it. I don't think that is the American policy, Colonel."

We filed out of the office. I went down the hall to Brigadier Aqa's office. My TERP met me at the door. Ramian, as he is called, is in his thirties. He'd been injured while working for the US Special Forces, and the ODA commander had landed him a job with my company. Ramian has been working inside the 201st Corps longer than anyone and is a great source of information on just about everything. Brigadier Aqa is the polar opposite of Wardak. It's impossible not to like the guy. Unlike Wardak, who's a Pashtun, Aqa is a Tajik. He's an older guy, with a belly and a bald head with soft features. Aqa prefers to speak in Dari. Aqa is a former member of the Mujahideen, and he'd ridden with the great Masoud in the Northern Alliance back in the day. Unlike Wardak, whose only military experience was serving as the commander of the Taliban Staff College, Aqa was a multidecade combat veteran who'd battled the Russians and later the Taliban. His warrior years were behind him, and the meeting with Aqa was purely social. Aqa has almost no involvement in the day-to-day operations of the Corps.

After spending an hour with Aqa the G3, I went down to the Operations Center. Colonel Fareed, the deputy G3, ran the Ops Center for the Corps. He's well educated, and his English is excellent. Fareed only has one arm. I was careful not to ask him how he lost it, but one day he volunteered. It was a bizarre conversation. We'd started talking about the Russians.

"Do you ever wonder how I lost my arm?" Fareed asked.

"Yes, but I didn't want to ask."

"Aqa took it."

"Brigadier Aqa, your boss, took your arm," I said.

"I'm a Pashtun from Kabul. My people sided with the Russians. One day, I was part of a vehicle convoy moving north when we were ambushed. The commander who ambushed our convoy was Aqa. His men shot me, and I lost my arm," he said.

"Does that make it difficult working for him?" I asked.

"No. He's a good man. He was doing his job and I was doing mine. It wasn't personal."

Whatever corruption is going on in the 201st, I don't think it involves Fareed, because he doesn't have any money. The salary for an ANA colonel is four hundred dollars a month. I knew he was broke, because one day I spoke to him and he was very upset. He told me his wife was very sick with an infection, and that the military doctor refused to see her unless he paid the doctor five hundred dollars, which he didn't have. I immediately went back to my B-hut and returned with five hundred dollars. Fareed seemed genuine in his response. He had tears in his eyes when I gave him the money. I didn't think it was a con, but in Afghanistan, one never knew for sure. Similar to Aqa, discussions with Fareed rarely involve the war. Fareed is enthralled with our new President. Discussions with Fareed are almost always political.

The last two hours of every workday are usually spent with the one person in the 201st Corps who knows everything that's going on operationally. Major Ibrahim is brilliant. In the US Army, he'd be the guy who'd win the white briefcase at Command and General Staff College. Explaining decision support templates, D3A targeting processes and RISTA planning with anyone else in the Corps is a waste of time. Ibrahim has no trouble understanding such things. He's the master of all things military, despite the fact that he only spends about ten percent of his time actually doing anything related to tactical planning. He spends most of his time on other pursuits.

A major pursuit is his tea boy. Major Ibrahim can never seem to get enough of the poor guy. When I enter the G3 plans shop, I often find it empty and have to knock on the adjacent sleeping room to get Ibrahim and his paramour back on task. Another even more consuming pursuit is Ibrahim's drug habit. He's very candid about his need for hashish in order to function, but I also suspect he's a consumer of Afghanistan's number one export, opium. The third pursuit, which towers over both the pederasty and the drugs in Ibrahim's world, is bird fighting.

Ibrahim is the proud owner of a champion fighting bird. Nearly every night, the bird goes into battle, and so far, it's undefeated. Ibrahim often invites me to attend the fights, but I always beg off. Ibrahim's winnings from his bird's triumphs are significant. He mentioned once that he won ten thousand dollars in a single bout.

I sat down with Ibrahim to review the attack plan for an operation in the Uzbin Valley.

"I've completed everything. The plan is on the commander's desk, waiting on his signature. Don't you want to hear about the fight last night?" Ibrahim said.

"Did he win?"

"Did he win? Did he win? He was amazing. He was heroic, the greatest bird the world has ever known. It was a tough fight. Many thought he was beaten. Many feathers were lost. I never doubted. He battled back. He's a genius bird. He pretended to be more hurt than he was. My bird drew the other in and then, when the opponent thought he had him beat and was moving in for the kill, my bird struck, with a vicious surprise killing blow. He drove his beak into the neck of the opponent and then, with his talons, ripped his heart out. It was magnificent. My bird is the champion of all birds."

"That's great, Ibrahim. At the rate you're going, you may want to just give up this military thing and become a full-time trainer."

"My bird doesn't need to train. It's a natural."

Chapter 5

Kabul, Afghanistan

I drove my dirty beat-up Isuzu SUV to the security gate at the Kabul Intercontinental Hotel. I unwrapped the scarf around my face and showed the guard my CAC ID card, identifying me as part of ISAF. The guard raised the barrier and waved me through. I headed up the steep hill to the parking lot next to the lobby entrance. I had a driver, but I didn't want anyone else to know who I was meeting. Plus, I like to drive.

I found Mike in the café outdoor seating area and joined him at a table. The Intercontinental is on a flat plateau on top of the highest hill in the city of Kabul, with a view of most of the city. The weather was warm and sunny. From our table near the edge of the hilltop, we could see a plume of smoke in the distance and two Kiowa Warrior helicopters orbiting above the source of the smoke.

"What's going on down there?" I asked.

"They hit one of the residences used by the UN," Mike replied.

I ordered a coffee and a club sandwich, and for several minutes we watched the battle play out in the distance. They were too far away to make out any of the details. At the edge of the hotel grounds, where the top of the hill ended in a cliff, a CNN crew was filming the battle. A war correspondent was wearing a helmet and body armor in the shot, with the plume of smoke in the background.

"Did you read my report?" I asked.

"Yes, I went through it last night."

"What are your thoughts?"

"It's not enough."

"What do you mean? It's full of details. Seventy-five percent of the fuel provided to the 201st ANA by the US military is being diverted and resold on the black market. Half of the troops are ghost soldiers. They exist only on the payroll accounts. That's a big rip-off on the American taxpayer. I even explained how the religious officer is skimming the death gratuities earmarked for the families of ANA soldiers killed in action. What more do you need?" I said.

"None of what you've provided is new. The kind of corruption you described is a way of life in Afghanistan. It's happening everywhere in all of the units. It's not a big deal. We think Wardak is up to something far more sinister," Mike said.

"I guess I'm going to have to change my methods, then, because I gave you all I could find."

"What are your sources?" Mike asked.

"The TERPs, mostly. They all seem to have a chip on their soldier when it comes to the ANA, and most of them have been around long enough to know where the skeletons are buried."

"TERPs are good, but you need someone on the inside. Who do you think knows the most about what's really going on inside the Corps?"

"Wardak, of course. Then his intel officer, who avoids me like the plague. The religious officer is a close confidant, and the brigade commanders would have to be in on it," I said.

"What about in the G3?"

"Brigadier Aqa doesn't seem to be involved, and if he knows anything about what the others are doing, I doubt he would talk. He's that kind of guy. Colonel Fareed is not involved. If he's a crook, he's a very bad one, because he's dirt poor. I doubt he knows much. Ibrahim is the one guy in G3 who I think would know what Wardak is up to," I said.

"Why do you say that?"

"You can't move a vehicle or a person in the 201st without Ibrahim knowing about it. He knows where every player is on the chess board, and he's the guy who writes the orders to move them. A lot of what he does is a secret between himself and Wardak."

"What about the chief of staff?" asked Mike.

"Major General Azimi doesn't seem to get along very well with Wardak. I doubt he's involved, but he might know something," I said.

"Do you think you can cultivate Ibrahim and Azimi as sources?"

"Probably, if I paid them."

Mike reached down to his feet and retrieved a small black backpack, placing it next to my chair.

"What's in the bag?"

"One hundred thousand dollars, a burner cell and the pistol you requested."

"I'm going to have to wait until Ibrahim's bird starts losing before this cash is going to do much good with him. General Azimi, on the other hand, should be able to deliver faster results."

"What's the deal with Ibrahim's bird?"

"It's a *chukar*—a fighting partridge. He's making serious bank betting on his bird, which, from the way he describes it, is the Mohammed Ali of birds."

"Ibrahim sounds like a character."

"If you can get past the gambling, drugs, animal cruelty and sexual depravity that borders on child rape, he's a great guy."

"Child rape?"

"Maybe not. I'm not really sure how old his tea boy is. He could be of the age of consent in this country for all I know."

"I think you should kill the bird and speed things along."

"I'll see what I can do. He's always inviting me to the bird fights. Maybe I should go."

I spent most of the drive back to Camp Blackhorse thinking of ways to assassinate a bird. The Army had spent millions of dollars training me if you combined just the costs of the courses I attended: Airborne, Ranger, HALO, diving, SERE, jumpmaster, demo, driving, tracking, sniper, SOT and the rest. Now I was going to put all that training and my years of combat experience to work assassinating a two-pound partridge. The idea made my chuckle to myself.

Lost in thought, the sound of a gunshot startled me. I hit the brakes, my heart raced, and my attention returned to the immediate surroundings. Just ahead of me was a HMMWV with a machine gun aimed directly at me. In my beat up Isuzu SUV, I must've gotten too close to the convoy for their comfort, which is why they fired a warning shot. I let the convoy get far ahead of me before moving again. Getting too close to American convoys was dangerous business. They were bullet magnets for the Taliban, and when they weren't firing at you, they were firing at someone else with you in the middle. I normally avoided them like the plague. I reminded myself to pay attention.

The next morning, I walked to the morning battle update briefing at the 201st Headquarters with a plan to attend the next bird fight. My plan was simple. When the opportunity presented itself and nobody was looking, I was going to put a bullet in the bird using the suppressed 9mm Mike had given me. When the BUB was over, I made my rounds. I spent a few minutes with General Wardak, then Aqa and Fareed, before heading to the plans shop. Ibrahim wasn't at his desk. Through my TERP, I asked his tea boy where Ibrahim was. He pointed to the sleep room.

I told the tea boy to get him. Weekends (Thursdays and Fridays) were especially hard on Ibrahim. Without the forced sobriety of work, his drug use went unrestricted. It was normal for him to look bad on Saturdays, but when he emerged from the sleep room in a bathrobe, he was at a totally different level of bad than I'd ever seen him before. His eyes were blood red, his long hair was unwashed and askew, he had a three-day growth of beard, and what emanated from him was pure emotional pain.

He sat down at his desk. I took the chair across from him and asked his TERP and the tea boy to leave the room.

"What's wrong, Ibrahim?"

Tears began to flow from his eyes. "My bird is dead."

"What happened?"

"He was killed. Murdered by a monster. The biggest bird I've ever seen."

"I'm sorry. That's just terrible. He was such a great bird."

"I don't know what I am going to do. I can't afford another bird, and I owe many people."

"What did you do with all the money you've been winning?"

"I don't know. It's all gone. I have a wife and three children. I have many debts. I have a very serious problem. You have to help me."

"I think we may be able to help each other," I said.

I met Mike several weeks later at the Thai restaurant at the French camp next to the Kabul Airport. It was a Friday afternoon and the restaurant was crowded. I had the prawn pad thai and a Heineken; Mike went with the cashew chicken and a Corona.

"Are you allowed to have alcohol? I thought your group fell under General Order number one," Mike said.

"We do. I'm breaking the law. I've adopted an outlaw lifestyle in my new role as a secret agent. Last night I even had a chocolate sundae at the Blackhorse DFAC. I'm throwing caution to the wind."

"Really? When did all this happen?"

"About the same time I became an assassin of small birds."

"Pat Walsh, killer of chukars. The avian world trembles at the mere mention of your name. That was a good move, by the way. Ibrahim is really coming through."

"Turns out I didn't have to do the deed. The bird died on its own."

"No kidding?"

"Yeah. According to Ibrahim, it went up against a steroid-enhanced Godzilla of a bird and died valiantly in the ring."

"Ibrahim's been a goldmine. Did you bring the recordings?"

"It's all on this USB."

"Can you give me the summary of what Ibrahim told you?"

"The Taliban destruction of Combat Outpost Bari Ali on May first was an inside job. It was ordered by Wardak."

"Why?" asked Mike.

"Wardak makes a lot of money collecting tolls from the trucks carrying supplies along Jalalabad Road. Everything that comes into Afghanistan from Pakistan comes in on that road. The Second Brigade has checkpoints on the eastern half of the road from Logar to the Khyber Pass, and the Third Brigade has checkpoints on the road from Kabul to the border with Logar," I said.

"Bari Ali is in Kunar Province. It's in a valley. It doesn't border J-bad Road," Mike said.

"No, it doesn't, but this big surge of thirty thousand troops Obama is bringing into Afghanistan is screwing up Wardak's operation. The reason the trucks pay the tolls is because they know if they don't, they'll be ambushed further down the road by the bad guys who are in cahoots with Wardak's guys. There are now so many American patrols out along the highway that it's no longer easy to set up those ambushes, and the truck drivers are starting to refuse to pay the tolls."

"That still doesn't explain why he wiped out Bari Ali."

"Wardak wants the new American troops reinforcing the camps. He doesn't want them patrolling and interrupting his business operations. That's why. Think about it. What's the first thing we did after the attack? We pulled in the patrols and began to evacuate the isolated combat outposts that were most vulnerable, and we reinforced the larger camps. The plan worked."

"How sure is Ibrahim that it was an inside job?"

"He's positive. How could anybody not be? The first shots were RPG-7s launched from inside the camp against the B-huts occupied by the US and Latvian troops. The NATO forces were dead seconds into the fight, which left only a few loyal ANA troops who resisted. Most of the ANA force disappeared after the attack and haven't been seen since."

"How did Ibrahim come by this information?"

"He helped plan the attack with Wardak."

"Was it Ibrahim's idea?" asked Mike.

"No, but Wardak quizzed him on US response times and reactions a few days before the attack."

"Are you getting any useful information from the chief of staff?" asked Mike.

"No, just gossip. He's a jealous outsider. Beyond confirming what we already know about who the conspirators are, he's not been much help."

"Keep at it."

"Why? With this latest, don't you have enough? We already knew Wardak was stealing tens of millions from the US taxpayers every month. Now we learn he's ordered the death of American soldiers. Isn't it time to put him in cuffs and take him to Gitmo?"

"Wardak is close to Karzai. He's a tribal loyalist. That's why he has the command closest to the presidential palace. It's not going to be easy to get clearance to do anything."

"Just in case, I'm going to start making contingency plans."

Chapter 6

Jalalabad, Afghanistan

Winter was fast approaching; the surrounding mountains were white with snow. The mountain range to the east and north was called the Hindu Kush, which translates to killer of Hindus. Over the years it'd been an effective barrier in keeping the invaders out, especially those from the Indian Subcontinent. The mountains are incredibly steep and are only passable through a few high passes. Once winter set in, all of the passes closed except for two or three of the main ones, like the Khyber.

The summer had passed quickly. My intel collection on Wardak had remained nonactionable, consisting only of widespread theft of the American taxpayers, but nothing that apparently violated whatever un-written understanding existed between the US and Afghan governments. My repeated requests to make Wardak go the way of Ibrahim's chukar bird had been repeatedly rebuffed by Mike.

Mike and I met at a place called Osama bin Laden's Tea House at Camp Casey in Jalalabad, which was at the far eastern boundary of Af-ghanistan, adjacent to Pakistan. I joined the Corps commander in a meeting with the Second Brigade commander and his Kandak com-manders. I was staying the night at Camp Casey before beginning the long drive back to Kabul. The tea house was an abandoned building once used by Osama bin Laden. It's surrounded by a beautiful garden that was still in bloom, even this late in September.

"What's it going to take to get a green light to do something about Wardak?" I asked.

"More than what we have, I can say that much."

"You know, if Wardak had been born in New York instead of Kabul, I think he might've become a Wall Street mogul. He's no different than those bankers, those financial masters of the universe who made billions selling toxic mortgage instruments, and who then, after the economy tanked, turned around and made even more money from TARP bailouts. If you look at what Wardak's doing, he's no different. He's also profiting from sabotaging his own country," I said.

"Still a little bitter about your homebuilding business, I see."

"You noticed. No wonder you're a spy. It's the powers of perception. Did I tell you about Wardak's latest business venture?"

"What's he up to now?"

"He's found a way to get paid twice for ghost soldiers. Now, he not only gets paid by collecting the salary of the nonexistent soldiers, but he's found a way to get conscripts to pay for the privilege of being smuggled out of basic training so they can desert and become ghosts. After he helps them escape, the deserters stay on the payroll and become ghost soldiers. Wardak double dips."

"That's very enterprising. How did you come by the info?"

"The chief of staff gave me the tip, but I went out and caught the operation on video. The troops are smuggled out at night through the front gate in the back of ANA trucks and then released down the road."

"The new RC-East commander loves Wardak. He says he really understands what the US is trying to accomplish and believes he's an excellent security partner," Mike said.

"Seriously?"

"The US ambassador and the ISAF commander share the same opinion."

"That's tragic."

"Wardak's untouchable. Karzai loves him too."

"What does the CIA think of him?" I asked.

"We have our doubts. The Bari Ali incident was inconclusive. The word of a grieving drug-addicted gambler in search of a payday isn't sufficient evidence to act."

I made the seventy-mile drive from the Pakistan border to Camp Blackhorse the next morning in my trusty Isuzu. I had my TERP and Mohammed, my driver, with me, which helped a lot at the checkpoints.

There were many missing and damaged guard rails on J-bad Road, and in some places the falloff was thousands of feet straight down. Between the checkpoints, convoys of speeding jingle trucks, rockslides and occasional ambushes, it has to be the most harrowing stretch of road on the planet.

The weather was turning cold. It was late September, and I'd just dropped the paperwork to go home during the Christmas holiday. I'd been in Afghanistan for seven months and my wife still wouldn't speak to me. When I showed up, I wasn't sure if I'd be allowed into the house. I was able to talk with the kids regularly, but that was it. The news from Trident was mostly good. We continued to tread water financially, which meant the bank hadn't foreclosed and salaries were being paid.

I planned on making my daily rounds after the morning battle update briefing at the 201st headquarters. The Eid holiday was coming up, and the religious officer was doing more talking than normal. He was speaking Pashtun, and the translator was having a hard time keeping up with his rapid-fire ranting. The man had a glass eye and a huge black beard. He looked like Captain Barbossa in *Pirates of the Caribbean*, only ten times crazier. I couldn't imagine he spoke with any moral authority. It seemed just about everyone knew that he was a crook who skimmed the death gratuities.

Ibrahim was at his desk and coherent, which was a pleasant surprise. He'd been slowly degenerating since I'd put him on my payroll. I was thinking I might be overfunding him. Because Ibrahim's English was fluent, my TERP made himself scarce when we talked. We went through the normal Muslim greeting in Arabic and then waited to be served tea before talking.

"Are you doing okay, Ibrahim?"

"Yes, but my children are sick. I need to take them to the doctor. Can I get an advance?"

"Sure." I reached inside my pocket and peeled off ten one-hundred-dollar bills, placing them on his desk.

"I have news. Giving you this information is very dangerous. I will need a bonus."

"Tell me what you have, and if I think it's worth a bonus, then you'll get one."

"I need two thousand, or I won't say anything."

"I won't pay two thousand unless you have evidence. I gave you that recorder for a reason."

"I have everything recorded. You won't be disappointed. But the recording exposes me. The price is five thousand."

"What happened to two thousand?"

"I reconsidered. This is very risky information I have."

"Come on, Ibrahim. I already pay you two thousand a month, and you've received so many bonuses you've been paid up to next year."

"Pat, this is worth five thousand."

"I only have three on me. It's either that or nothing."

"Okay, three thousand," he said. I paid him.

"General Wardak has ordered the movement of the Kandak defending Camp Keating back to Jalalabad. The forces will evacuate the camp over the next three days."

"That's not good. That's going to leave the Americans alone to defend the camp. Last I heard, there were about one hundred ANA and seventy US. Is that still the case?"

"One hundred and sixteen ANA and fifty-eight US."

"Why is he breaking his commitment to the RC-East commander?"

"I don't know. But it's not just the RC-East Commander he's going against by evacuating. It's President Karzai himself. The US put pressure on Karzai to maintain forces in Keating, and the president ordered General Wardak to support the Americans."

"Why is it such a big deal?"

"Keating guards the only mountain pass between Afghanistan and Pakistan in Nuristan. The opium crop has been harvested, and the route it takes to markets in Europe and the US goes through Pakistan. The US is using the increased troop numbers to cut off the distribution routes into Pakistan. The Taliban needs an open pass to move the opium. If Wardak is removing forces on the border against the will of the president, it must mean a Taliban attack is imminent to open up a supply route."

"Why would Wardak go against Karzai's wishes?"

"The Taliban rely on the opium money. They'll attack with or without the ANA troops defending the camp. Saving the lives of one hundred ANA will please Karzai. Plus, most likely Wardak is being paid by the Taliban. About a third of the opium grown in Afghanistan is from farms in the 201st area of operation."

"You think he benefits twice, then."

"Yes."

"That's a lot of speculation. What's on the tape?"

"It's a conversation between Wardak and me. He instructs me to prepare orders to the Second Brigade commander. I ask him why we are withdrawing, and he refuses to answer. I press him. I tell him we have specific orders from MOD not to withdraw and to support the Americans, and he loses his temper. He says to hell with the Americans. They can all die. His responsibility is to his people."

"And from that, you believe he's being paid by the Taliban and that an attack is imminent. That's pretty thin."

"I know him better than you. I'm positive that's what's going on."

I handed off the information and the digital recording to Mike. Later in the week, when the ANA troops boarded trucks and headed south back to J-bad, the new RC-East Commander raised a big fuss. The RC-East Commanding General personally flew to Pol-e-Charki and confronted General Wardak. I was present during the meeting. At the conclusion, General Wardak explained it was all a misunderstanding and that he would return the troops to the camp as soon as possible.

Two weeks went by and the ANA had still not reinforced the camp. Each day, Colonel Chu, the RCAT commander, would press Wardak on the issue, and each day he was reassured that the movement was in the works but was being delayed by logistics issues that kept cropping up.

In the early-morning hours of October 3, three hundred Taliban fighters assaulted the Camp Keating perimeter. The Taliban fighters had marshaled in a mosque only three hundred meters from the camp. The Taliban advanced under the cover of a rainy, heavily overcast night that prevented the use of air support. The Taliban attacked with the element of surprise against a sparsely defended perimeter. In a brutal, bloody battle, the Taliban came very close to completely overrunning the camp. When the fighting finally ended nine hours later, thirty-five of the fifty-eight US soldiers had been either killed or wounded. The heroism of the American forces who fought to defend Camp Keating that night was historic. Although the Taliban never succeeded in capturing the camp, the American losses were so severe that the camp was evacuated the next day. If the purpose of the attack was to remove the American presence and allow unmolested travel between Pakistan and Afghanistan, the Taliban mission was a huge success.

It was a cold rainy morning. I was in the dining facility, eating breakfast. Bud, the deputy RCAT Commander, sat across from me with his breakfast tray.

"There's a big fight happening in Nuristan. Keating got hit early this morning," Bud said.

"How are they holding up?"

"They're outside of artillery range. It's no-go weather for CAS and attack air. We think the camp has been overrun."

"What's being done?"

"The weather should break soon. Reinforcements from J-bad are already loaded up in helicopters, and CAS should be on station in the next hour or so."

I looked across the table at Bud. He was an F-14 pilot, a tough guy who had been a lineman on one of the better teams ever fielded by Navy. A decent guy, who looked like he had the weight of the world on his shoulders.

The Blackhorse dining facility had a macabre tradition. In an effort to honor the fallen, every soldier assigned to the camp who died in country had his picture mounted on the wall. The pictures were at shoulder level and stretched all across the usable wall space in the small DFAC. I counted them once. There were forty-three photos. That was a huge sacrifice to make for the likes of Wardak and his fellow criminals. At that moment, I decided not to wait for the green light from Mike and to go ahead and do something about Wardak on my own.

I skipped the battle update briefing that morning. Instead I took my SUV and drove into Pol-e-Charki camp. I drove around the camp, to the various units, searching, until I found what I was looking for. I liberated an RPG launcher and two RPG-7 rounds from the back of an unoccupied ANA HMMWV. I also found an AK-47 and four magazines of .556 ammunition inside another vehicle. I threw the weapons and ammo in a green duffle bag and drove out of the camp onto J-bad Road, headed toward Kabul.

The rain slowed traffic to a standstill in downtown Kabul. I parked the SUV in a narrow space on Wazir Akbar Khan road, less than fifty yards from the Masoud Traffic Circle. I'd followed Wardak home to his villa on the south side of Kabul near the Intercontinental Hotel on several occasions. I knew his security team altered the route each day, which was good tradecraft for a personal security detail. However, every possible route had to pass through the Masoud Traffic Circle. It was unavoidable. I slung the heavy duffle bag over my shoulder, pulled a hat down over my eyes, tightened the scarf around my face and ventured out into the rain.

It took me forty-five minutes to find a suitable truck. I settled on a one-and-a-half-ton box truck with the cab behind instead of over the engine, which are far more common in Afghanistan. I smashed the driver side window and let myself in. With my pocketknife, I stripped the wires and drove away in a matter of minutes.

By one in the afternoon, the rain had slowed to a drizzle. I was double-parked next to my SUV, looking into the traffic circle. Inside the circle there were two police directing traffic. The traffic was heavy, and the vehicles were moving at less than five miles per hour. There were two lanes of traffic inside the circle. In the center was a large pillar built to recognize the hero Masoud, the lion of the Northern Alliance. I emptied the duffle bag and loaded an RPG-7 into the launcher, then I chambered a round into the AK-47. I tucked the CIA issued SIG P226 into my belt as a backup.

By 3 p.m., I began to doubt myself, thinking I might have missed him. Wardak drove a white armored Lexus 470. He usually had a security vehicle ahead of him and one behind. The security vehicles were armored Chevy Suburbans. His security detail was all Afghans.

I was about to pack it in when I spotted a black Suburban entering the traffic circle, followed by a white Lexus SUV. My target was entering the ambush site. I pulled forward to the entrance of the traffic circle and waited. Cars were lining up behind me. It didn't take long before the horns began to blare, still I waited. The lead black Suburban passed me on the outer lane of the circle, I spotted Wardak's SUV behind it. I charged into the traffic circle, cutting off the trail Suburban and got right on Wardak's rear bumper. The Suburban behind me was flashing his lights and blaring his horn, but I stayed in position behind Wardak.

The white Lexus turned off onto the next road. A police officer was directing traffic, and he signaled for me to follow. The road was less congested, and I followed Wardak's Lexus at thirty miles per hour while blocking the trail Suburban from passing me. I saw the lead Suburban turn right at the next intersection, and that's where I made my move. I checked my seat belt, and then hit the gas. I was going fifty when I hit the Lexus on the passenger side as it was turning the corner. My chest strained against the seat belt, and the screech of the steel on steel collision filled my ears. I kept my foot on the gas and pinned the sliding Lexus against a parked van. I pushed open the door, slung the AK over my shoulder, grabbed the loaded RPG and extra rocket and jumped out of the cab.

As soon as I hit the ground, I fired the RPG-7. The first round went into the bulletproof windshield of the trail Suburban. The Suburban erupted into a ball of flame. The engine on Wardak's heavy armored Lexus was racing as the driver gunned it to get out of the vice it was caught in between the box truck and the van. I could hear the groans of the metal on metal. I finished reloading the RPG just as the Lexus sprang free. Standing in the middle of the open street, I fired the 40mm rocket into the rear of the retreating Lexus at a range of seventy-five yards. I dropped the RPG launcher and ran toward the flaming SUV with my AK at the ready.

Beyond the Lexus, I could see that the lead Suburban had stopped. Two men had taken up firing positions on either side of the vehicle. I engaged one with an automatic burst from my AK. I watched one of the guard's duck for cover and began to receive return fire from the second. I used the burning Lexus SUV twenty yards ahead of me as cover as I advanced.

The rear passenger door to the Lexus opened. A security man from the lead Suburban made a dash across the open road to get to the first man I'd engaged. I cut him down with a burst from my AK and switched magazines. When I got to within five yards of the burning Lexus, I moved to the passenger side. Bullets whizzed by my head fired from the direction of the lead Suburban. I fired a burst of AK rounds and dashed to the Lexus.

A security guard lay dead on the road next to the vehicle. I pulled the front passenger door the rest of the way open. Inside the smoky Lexus, I found Wardak stuck in the rear passenger seat. His face was covered in blood, and he was struggling with the seat belt. He was only able to use one hand and couldn't free himself. He stopped what he was doing, and he looked directly at me. He didn't say a word. I brought the rifle barrel over the front seat and emptied the rest of the magazine into his face.

I'd lost track of the first man I'd engaged from the lead Suburban. I slapped my last magazine into the AK and slowly moved around the Lexus. A round pinged off the vehicle's armor. I fired a quick burst and dropped below the smoldering vehicle. A fusillade of rounds impacted against the side of the SUV.

As soon as the firing stopped, I ran across the street and slid behind the cover of a parked vehicle. I advanced at a crouch concealed behind the line of parked cars. Through a car window I spotted the guard standing behind the passenger door of the suburban, looking the wrong way. I stood up straight and stealthily raised my rifle above the hood of the car and took aim. I let loose with a five-round burst. The guard fell back into the suburban.

I dropped the AK and ran back down the street toward my Isuzu SUV where I'd parked it earlier. I was surprised the police hadn't blocked the street yet. The sound of sirens was already drowning out the normal chaotic street traffic, so I knew I didn't have much time. I tried to stay under the storefront awnings to avoid the overhead cameras on the huge surveillance aerostat that floated above Kabul on a half mile long tether. Once I reached my vehicle, I headed back into the Masoud Traffic Circle and back to Camp.

I was back at Camp Blackhorse by four thirty in the afternoon and resumed my normal routine. I went to the gym, lifted, ran on the treadmill, showered and headed to my B-hut to work on Jessica's daily task list.

When I got back to my room, where I'd left my cell, I noticed I'd missed five calls from Mike. I called him back.

"Where've you been?" he barked.

"I was at the gym."

"We need to talk."

"Where and when?"

"Tomorrow. Meet me at ISAF headquarters."

"Where in ISAF?"

"Out front, by the security checkpoint. Meet me at ten."

The next day, I attended the morning battle update briefing. The Corps Commander wasn't in attendance, and there was no mention as to why he was missing.

I arrived early and waited for Mike in front of the ISAF headquarters building. I watched him as he approached. He was limping more than normal. As he got closer, I could see he was very tense.

"Follow me," he said, before leading the way through security. We went into the building and then down a flight of stairs and through a maze of corridors until we arrived at a nondescript office with a security guard in civilian clothes posted outside. Inside the office stood a thin man of medium height with curly hair, he looked to be about thirty. He was dressed in khaki pants and matching shirt with a gray hunting vest. He looked like he was about to go out on a safari.

"Pat, this is Tom Kerry. He's my boss, the chief of station in Afghanistan."

"Nice to meet you, Tom." I offered him my hand, but he didn't respond. Apparently, Mike wasn't the only person upset with me.

"I don't have much time, so I'm going to get straight to the point," Tom said. "Did you kill Lieutenant General Wardak?"

"I put about twenty 7.62 rounds into his face, so yeah, I'm pretty sure I got the job done," I said matter-of-factly.

"You'll tread very carefully, if you know what's good for you," he said, with his finger pointed in my face. "Do you know what you've done to US-Afghan relations?"

"I killed a man who's responsible for thirty-five American casualties. Now they should understand that when they screw us over, they'll pay a price. If anything, that's an improvement in US-Afghan relations," I said.

"Who told you to kill General Wardak?" he yelled.

"No one," I said.

"Mike didn't know about it?"

"No, he didn't."

"It wasn't an approved attack, that decision was never made," he said with an expression of disbelief.

"I realize that, but you people seem to have difficulty making decisions. We had solid intel that the camp was going to be hit, and what did all of you great decision makers do? Nothing. How do you explain that to the families of the soldiers who died yesterday? Next time do your job, and I won't have to do it for you," I said.

"There'll be no next time, Mr. Walsh. You're going to be on the next plane out of here, and whether or not that plane lands you in a black site prison is going to depend on me." He snarled.

I closed the gap between us and put my chest close to the smaller man's face "Nothing personal, sparky, but you're going to need a lot more firepower than that guy outside the door if you think you're going to be taking me anywhere," I said.

Tom's face got red, and he slammed the tabletop next to him with an open hand. It made a loud slapping noise. "Mike, come with me." The two left the room, leaving me alone to consider my fate.

The saving grace was the room had a coffee machine. I brewed a fresh pot of coffee and waited a full three hours for the door to open again. Mike returned to the room alone.

"What happened to Tommy the terrible? Is he still all pouty and indignant?" I asked.

Mike just shook his head. "Let's go," he said. We walked out of the building together.

"Can we grab lunch? I'm starving," I said.

"How can you be hungry? Do you realize how close you just came to permanently disappearing?"

"I'm hungry because I missed lunch. Are you going to tell me what just happened?" I said.

"What just happened is that the ISAF Commander intervened and saved your butt. He knows who you are. Apparently, you worked for him when he was the JSOC Commander. He decided that officially, Wardak was killed by the Taliban, and that you're going to go back to your job, where you'll complete your one-year contract. And after that, you're going to leave Afghanistan and not come back," Mike said.

"What did little Tommy, your baby boss with the Boston Brahmin accent, have to say about that?" I asked with a smile.

"The boss fought hard to put you in a cell in Eastern Europe, but the ISAF commander brought in the ambassador, and between the two of them, they got Tom to accept the decision."

"It sounds like if I hadn't decided to off Wardak on my own, he'd still be running the 201st."

"Yeah, that's about right."

"I would've felt bad about killing Ibrahim's bird, but with Wardak, I have no regrets."

"It was a good call, but promise me you'll stay out of trouble between now and March," Mike said.

"Definitely. Should I keep paying Ibrahim?"

"No, don't do anything. Your secret agent status has been revoked."

"All right, then. Take care of yourself, Mike."

"You too, Pat, you too."

Chapter 7

Dabiq, Syria

The bodies of all eighteen Syrian officers and pilots were arrayed on their knees. They were each staged facing Mecca as if in prayer, with backs to the sky and a severed head perched on each. The victims' blue aviation coveralls were soaked with blood, and flies were beginning to swarm. The butchers, clad in desert camouflage uniforms and body armor, were loading into waiting pickup trucks. Among the last to load was Mohammed Emwazi, a man known in the West as Jihadi John and to his friends as Ahmed. He was hurriedly directing the cameraman to capture some final shots before he too could depart.

Ahmed snatched the memory card containing the footage from his cameraman and hurried toward the road, where a white Nissan Patrol awaited. Although it was late in the afternoon on a cool mid-November day, the Kuwaiti jihadist began to sweat as he approached the vehicle. He feared Abdul-Rahman, and his anxiety grew with each step. When he reached the SUV, the fully tinted rear passenger window descended, slowly revealing a very displeased face that made him perspire even more. Ahmed had been taking orders from Abdul-Rahman for the past ten months and had yet to learn a single thing about his history. Abdul-Rahman kept his distance from those beneath him.

Abdul-Rahman Al Ghaneem was also a Kuwaiti. In Arabic, his first name meant "servant of the most merciful," and his family name, Ghaneem, meant "prosperity." Although he was very rich—his family owned one of the largest holding companies in Kuwait—Abdul-Rahman was anything but merciful. He was short of stature, thirty-four years old

51

with a hawkish beak for a nose, intense dark eyes, closely manicured black beard, powerful muscular body, and an aloof superior manner so common to the highborn in the region. Born outside the wall of Kuwait City to a prominent trading family in Jahra, Kuwait, Abdul-Rahman was the fourth son from his father's third wife. His birth order and standing within the family made a prominent role in the family business impossible, which is why he chose to serve in the military.

Jahra is an ultraconservative city located forty-five minutes to the north of Kuwait City. Hostile to outsiders and tribally loyal to the Al-Sabah royal family, it was the recruiting grounds of choice for the Kuwait National Guard (KNG) and other elite security forces within the emirate. Abdul-Rahman was a major in the KNG Counter-Terrorism Battalion. A graduate of the Royal Military Academy Sandhurst, the US Special Forces Q course, and the US Marine Corps Staff College, Major Abdul-Rahman was the recipient of the finest training available to a Kuwaiti Special Forces officer.

Abdul-Rahman's family name and background were not known to Ahmed; he only knew the man was to be feared. It was Abu Bakr al-Baghdadi, the caliph himself, who'd placed Ahmed under Abdul-Rahman's control, and he had no doubts about what would happen to him if he failed in his duties. The group beheading of the airmen was supposed to be the warm-up to a grand finale, which was scripted to be the confession and ceremonial decapitation of the captive American aid worker. Unfortunately for him, something went wrong with the plan, and it was now Ahmed's duty to explain it to the boss.

Hours earlier, while loading the prisoners onto the trucks, misfortune had struck. The docile behavior of captives in Ahmed's videos was always helped along by the secret administration of drugs to the prisoners. Sprinkling sedatives into a starving prisoner's food was a tried and true method to create a compliant captive. Ahmed was not sure if Kessig, the American, had gotten the wrong dose or the wrong drug. What he did know was that the former American Ranger turned out to be anything but compliant.

When the guard had lowered the tailgate on the Toyota pickup truck and ordered Kessig to load, the prisoner had struck. Despite having his hands bound behind his back, the wiry American managed to swing his hands under his feet and place a stranglehold on the guard. A second guard quickly ended the attack with an AKM rifle shot to the head, saving his friend, but also ending any possibility of filming the script as planned. The 7.62mm rifle round fired at point-blank range made it impossible to film a close-up of the American. Ahmed was not even sure if it would be possible for enemy intelligence to identify Kessig when his latest opus was released to the public.

Abdul-Rahman grew impatient listening to the groveling explanation Ahmed provided. The obsequious whining tone in which he blamed the guards for his own leadership failure was difficult for Abdul-Rahman to stomach. Having heard enough, Abdul-Rahman violently opened the door into Ahmed's chest, knocking him hard to the ground. While Ahmed was pushing himself up with his skinny arms to stand, Abdul-Rahman kicked him in the face and then proceeded to kick him in the ribs and back until the cowering jihadist rolled into a ball and begged Abdul-Rahman to stop. Abdul-Rahman considered the failed IT salesman a pathetic excuse for a soldier and was badly tempted to shoot the British Kuwaiti on the spot, but instead he gave him a parting kick to the ribs before walking back to his vehicle.

Abdul-Rahman had no illusions about the quality and motivations of his troops. He knew for the most part they were neither soldiers nor true believers. He had worked with enough of them to know they were misfit serial failures drawn via YouTube and other social media to the romantic images of a global caliphate. The images of sex slaves, brutality, military victory, and a master religion were the dominant themes in his recruiting videos. Brutality was catnip to his audience. The caliphate was a magnet for the cruel and maladjusted. Poorly educated, unemployed, sexually repressed men dominated the ranks. The lack of any kind of selection process and even a remote semblance of discipline and training culminated in a Daesh force that was a complete menace to humanity.

Abdul-Rahman stemmed his anger, realizing he would have to spare the British Beatle, as Ahmed and his three British companions were called. The shocking effectiveness of the perverted work Ahmed was doing was critical to his objective, and he couldn't let his personal disgust interfere with the mission. More than a thousand misfits a month had begun flowing into the caliphate since Ahmed's first production had hit the internet back in August. There was no disputing that the skinny IT geek knew how to hit the right notes to resonate with the target audience. Ahmed was the Leni Riefenstahl of the caliphate. With that in mind, Abdul-Rahman jumped back into his vehicle and began the long drive back to his hometown.

Chapter 8

Kuwait City, Kuwait

Abdul-Rahman was dressed in an immaculate white *kandora* with an equally immaculate white *gutrah* around his head as he relaxed in the waiting room, nibbling on dates while sipping Arabic coffee outside the private office of Sheik Meshal al-Ahmad al-Jaber al-Sabah. Sheik Meshal was the younger brother of the emir of Kuwait and was the deputy chairman of the Kuwait National Guard. The KNG is the only military force allowed to be stationed within the confines of Kuwait City. The palace is in the urban center of the city. Bland and unimpressive from the outside, the huge building consumed most of a city block. While the architecturally uninspired exterior was clearly lacking in curb appeal, the inside was magnificent. The three-story domicile houses more than one hundred cavernous rooms lavishly decorated and furnished in marble and gold.

The palace has only recently reoccupied, and this was Abdul-Rahman's first visit to the sheik in his newly renovated home. While he was sure the seventy-three-year-old sheik was aiming for an exotic *Arabian Nights* theme with his choice of décor, he seemed to have just missed the mark and managed instead to capture something more akin to what Abdul-Rahman imagined a 1920's French bordello would have looked like. The sheik had a reputation for liking the ladies, and from this perspective, it was possible the décor was not an accident after all. His latest marriage, to a lovely nineteen-year-old girl, was his sixteenth. Although limited by law to only four wives at a time, the sheik was quick to divorce and remarry. His favorite wife had been with him for thirty-seven years, but the remaining three changed with the seasons.

While being ushered into the sheik's office, Abdul-Rahman took note that he was meeting him alone, as was their routine. Unlike the gaudy décor in the rest of the palace, the office had the look and feel of a British private men's club. Subdued lighting with mahogany wood-paneled walls, deep red carpet, solid leather furniture, and a scattering of scenic paintings featuring hounds, foxes, and of course the mounted hunters. Abdul-Rahman had known the sheik since he'd served as his personal assistant while still a junior captain. He was distantly related to the sheik on his mother's side, and that, along with his military record, was the justification for his trusted position.

When they got through the perfunctory greetings, the sheik got right down to business and asked Abdul-Rahman about his travels. Abdul-Rahman picked up the fruit drink sitting on the coffee table in front of him and observed the keen interest from the sheik, who was seated across from him. "Cee Dee, the Shia threat along our northern border has almost completely vanished. Daesh has claimed large territories in the north and west of Iraq, and the major focus from the Iranians is the defense of Baghdad. Daesh continues to grow in number despite the co-alition bombings. The morale is high, and they're continuing to expand into territories to the north and east. The coalition air campaign was very effective at first, but Daesh have adapted and are shifting tactics away from vehicle assaults that can be easily targeted from the sky. Instead they're relying more on dismounted and night operations. They've taken control of Mosul and will soon lay siege to Baghdad. In Kobani, the Daesh casualties have been enormous; the air strikes guided by coalition special forces have made it very unlikely Daesh will succeed. In Syria, the Alawites are being slowly bled to death; both sides lose hundreds each month. But a thousand new Daesh fighters arrive every month, while Assad's forces enjoy no such benefit. The Alawites are slowly shrinking out of existence. At this stage, it's only the Iranian revolutionary guard and Quds Force who are offering any resistance on the ground. The Syrian air strikes continue to be effective, but the Alawites' days are numbered. They just don't have the personnel necessary to sustain a war of attrition."

"What about Abu Bakr al-Baghdadi?"

"Cee Dee, he moves daily to avoid the coalition attacks. I met him in a village near Raqqa, and he was in good spirits. He's obsessed with removing the infidels and apostates from the Levant, he's well advised in military matters, and those around him are loyal. As the caliphate grows, so do his ego, ambition, and paranoia. He's very open about his desire to conquer the Arabian Peninsula including Kuwait. The areas he controls are very dangerous; bands of young men rove like wild dogs. As time goes on and his force gets bigger, the quality declines, and it gets less disciplined. If Daesh were ever to run out of enemy, I'm sure they'd turn on one another within days."

For a few minutes both men sat quietly. Abdul-Rahman glanced at the large-screen TV that always seemed to be showing a soccer match of some sort. The sheik thanked Abdul-Rahman and said he must go; he had another appointment. He could see on the young major's face the conflicting emotions he had about his role. He knew Abdul-Rahman suspected that he was operating independently from his brother, the emir, on this project. The sheik stood and embraced Abdul-Rahman and walked him to the door with his arm around the younger man's shoulder as if to reassure him.

After Abdul-Rahman left, Sheik Meshal sat quietly processing the information. There was really nothing new, but it always helped to hear the news reports confirmed by someone he trusted. Sheik Meshal was worried, because he was playing a dangerous game. Many months earlier he, Prince Bandar from Saudi Arabia, and Sheik Rasheed from UAE had hatched a plan to strike a blow against their greatest threat, the Shia of Iran. With the withdrawal of the Americans from Iraq, the nation on the northern border of Kuwait was gradually becoming a satellite state of Iran. Sheik Meshal and his like-minded accomplices funneled hundreds of millions of dollars to the fledgling caliphate to counter the influence of Iran in Iraq. Although he'd never had complete control of Daesh, the sheik's influence on Abu Bakr al-Baghdadi was declining rapidly. Earlier, when they were fighting only in Syria, the money Sheik Meshal had funneled to them had been essential and provided him a modicum of control. Once Daesh had seized the Iraqi oil fields, outside funding had become less important, as had the people who were supplying that funding.

Managing the propaganda campaign through Abdul-Rahman allowed the sheik to maintain influence over Daesh and promoted an awareness to the Western powers that intervention was necessary. Sheik Meshal's aim was Sunni control over Iraq. The risk of an Iranian puppet Shia state to Kuwait's north was too dangerous for the sheik to accept. He viewed Daesh as chemotherapy and the Iranians as the cancer. He was not a supporter of the extremists; he was a pragmatist seeking a counter to Iran. Since the three royals had developed the plan, they'd managed to keep their activities secret and had grown to call their little group the "council." The multitude of economic and security meetings within the GCC allowed them to meet regularly without drawing unwanted attention as all three men held prominent roles within their respective governments.

Chapter 9

Abu Dhabi, UAE

I left Afghanistan in March of 2010 and moved to Abu Dhabi, United Arab Emirates. I found a job with a locally owned start-up trading company that resold military goods from global defense manufacturers to the UAE Armed Forces.

My job as COO at Falcon Trading turned out to be a huge success. After only a few years, the company was exploding, and I was beginning to make serious money. The CEO was an Emirati. He was a good guy, somewhat eccentric, who rarely interfered with the business. The owner was a billionaire sheik, the brother of the president. He had almost nothing to do with the business directly, but his ownership was still very helpful. Initially, I'd taken a pay cut from my last job in Afghanistan, but within a few years I was able to pay off the bank loan on the subdivision in North Carolina. We even had enough free cashflow to put Stan and Jessica on path to finish the subdivision. My marriage remained a disaster, but the absence of financial peril for the first time in ages was enough to make me content in exile.

It was a Friday afternoon and I'd just finished washing the deck of my boat. I named it the *Sam Houston*, because he was a hero of mine. I was sitting at the table on the flydeck of my recently acquired 2012 Azimuth 64, drinking a Sam Adams and watching the Red Sox game on an iPad. I heard someone walking toward me on the slipway and looked up to see who it was. It took a few seconds before I recognized the visitor as Mike Guthrie. His telltale limp gave him away. I gave him a wave and walked down the stairs to the main deck to meet him at the gate of the aft deck.

"Welcome aboard," I said as we shook hands.

"Long time no see. What've you been doing with yourself? Robbing banks?" Mike said as he gestured toward the boat.

"It's a bit ostentatious, but rents in this town are outrageous, and I figured if I was going to spend crazy money on a place to live, I might as well be able to drive away with it when I'm done."

"You don't need to rationalize it to me. I love it."

"Do you want the nickel tour?" I said.

I took Mike through the glass triple doors into the salon. I showed him the home entertainment center with the pop-up big-screen TV and the three leather couches that surrounded it, then I walked him through the galley to the helm and showed him the controls and the sun deck through the front windshield. Below deck, I gave him a tour of the three staterooms and the engine room housing the twin CAT 18 engines. Then I took him up to the flybridge above the main deck.

"Do you want a beer?" I asked.

"Sure."

I grabbed two bottles of Sam Adams from the refrigerator next to the gas grill. I passed one to Mike and took a seat opposite from him at the table. Intercontinental Marina is a small marina adjacent to the Intercontinental Hotel in Abu Dhabi. Behind where I was docked was a parking lot. On the starboard side of the boat was the Fish Market Restaurant and the Bayside Beach Club and on port side was the hotel. The bow of the yacht was pointed toward the narrow gap in a stone jetty that leads to the Arabian Gulf. I watched as Mike took it all in.

"How's work?" Mike asked.

"It's good. The transition from end user to seller is easier than I thought."

"You're obviously doing well," Mike said.

"I'm getting by. Are you still with the Agency?" I asked.

"I'm working out of Langley. I manage the Middle East Desk at DCO."

"What's DCO?"

"Directorate of Clandestine Operations."

"How's my buddy Tommy doing? I can't remember his last name— the little guy who talked like William F. Buckley."

"He left the Agency and joined the administration. He's a higher-up in the national security advisor's staff."

"Figures. I'm not in trouble again, am I? Falcon follows the rules regarding export restrictions. I'm not sure what I could've done to wind up on your radar."

"What makes you think you're on my radar?"

"Because you don't have a social life and you're here," I said.

"Guilty as charged. I have a proposition for you," Mike said.

I have a terrible poker face and Mike picked up instantly that this wasn't a conversation that I wanted to have.

"Just hear me out. I've been in the UAE for the past two weeks, meeting with members of the government, including the owner of your company, who's also the head of national security, and his brother, the crown prince. The UAE leadership is very concerned about what we Americans call ISIS and what they refer to here as Daesh. The United States, of course, shares the same concern.

"After we withdrew from Iraq in 2012, chaos ensued. Now a third of Iraq is controlled by the Kurds, a third is controlled by Iran through a proxy government, and the other third is run by the ISIS caliphate. The southernmost ISIS-controlled city in Iraq is Fallujah, which is only a day's drive from Abu Dhabi.

"The situation is even worse in Syria. Assad is barely holding on with support from Iran and Russia, and ISIS controls most of the major population areas. The big bosses in UAE are asking the United States for help. Beyond a few special operators, the president has no intention of putting boots on the ground. Although, we have been providing air support against ISIS targets in both countries.

"The GCC countries are asking the United States to step up our efforts to supply weapons, ammunition, and equipment to the anti-ISIS forces. We've been trying, but have had little success in this area, especially in Syria, where many of the recipients of our supplies have been radical elements who aren't much better than the guys we're trying to get rid of. The most effective force has been the Kurds in both Syria and Iraq. We've been reluctant to supply these forces, out of deference to Turkey. But the situation has now become desperate enough that the Agency's been given the green light to supply the Kurds, with the caveat that it must be kept secret."

"Which is why you're telling me all of this," I said.

Mike went on, "We're going to funnel the purchases for the Kurds through UAE. Your UAE employer, Falcon, will buy from the manufacturers and suppliers. The UAE government will provide the end user certificates necessary to export the goods and bring them into the UAE. Once the products arrive at Al Dhafra Air Force Base, Falcon will sell the goods to your personal company, Trident.

"The US government will pay you for the goods and you'll deliver them to the Kurds. This has all been cleared at the top level, both in the United States and in UAE. The export licensing will all be approved with UAE as the recipient. The end user certificates will all be provided by the UAE armed forces GHQ; we'll give you the contact info. This is a project that'll make you a lot of money, and it will also allow you to do something very important for your country."

"I see you've shifted from altruism to greed to motivate me," I said.

"I think you should do it for both reasons. This is a very sensitive operation that requires full deniability. There are very few arms-trading companies in the Middle East managed by people we trust and who can keep a secret. There are only one or two countries in the Middle East who would support us on this project. The UAE is one of them. By a sheer stroke of luck, the one company in the Middle East managed by an American happens to be in the UAE, and that manager happens to be someone I've had good experience working with in the past. So, this is your lucky day."

"Weapons, money, Middle East—what could go wrong?" I said.

"So, are you in?"

"No, I don't think this is something I want to do."

"Why not?"

"I haven't had a lot of great experiences with the US government. I'm one of those guys who peaked as a captain. The political stuff is just not for me. I always end up in trouble. Look what happened in Afghanistan."

"I know about what happened to you when you were at the Pentagon. That was a rough deal. But the private sector can be just as rough. Look what happened to your building company during the mortgage crisis. Afghanistan was a success story; no harm came to you. I looked out for you then. I'll look out for you on this project as well."

"You and I have history. We served together, and I trust you. The rest of the bottom-feeders in Langley and D.C., not so much. I don't want the exposure."

"Give it some thought. This is a golden opportunity, not only to make a difference, but also to make some serious money."

"I'll think about it, but I really don't want to get caught up in more government silliness. I'm pretty happy the way things are at the moment."

Chapter 10

Abu Dhabi, UAE

I was wearing a pair of Bose headphones, kicked back on a ham-mock, with a Kindle to my face, when Steve Tidman slapped me on the leg. I could feel the plane starting to descend. Steve was a loadmaster, and he was signaling me to prepare for landing. I got out of the ham-mock, unclipped the carabiners that connected it to opposite sides of the C-130J Hercules, moved over to the nylon cargo seats lining the walls and buckled up.

When we first started running supplies to the Peshmerga in North-ern Iraq, we used chartered cargo planes. The charters had proven unreliable and expensive, and we also had issues with operational security and pilferage. Nine months ago, I bit the bullet and invested in two C-130 Hercules cargo planes. The Hercs were perfect for our needs. They have a range of twenty-one hundred miles and can land on a three thou-sand-foot dirt airstrip with a forty-two-thousand-pound payload. The Trident mini fleet stayed busy shuttling cargo from Abu Dhabi to North-ern Iraq and sometimes picking up deliveries in Europe and Asia. Mike helped out, by arranging for the UAE government to provide Trident with a dedicated hangar and landing rights at Al Dhafra Air Force Base in Abu Dhabi.

I felt the plane touch the runway. It took another fifteen minutes before the plane finished taxiing. The tail ramp opened, and I was greeted by bright sunshine and a wave of hundred-degree heat. Before exiting, I went forward and thanked the two pilots, Frank Belonis and Jack Carpenter. Both have thousands of flying hours with the four-engine turbo prop and years of experience landing in dangerous places with the Air Force Special Operations Command. Steve Tidman was also former AFSOC. The fourth crew member on this aircraft was David Bell. Dave is a retired green beret. Having someone on board with regional language skills and the ability to provide security had proven to be useful on the Iraqi leg of some of our deliveries. The second aircraft crew is a mirror image of the first.

I looked inside the hangar and could see the other crew moving air pallets that were part of the next shipment. I walked into the hangar to have a closer look. The boxes stacked on the aluminum pallets were tied down with green nylon webbing. On the boxes were company markings that read "Raytheon" and the words "Javelin" and nomenclature of either the missiles or the control launch units.

We didn't have any say over what we delivered. The CIA told me what to buy, and I'd go into the market in my role as Falcon COO and negotiate the purchase. Most items required export licenses, which meant I had to provide the manufacturer an end user certificate signed by the UAE government. Technically, it was the UAE who was importing the goods, but once they arrived in UAE, they were transferred to Trident and delivered to the Peshmerga in Iraq.

After I delivered the goods, I submitted an invoice to a contract office that managed black programs at the Department of Defense and got reimbursed. I then paid Falcon, who in turn paid the suppliers. The money was as originally advertised, and up until recently the risks had been manageable.

I slid into my Ford Explorer and was pulling out of my parking space next to our hangar when the phone rang. It was Mike Guthrie and I answered it on the Bluetooth.

"Mike, thanks for getting back to me," I said.

"I tried earlier, but your phone was off."

"I just landed. I was in Iraq."

"Everything okay on your end?"

"The trip was fine. I wanted to talk to you about these Javelins."

"We had this discussion six months ago, when the order began. What's left to discuss?"

"I wanted to know if the situation has changed."

"No change, continue as directed."

"Do the big bosses still want to go through with it now that the operation has been leaked to the press?"

"The administration were the ones who leaked it, Pat."

"Why would they do that?" I asked.

"The press reports on the support to the Syrian rebels fighting Assad and ISIS have been horrible, embarrassing even. DoD spent half a billion dollars training and equipping a battalion-sized force of supposed Syrian resistance fighters, and the moment they were finished, all but thirteen disappeared. The arming of Syrian opposition groups has been a total failure. The only bright light has been the successes of the Peshmerga, and the administration wanted the word out that they had a hand in it. They needed to counter the bad press."

"Is this program still classified?" I asked.

"Yes. Your name and Trident's role are being protected."

"That's what has me worried. I'd appreciate it if you could keep me out of trouble with the government. The legal term for our violation of the export laws is called diversion. Breaking export laws is a big deal. It's a ten-year felony last time I checked."

"You're covered."

"That's good to know, because when the Peshmerga start using Javelins to bust Leopard tanks owned by Turkey, our supposed NATO ally, I'd prefer to stay out of the news."

I drove into the underground parking lot of the Falcon Office. We're located on the ninth floor of an office tower in the Abu Dhabi Exhibition Center (ADNEC) complex. Falcon is a small company with only twenty-five employees. I passed through the biometric hand scanner and entered the office. My office was next to the CEO's, who had the corner. Ahmed Al Junaibi, the Falcon CEO, only came to work two or three days a week, and I was hoping to catch him today. It was still morning, and the office was empty except the admin team. The sales staff was out with their customers, who were the various organizations within the UAE armed forces. The Falcon employees were a diverse group. About a third were Emirati, and another third were Arabs from Palestine, Jordan, Lebanon and Egypt. The support staff were from Asia, mostly India, the Philippines and Pakistan.

I checked the CEO's office, but he wasn't in, so I continued to my own office, which had an excellent view of the Arabian Gulf. No sooner had I parked myself at my desk than a stream of admin personnel came in for signatures. Proposals, payments, invoices and contracts. The morning was all paperwork with admin, and the afternoon was all deal talk with the sales staff. I'd already put in ten hours with the trip to Iraq and back, and by the time I was finished at Falcon, it'd been an eighteen-hour day and I was beat.

On my way to the marina, I called ahead to my crew to get dinner going. I'd skipped lunch and was starving. My crew consisted of two thirty-something Filipinas. Jenny Lyn, my first mate, was a terminally pleasant, very pretty Filipino woman with a contagious smile that never seemed to go away. When I hired Jenny Lyn, she had no nautical experience, but she was a quick study. I sent her to a boat handling course and after only a short while, she'd become an expert at the helm. She also managed the cooking and cleaning.

I hired Mia because she was Jenny Lyn's friend and she'd lost her job. Mia was a mechanical engineer who used to work for the National Drilling Company before getting laid off when oil prices crashed. Mia kept the twin Cummins engines and generator operational, along with the rest of the electromechanical systems on the yacht. Like Jenny Lyn, Mia was pleasant company. They both had rooms next door at the Intercontinental, as did I, but they seemed to spend every waking hour on the boat. I hadn't started off with a middle-age fantasy of a plan to hire two goddesses for my boat crew, it just turned out that way. I initially hired Jenny Lyn to clean part-time, and then she managed to insinuate herself into everything until she became indispensable and wound up working full-time as a first mate. When her friend Mia lost her job, I was having generator problems. Her interview was a repair job that she'd passed with flying colors.

Both ladies were working in the galley when I entered the salon.

"How was your day?" they asked.

"Good, what are you cooking, that smells great."

"It's a pork stir fry," said Jenny Lyn.

Mia handed me a cold beer on my way downstairs to shower.

Chapter 10

Mosul, Iraq

The day-to-day grind at Falcon Trading could be a draining experience. The Arab workforce at Falcon is capable and outwardly very convivial, but below the surface, there's a layer of hostility that can rise to the surface at the slightest provocation. Drawn to conspiracy theories and intrigue as the workers are, these provocations occur far more than I wished they did. As much as I respect what the team does, sometimes dealing with their never-ending petty grievances can be taxing. One of the reasons I strap-hang on the delivery plane to Iraq at least once a week is because I find the upbeat teamwork and comradery of the ex-military flight crews refreshing. There's something about the spirit and can-do attitude of the American service member that I find uplifting.

On this day, we're delivering Ukrainian 12.7mm machine guns, tripods and ammunition. The loadmaster on this crew is Bill Sachse, and the green beret and local liaison is Dmitri Migos. The two pilots are Joe Ferguson and Joe Kilpatrick.

We landed at the International Airport in Mosul at three in the morning, and Migos and Sachse were offloading the pallets with the remote-control forklift when I got a phone call.

UAE is part of the coalition providing air support and special forces against ISIS. The unit providing the special forces are from the UAE's Special Operations Command. Jimmy Klinghofer, a guy I'd served with in the Army, was the senior advisor to the SOC commander, Brigadier Khalid. Through Jimmy, and also because Falcon did some business with SOC, I'd come to know the commander fairly well. It was Brigadier Khalid who was calling.

We went through the traditional Arab greeting, and then Khalid got to the point.

"My chain of command has informed me you're in Iraq and that you work closely with the allies. We have two operators who broke contact with their patrol last night and missed extraction. The closest forces available to help are the Peshmerga. Can you make request on my behalf to the local commander for assistance?"

"Of course. Are you in contact with the lost element? Can you give me their location?"

I asked Migos to help, and he managed to get us a ride to the nearest Peshmerga commander, a major named Ali. Before leaving the airfield, I tossed two duffle bags into the back of the SUV that was taking us to the headquarters.

We managed to reach the two Emirati commandos by cell. This is where Migos's language skills were invaluable. He was able to speak Kurmanji to the Kurds and Arabic to the Emiratis. Eventually, he was able to work out a linkup point and procedure with the two stranded operators. The commander offered us a detachment of ten soldiers and four M1151 armored HMMWVs, each with a .50-caliber gun mounted on top in an armored cupola for the task.

"Migos, I know you didn't sign up for a trigger-pulling job when you joined up, but I could really use your help with this."

"I've got your back," he said while he opened up the first of the go-bags.

I kitted out the go-bags myself. I made them in case a plane ever got grounded in a hostile situation and the crew needed to defend themselves. Each bag contained the equipment needed for a single operator—plate carriers, helmets, eyepro, lights and strobes. A tactical comms package, ammunition, weapons, first-aid kit, night vision, food and water, the whole works. For good measure, I even included grenades and an M72 LAW rocket.

We drove away from the airport, out into the desert toward the village where the SOC troops were hunkering down. I was in the back seat of the lead HMMWV with Migos next to me, tracking our route with a handheld GPS. We were on a dirt road still two miles from the village when we came under fire. Green tracers from a machine gun streaked over our vehicle. Seconds later, the crackle of gunfire reached my ears. Our HMMWV driver swerved off the trail and parked in defilade behind a sand dune. The trailing HMMWVs found cover the same way.

"Tell them to return fire," I said to Migos.

"This is as far as they go," Migos said after relaying my message on the radio to the convoy commander who was in the vehicle behind us.

"You stay with them, if the driver tries to take off with this vehicle shoot him. I'm going to the linkup point on foot. Stay up on the radio."

"Wilco, boss."

I grabbed my M4 out of the holding rack and snapped the PVS-31 night vision goggles down in place in front of my eyes. The terrain between my location and the machine gunner was open desert, with small sand dunes just high enough to mask a HMMWV. I used a small wadi to move laterally away from our line of HMMWVs and then made my move toward the machine gunner. I was banking that the man was focused on the vehicles and didn't have night vision. It was a half moon and although the visibility was good enough to spot a column of vehicles on a trail with the naked eye, I didn't think it would be good enough to see a lone man until he got within a few hundred yards. My real concern was that the machine gunner was part of a larger defending force.

It took me about thirty minutes of weaving between sand dunes using the low ground to get within two hundred yards of the first technical vehicle. As I'd feared, the vehicle wasn't alone. The ISIS terrorists had a line of four pickup trucks with machine guns mounted on the back—in defilade behind sand dunes oriented toward the road leading to the village. Rising up above the dunes were the 12.7mm machine guns and the top half of a lone ISIS fighter standing behind each gun.

Behind the ISIS blocking position, I could see the lights of the small village. The linkup point was on the opposite side of the village roughly fifteen hundred yards from where I stood. I went wide to my left to get to the flank and rear of the first pickup truck. I could see the back of the machine gunner clearly through my night vision as I walked forward in a crouch with my carbine in the ready position.

As I approached, I triggered my weapon laser, and an infrared dot appeared on the gunner's back. I crept forward and managed to get within twenty yards before the gunner turned. I was close enough to see the man was wearing body armor, so I raised the laser dot up to his face and pulled the trigger twice, then I pivoted and shot the machine gunner on the technical that was fifty yards to my left.

Turning my attention back to the first pickup, I shot the driver through the rear window and then sprinted toward the second pickup. I could see the driver climbing onto the back to man the machine gun, and I dropped him with two shots to the chest. When I got to the tailgate of the second pickup, the third and fourth technical came into view. Both machine guns were turning in my direction.

I dropped flat onto my stomach and shot the third machine gunner from the prone, then I rolled to my right, behind the second technical vehicle, just as the area I'd fired from was torn up by machine-gun fire. I high crawled on my elbows across the desert sand towards the third technical. I was using the third pickup truck to screen me from the fourth until my cover suddenly disappeared when the third vehicle backed up. I shot the escaping driver through the windshield and rolled into a shallow depression to my right. Fortunately for me the fourth vehicle was also on the move. The fourth machine gunner was firing erratically, tracers were spraying everywhere as the gunner tried to find his mark while bouncing around in a pickup that was backing up over uneven ground. I triggered my PEQ laser and shot the gunner with two quick rounds at a range of seventy-five yards. Then I emptied the rest of my magazine at the driver as he continued to back away. I was changing magazines when the pickup careened off the trail and came to a halt.

I went back to pick up number two and jumped into the empty cab. I started it up and followed the road to the village. I stopped two hundred yards from the village and contacted Migos to notify the SOC team that I was in a technical, heading into the village. They told him to bypass the village, to drive around it clockwise. They would meet me at the opposite end at the twelve o'clock. When I got within five hundred yards, I turned on my IR strobe. The team responded with two flashes and that was my signal to move forward.

I pulled to a stop, and both guys jumped in the back. I contacted Migos on my comms and told him I was heading back and to warn the Peshmerga not to shoot. It only took fifteen minutes to race back to the HMMWVs, and transload into the Peshmerga vehicles for the trip back to the airfield.

When we returned, Sachse and the pilots had already finished off-loading and the plane was ready to go. Migos called Major Ali to thank him for his help and I notified Brigadier Khalid we were bringing his guys back to UAE. Brigadier Khalid was immensely grateful.

I didn't give the incident in Mosul any thought until two weeks later. It was a Friday evening, and I was on my usual perch on the fly-bridge of the *Sam Houston*. It was after eight o'clock, with a warm spring breeze coming in off the shore. I was sitting on the couch next to Jenny Lyn with my feet up and a glass of Macallan 18 in my right hand. The boat's sound system was playing James Taylor's "Carolina on My Mind."

"What are we going to do about dinner?" I asked.

"I can cook something if you want," Jenny Lyn replied.

"No, let's go out. Ask Mia where she wants to go." Jenny Lyn and Mia loved to dance, and I tried to take them out one night each week. The options in Abu Dhabi broke down into three general categories: preten-tious, smoke-filled Arab clubs with celebrity deejays and escalating levels of VIP tables, each more ostentatious and outrageously expensive than the last; British bars with live bands and overdressed, highly intoxicated mem-bers of the commonwealth; and Filipino dive bars with live bands, greasy food, cheap alcohol, and fun-loving Pinoys. In the proper mood, I liked them all. Jenny Lyn headed downstairs to consult with Mia.

I watched as a black SUV pulled up to the entrance of the marina and a lone man emerged from the passenger door. Even in the dwindling light, I recognized the passenger immediately.

"Permission to board, Captain."

"Tabless bitch, recite the third stanza, or I'll keelhaul you."

"Never shall I fail my comrades. I will always keep myself mentally alert, physically strong, and morally straight, and I will shoulder more than my share of the task, whatever it may be, one hundred percent and then some." Mike walked up the stairs to the flydeck, and I shook his hand.

"Impressive that you can still remember all that. It's a miracle that so many years of practicing the dark arts hasn't erased such thoughts. Have a seat. Can I get you a drink?"

"Whatever you're having is fine, thanks," Mike replied. I got up and poured a healthy scotch for Mike and took the seat next to him over-looking the water.

Jenny Lyn popped her head up the stairs and said hello to Mike. "Mia wants to go Yacht Club. She wants to eat sushi."

"Sounds good. Can you call and get us a table for ten, and can you give Mike and me a moment?" I said.

"Okay," said Jenny Lyn as she disappeared.

"Wanna join us for dinner?" I asked.

Mike shook his head. "I can't. I have to fly back to the United States tonight."

"I'm your last meeting. What should I make of that?"

"Nothing bad, I can tell you that much. I spent most of the afternoon with the UAE government, including the crown prince and his military aide. Most of the time was dedicated to the fight against our common foe. We spent some time discussing your operation. That mission you pulled off rescuing those two SOC operators made an impression. You have friends in high places with this government."

I took a sip of scotch. "That was never my goal. The SOC commander asked for my help, and I couldn't refuse."

Mike put his drink down. "What surprised me about the operation was how ready you were. You went from civilian cargo hauler to commando in a split second. How is that?"

"I work with the best. Each C-130 is crewed by two retired AFSOC pilots and a retired AFSOC loadmaster. I have one former Green Beanie on each aircraft with language skills to help with the locals and troubleshoot problems on the ground. Each plane is equipped with a full complement of electronic and nonelectronic countermeasures. I even have go-bags for crew members to use during emergencies. When the call came in, the kit was available, and I made use of it."

"We had a Predator over the area. The footage of that mission circulated around. When the deputy director of operations saw it, he went ballistic and ordered a full review. From our count, you went head-on against eight ISIS fighters. You took the riskiest course of action, and that raised some eyebrows. Why didn't you attack with the armored HMMWVs?"

I wasn't liking the direction the conversation was taking. "Migos had to keep the Peshmerga from running away at gunpoint. A mounted attack wasn't a possibility. It wasn't that big of a risk. The bad guys didn't even have night vision. What I can't understand is why the government doesn't take a couple thousand of our best and just wipe them off the face of the earth. They don't appear to be very well trained."

That last comment got a grin out of Mike.

I went on, "I'm serious. You see the stories about what they do to those Yazidi girls. It's all so very unnecessary. Those guys have no skills."

"What you're saying makes sense. It really does. But let me tell you what the shrinks at Langley who the DDO called into the review had to say about it. They looked at your file, including psych evals from all the way back to when you were a junior officer—the selection psych eval for the regiment and later for the unit. Then they reviewed the tape, which covered everything from your call with the SOC commander until you returned to Abu Dhabi. They didn't report anything particularly damning, but they made some observations.

"You have a tendency toward risky behavior, and it's escalating. They think you take risks physically and financially that are well outside of the normal range even for a field agent, which is something you're not. You're an asset and not a field agent, but you should understand the risk thresholds for an agent are extremely high. Last year you gambled all of your cash resources speculating on oil futures.

"Second, you appear to be putting all your affairs in order. You've transferred most of your assets to the Trident Trust, which belongs to your kids, and to the Trident Foundation, which is apparently some kind of a charity. On the operational side, you make weekly jaunts to Iraq, even though your presence isn't required.

"Bottom line, Pat, the Langley shrinks think there's a distinct possibility that you're looking for ways to punch your ticket, that's why I was sent here to talk to you."

I was speechless. We both spent the next minute nursing our drinks until Mike broke the silence.

"You're a friend, Pat. I know your Army career, marriage, and business didn't turn out the way you planned. We have a specialist who'll be coming out next week to talk to you about things. I'm here in person because I wanted to make sure you agree to meet with her."

"This is the most ridiculous thing I've ever heard. You guys should stick to what you know and stay away from psychology."

"It's a serious subject, and I need you to play along even if you think it's unnecessary."

"I knew you guys kept tabs on me, but I had no idea of the extent. Since you know so much, you must be aware that I made a killing on that oil deal.

"As to your second accusation of getting my affairs in order, that's just responsible financial planning. Managing money is a full-time job, and it's not something that I have any interest or expertise in doing. The Trident Trust and the Trident Foundation portfolios are handled by bankers in Manhattan, so I can run Falcon and Trident Corp. That's a division of labor, not a suicide note.

"As far as the operational stuff goes, I need to set the example for the crews, and sometimes I like to take a break from the office work at Falcon."

"You make some good points. Unfortunately, it was the deputy director who ordered the psych review, and I don't have the authority to call it off. You're an important asset, and you've been in play a long time. You need to respect that periodically, we need to look under the hood and check the fluid levels on our investment. Dr. Schneeberger is going to arrive in Abu Dhabi early next week. I want you to meet with her as much and as long as she needs."

I threw my hands up in defeat and then changed the subject. "Are you sure you don't want to stick around, Mike? After a few drinks, Mia can be very provocative. Who knows? You two may hit it off."

"What's with you and Jenny Lyn anyway? The deputy director ordered you to be shrinked because of the UAV footage, but I was going to order it based on your breaking the rule of the three Fs."

"Okay, I'll bite. What's the rule of the three Fs?" I asked.

"If it floats, flies, or fornicates, you rent. You never buy. I'm looking at you with a yacht, a fleet of cargo planes, and now a harem. It's worrisome. Rules exist for a reason." At that, we both laughed.

I woke the next morning at six after my usual four hours of sleep. I turned on the TV and caught the last three innings of the Red Sox game, something only made possible by the time-zone difference. I walked across the parking lot to the Intercontinental Hotel gym. I always enjoy my morning routine at the gym. Today was a chest and shoulder day. After ninety minutes it was off to my hotel room for a shower.

I selected a navy-blue suit and a white oxford shirt, gold cuff links, a solid red Kiton cashmere-silk tie and a stupidly expensive watch. I hate wearing suits and jewelry, but sometimes I have to play a role. UAE is the land of the superficial. The quality of a man's clothes, watch and car mean far more than they should. At precisely eight o'clock, I stepped out of the main entrance of the Intercontinental and into the back of a black Mercedes 550 sedan and began the seventy-five-minute trip to Dubai.

I had a breakfast meeting with Andre and Nizie. Most of the ammunition and small arms we supply is from Cold War stocks in Eastern Europe. Despite the huge quality advantage held by NATO weapons, the AK-47 rifle and PKM are staples in the Middle East and Africa. Over the past year, Trident has delivered tens of thousands of rifles and machine guns and millions of rounds of small-arms ammunition. Ammo consumption was huge, primarily because the preferred rifle marksmanship technique employed by our customers was spray and pray. Sometimes I think it's a waste to even mount sights onto the weapons.

Andre and Nizie were my primary Eastern European arms connection. Andre Yuripov is a Russian Ukrainian who represented the Ukrainian export company that had the authority to distribute most Ukrainian defense products.

When the Soviet Union broke up, portions of their defense industry were unevenly distributed across the former Warsaw Pact countries. Many of the major defense companies, like Anatov and Sukhoi, were in Ukraine, which made them an excellent source. I was usually hesitant to buy from the Russians or Belarussians because with Trident's activities in Syria and Iraq, it didn't make sense to give the Putin government a veto over every sale. The remainder of the Eastern European manufacturers were under the European Union, which prohibited the sale of defense goods heading to the war zone. The Ukrainian government was in chaos, and the lack of a controlling central government allowed the factories and export agencies the power to sell to anyone they wished.

Nizie is a Palestinian. He has a home in Jordan and another in Gibraltar. Nizie is what I like to refer to as an IMM, an international man of mystery. I'd guess Nizie's age to be in the early seventies. He's of medium height and build, with white hair and a mustache. He's always smiling, and he has alert eyes and a glad-handing demeanor. He likes to dress in Savile Row suits and lots of gold. Nizie is a professional middleman who specializes in connecting buyers with sellers. He works off a commission paid by the seller, which is typically below five percent, although he's not above getting a cut from the buyer when he can.

While he's rumored to be on the US no-fly list for selling weapons to Hamas, Nizie is infamous for being the guy who brokered the sale of the Tetra IED jamming devices to Saudi Arabia. The Tetra deal is a frequently told story in the industry. It's been told so much, it's become something of a fable, with a lesson for newcomers to the business in the region.

In 2005, the Saudis purchased twenty-five hundred Tetra vehicle IED jammers for the Saudi national guard. IED jammers are often mounted on vehicles and are used to block the radio signal enemy forces use to detonate roadside improvised explosive devices. Months after the delivery and final payment, an employee from a US defense firm with the contract to mount and install the devices became curious and took apart one of the units. What the contractor discovered was that the Saudi government had been swindled and had spent $155 million on vehicle-mounted golf ball finders. Everyone involved within the Saudi government went into cover-up mode, and the US contractor who'd discovered the problem was immediately fired. The devices were then buried in the desert, and every official record of the sale was destroyed.

The lesson of the story is that, in the Middle East, mistakes are never fixed. They're erased, along with every person connected to them. If you have a contract to install devices onto trucks, then install them, don't test them. And whatever you do, don't ever tell a senior person in an Arab government that he's made a mistake.

I like to schedule meetings with Andre and Nizie in the morning. Both are heavy drinkers, and I've always thought meeting in the morning gave me an advantage. Nizie is a natural storyteller. He's had encounters with many of the most famous people in the region, and his tales are wildly entertaining. Andre, on the other hand, is a typical former Soviet military officer. Zero personality, zero sense of humor, and the social graces of a silverback gorilla. What I've always liked about Andre is that he's a straight arrow. In a business filled with cheats and con men like Nizie, Andre is the rare straight shooter. Although a knuckle-dragging thug, Andre's loyal and reliable. Nizie, who by all appearances is a genteel, sophisticated man of culture and good breeding, has the morals of an alley cat.

I exited the Mercedes and entered the lobby of the Grosvenor Hotel in the marina area of Dubai. The Grosvenor is a forty-four-story five-star hotel that caters to the Russian population. I went to the thirty-seventh floor and knocked on the door to Andre's suite. After the perfunctory greetings, we sat down to breakfast in the living room.

After we finished eating, I turned the conversation to business.

"Do you have any updates on when the Mi-17s will be ready for inspection?" For the past three months, Andre had been working on the procurement of eight Mi-17V-5 helicopters. The HIP is a Russian twin-engine medium-transport aircraft. I'd been given instructions to purchase eight aircraft, with three to be fitted as gun ships and five as transports. The seventeen-million-dollar helicopters were to be the start of the Peshmerga Air Force.

"The aircraft are in Bulgaria, and they're ready now. I've already had one of my guys look at them. I'm sure you'll be happy," Andre said.

"Who's the seller?" I asked.

"They belong to the Bulgarian government," replied Andre.

"What about the guarantees?"

"There are none. This is a cash-and-carry deal. You'll conduct an onsite acceptance test in Bulgaria and pay one hundred percent. We'll then ship the aircraft and spare parts in two loads on an Anatov 124 that we've leased to a location of your choosing, which I assume will be in the UAE."

"Does the hundred-and-thirty-six-million-dollar price tag include shipping?" I asked.

"Yes, it does."

"Okay, the inspection team will be in Sofia on Tuesday. They're going to need two weeks to complete their work. Please coordinate the local transportation and access to the aircraft. I'll have a contract sent from the Falcon main office to you next week. It will be a conditional contract, based on passing the inspection, but it should be enough for you to take care of the export licensing and shipping," I said.

After the business was finished, we returned to small talk. While gazing out at the magnificent view of the Palm Jumeirah, I said, "There's one more matter we need to discuss. Last month, one of our competitors submitted a proposal to GHQ DGP. It was a proposal for eight Mi-17s.

I don't mind telling you that I'm confused by this action. The requirement was given only to us by the UAE government. This sale isn't going through GHQ. It's part of a sensitive foreign aid package that's been routed through a different part of the UAE government. You know this, because I've told you this before.

"I want to know who leaked it. Because there's no one from GHQ who could've given the requirement to our competition. Outside of the UAE national leadership, only three people even know about this: me, you, and Nizie. I haven't even told anyone else in Falcon about this project," I said to Andre.

I paused for a minute to let the facts sink in before going on. "In the past year, I've given you guys almost two hundred million dollars in business. This deal is another hundred and thirty-five million. I don't understand why you would do this. Why would you try to go around Falcon on this sale?"

Before Andre could respond, Nizie chimed in with the expected obfuscation of how others could have found out about the deal. He wasn't my audience and so I tuned Nizie out and focused instead on the spectacular view. Tomorrow, I was planning to take the boat out fishing. As I looked out at the Palm Jumeirah, I could see some watercraft, which reminded me of how much I loved being on the water, away from the sordid complications of this business.

I stood to leave, and Andre and Nizie joined me. As we walked to the door, Andre grabbed me by the shoulder. "I'll take care of this," he said.

I looked over at Nizie, and behind the fake smile, I could see the tension in his eyes and sweat forming on his upper lip. I looked to Andre and said, "I wouldn't have finalized the sale for the helicopters if I had any doubt that you were going to plug the leak." Andre was former Spetsnaz; nobody would ever accuse him of being a great thinker. Like me, he was a fighter. Andre was a solid guy, both physically and in terms of character. He was in his early forties, with classic Slavic features and arms as thick as my legs. When I looked at him, I could see the steely resolve of a man betrayed.

Nizie, of course, thought he could talk his way out of anything, so he kept talking. He kept up the charade, but as we neared the door, there was little doubt in my mind that Andre was going to question and possibly kill Nizie. I could see it in Andre's body language that he was distancing himself from his partner. It was sad. Nizie was an affable fellow, but his greed and propensity to talk were serious problems, and while this was a manageable situation, the next time might not be. There are no second chances in this business. Nizie had to go.

I said my goodbyes to both Andre and Nizie and left the hotel room. I called my driver on the elevator down, and he was waiting for me as I exited the lobby. My next stop was the Shangri-La Hotel on Sheik Zayed Road in Dubai's financial district. The meeting with Andre and Nizie had gone as expected. Nizie was a gifted liar, and if for some reason he could convince Andre to remain partners with him, I'd cancel the helicopter deal and never again work with either of them. The most likely scenario was that Andre would force Nizie to retire and disappear; the worst-case scenario was that Andre would bury Nizie in the desert. I hoped that wouldn't happen, but I couldn't exclude it as a possibility. The proposal submitted by Falcon's competitor was a serious security concern. Several of the junior staff members within DGP were on the payroll of Falcon's competitors. If any of our competitors were to see the proposal, then before long, there would be local UAE companies asking questions of the UAE armed forces senior leadership, attempting to compete for a contract on a secret CIA – UAE project.

I arrived at the Shangri-La and made my way through the lobby to the elevators in the back. In any other city in the world, the Shangri-La would stand out, but among the many luxury hotels in Dubai, it was fairly average. I took the elevator to the club lounge on the forty-sixth floor. It was late morning and the breakfast buffet was still set up. In the far corner, I spotted my next appointment. Shu Xue Wong, the Middle East vice president of business development for CASIC.

China Aerospace Science and Industry Corporation (CASIC) is the largest Chinese aerospace firm. Like many Chinese defense firms, it's owned by the military, and most of the senior employees are military officers. Susu, as she liked to be called, is an extraordinary woman. She's a sales executive for CASIC, a colonel in the People's Liberation Army, and—I'm pretty sure—an agent with Chinese Intelligence. She speaks English and Arabic fluently, along with some other languages. Susu's looks are a distraction. She has the face of an angel and a black mane of hair that goes down to her waist. Well into middle age, Susu could still make the best of men betray their country. I was first introduced to Susu through our chairman at Falcon. A former deputy chief of staff of the UAE armed forces, like most men, our chairman is putty in Susu's hands.

Susu stood as I entered the club lounge and made a beeline to meet me. She met me halfway and gave me a warm hug, then took my arm and walked me to her table next to the window overlooking the city and the Arabian Gulf. The waitress poured me a hot cup of ginger tea.

"So, tell me, Pat—what have you been up to? You are so busy. I never see you anymore."

"Global domination is a very demanding job. I have so little time to report my activities directly."

The amount of intelligence collected on my activities, including what I was getting from Mike, was rapidly becoming a sore spot. The Emiratis, Russians, Chinese and Israelis all kept tabs on me. It was beginning to make me paranoid. Most frustrating were the hacks. I hired a service that could sometimes trace them, and they usually led back to China. The United States was probably doing the same, but my tech firm of former MI6 hadn't caught them yet.

I have pretty good habits, but unless you live in a SCIF it's impossible to keep state actors from being able to read your email and electronic messages. My biggest problem with cybersecurity is my boat crew. The Filipinas are constantly on their smartphones, downloading apps, videos, and coupon offers. All the hackers have to do is send a phishing message offering a free lunch, and the next thing you know, my crew's phones are turned into microphones and cameras.

It's so bad, I now avoid doing business around the girls' devices. Let the government intel stiffs spend hours reviewing video of Jenny Lyn and Mia chasing Pokémon characters around the marina with their iPhones; it serves them right. The paranoia has me buying bug finders and stashing weapons. It's not healthy.

"You know I'm always interested in how I can help you," said Susu.

"I appreciate that. I'm an open book to you. By the way, if your tech support guys pass on to you any of the video from my boat crew's latest data breach, I just want to explain. I just got back from the pool, and the water was very cold."

Susu giggled. "I have not had the pleasure of viewing anything of the sort."

We sat quietly for a minute, looking out though the panoramic window. Through the window reflection, I could see that the staff was closing the breakfast buffet, and no other guests were in the club lounge.

"I have several requirements that I'm hoping you'll be able to support. The end user for all will be the UAE armed forces, but they'll be purchased by Falcon and redirected to the Peshmerga. That's information I don't usually share, but I think you'll need to know it to get approval."

"What do you have on your shopping list?" asked Susu.

"We're looking for three air-defense surface-to-air missile systems, one medium-range LY-80 missile system, and two short-range FM-90 missile systems. With each system, we want eighteen missile vehicles with the accompanying radar and command-and-control vehicles. I also need twelve medium-range surface-to-surface missile systems capable of firing the A-100 with two fire-direction vehicles. For both the surface-to-air and surface-to-surface systems, we'll require the support vehicles, training, a twelve-month stockpile of munitions and spare parts," I said.

"That's a big ask. I'll need to take this back to headquarters before I can give you an answer. Air-defense systems in that part of the world are politically sensitive."

"I understand, but if we don't buy this equipment from you, we'll buy it from somewhere else. Plus, maybe having the systems along the northern border with Turkey might be a deterrent that'll keep that powder keg from exploding."

"This is very advanced equipment. Do you think the Peshmerga can operate and maintain it?"

I smiled. "No, we don't think so. These are standoff systems that we can run using expat technicians. We think the situation is stable enough that we can utilize contractors for these tasks.

"The reason we need the air-defense systems is to protect a couple of key airfields that will house a couple of small aviation units we're building. These are just small rotary-wing units that will enable the Peshmerga to pursue some of the ISIS high-value targets and conduct night raids. We need the surface-to-surface missiles for suppressing enemy air defense missions as well as lethal fires. This is a high priority. I need an answer in the next week as to whether or not you can support. I'll also need a delivery timeline of six months or less."

"Okay, I'll do my best," said Susu.

"Thanks. I look forward to hearing from you," I said. I looked at my watch and noticed the meeting had lasted ninety minutes.

"Can you stay for lunch?"

"Not today. I have another meeting."

"You're a rich man, you have good health, and you work every day and most nights. This is the weekend, and you're working. Why don't you slow down and enjoy?"

"I'll tell you what. If you agree to run away with me, I will. We can buy an island in Thailand, drink mai tais on the beach, and enjoy our golden years."

When Susu laughed, her eyes crinkled, her cheeks dimpled, and her smile dazzled.

"It's a standing offer. It's time for both of us to start thinking of an exit plan from this work," I said.

We both stood up. I gave Susu a long hug. Still feeling the glow of effervescence that radiated seductively from the most beautiful woman I'd ever met, I headed through the club doors to the elevator.

My next meeting was at the JW Marriott Marquis, just a few miles down the road back toward Abu Dhabi. The Marquis, at seventy-six stories, is the tallest hotel in the world. Marriott is headquartered in Maryland, so it's the hotel of choice for many of the Beltway bandits who are slaves to the Marriott loyalty plan. While being driven to the hotel, I texted that I'd be arriving in five minutes.

As the valet opened the door of the car, I spotted Jim Granger and Robert Hurd. Both Jim and Bob work for Fleer Corporation. Jim's a vice president of operations and Bob is the director of international sales. Normally, I would've driven my Explorer and attended the day's meetings with Andre and Susu in blue jeans. But even though I'd never met either Jim or Bob in person, I knew both were retired senior military officers from the old school and would expect me to be wearing a suit.

I also noticed Ambassador Tobin exiting the lobby doors to join the greetings and introductions. Ambassador Tobin was a retired State Department foreign service officer. His last posting before retiring had been as the US ambassador to the UAE. Tobin was part of the Cahill Group, a company started by former US senator and former secretary of defense

Cahill to assist US-based defense companies with international sales. The big sell of the Cahill Group is the ability to expedite export licenses on sensitive US defense systems to foreign governments. Ambassador Tobin and the Cahill Group are on retainer from the Fleer Group as consultants. It was in that role that the ambassador had introduced Fleer to me. As with so many introductions, I had filed the information away should a need arise, and sure enough, less than three months later, a requirement had come up that I thought the Fleer Group would be perfect for.

After the greetings and introductions, the four of us went into the lobby and rode the elevator to the mezzanine, where a small conference room was reserved. Once we sat down, the group spent a few minutes going through the time-honored tradition of "do you know", identifying mutual relationships with other military officers.

Both Jim and Bob were retired flag officers. Jim is a retired Army major general, and Bob is a retired Navy rear admiral. Ambassador Tobin sent me a biography on both officers. Jim has steel gray hair, cut military short, a strong face, and piercing blue eyes. He's average height with a slim build. On the lapel of his blue pinstripe suit jacket, Jim wore a miniature combat infantryman's badge, a Ranger tab, and a master parachutist badge. On the ring finger of his right hand, he wore a West Point ring. Jim was a graduate of the class of '67, a group that had been fated to have the highest casualty rate of any class ever to graduate from USMA.

Bob was six-four and weighed about 275 pounds. He was bald, with heavy features, brown eyes, and a fleshy, jovial face. Bob had been an all-American tight end at Annapolis and graduated in 1981. Following graduation, Bob had gone to Navy Nuclear School and become a submarine officer.

The four of us sat around the conference table making small talk for the next few minutes. Bob then turned on a laptop and projector and launched into a twenty-minute briefing on Fleer. After the briefing, I asked the others what they knew about Falcon. I then took a few minutes to tell my story and the story of the company. At the end, I opened a leather binder and removed some documents. I handed each of the men at the table a nondisclosure agreement. "Before I can go on, I'm required to have you sign this NDA. You'll notice that it's a US Department of Defense NDA and not from Falcon. You each have two copies already signed by DoD legal, so all I need from you is a countersignature. You keep one copy, and I'll take the other. This NDA covers only a single project, one that we're calling Monument Men. Please take the time to read it and then sign. If you choose not to sign, I'm afraid this meeting will come to an end." Once all three had signed the documents, they passed one original to me.

"Did any of you guys see the movie *Monument Men*? It was set in the closing days of World War Two. There was a group of American art experts who were sent out to the battlefield to recover as much of the artwork stolen by the Nazis as possible. The government contract I've received, and on which I'm seeking to enlist Fleer as a subcontractor, has a similar premise. There are billions of dollars of American-made, high-tech, high-value weapon systems that've been stolen by ISIS. Most of it's non-operational because of a lack of maintenance and spare parts. With ISIS in retreat, there's a danger of the equipment falling into the hands of other bad actors. We've been contracted to recover as much of the equipment as possible and place it back under the control of the US government. My interest in Fleer is simple. You manage the APS-5 Army prepositioned stocks in Kuwait. I have authorization in my hands granting you authority to sell me spare parts, material, and even ammunition from the APS-5 inventory, which you will then have to replenish."

I handed Jim an original letter of authorization and a contract amendment, both signed by the DoD contracting officer responsible for the Fleer APS-5, detailing what I had just said. I then passed a purchase order to Jim with a long list of parts.

"You can see that we're initially going after the abandoned M1A1 Abrams tanks and the M109A5 self-propelled 155mm armored artillery systems. That first parts list is a little over thirty million dollars. The company that's making the purchase is not Falcon. It's an American company I own named Trident. Trident has a US government IDIQ contract with a healthy yearly spend. That IDIQ will be the contracting vehicle we'll use to make these purchases. The pricing is the US government prices plus a twenty percent markup for Fleer. All the shipments are ex-works Kuwait. I'll need your input, but the way I see this working is that I'll give you a purchase order, you'll provide me details of availability, and then, using our aircraft, we'll fly the parts up north. We shouldn't need any export clearance, because the process end-to-end is all American. What are your thoughts?"

I could see that all three were surprised. Ambassador Tobin spoke first.

"This isn't what we expected. I was thinking it would be more of an introductory meeting. It's a welcome development, but I'm trying to figure out who you're working for. I was under the impression that you worked for the crown prince."

"Ambassador, in my capacity as the COO of Falcon, I work for his brother, who owns the group of companies that owns Falcon. Although to be honest, I hardly know the man. In my capacity as the CEO of Trident, I work for myself. Since Trident has numerous contracts with the US DoD, primarily involving overseas contingency support, it's fair to say that Trident works for the US government."

The next to speak was Jim. "We can't execute these documents until they're authenticated, and a lot of that authentication will be on you personally. We need to know your background, what agency has oversight over Trident, FCPA policies, and so on. For compliance reasons, we have to do a full due diligence check on Trident, and we'll need references."

"Jim, my estimate on the value of this entire project to Fleer is north of three hundred million dollars. The good news is I'm giving you the opportunity to make money for your company while also doing something important for your country. I'm fine with a due diligence process, but it has to be fast. Trident has already been vetted and has a large existing contract with the US government, so there shouldn't be much of a delay in obtaining approval on that end. I understand the reference stuff is important. The deputy CENTCOM commander will call you today or tomorrow and address any questions you may have."

The next question came from Bob. "We came to this meeting thinking you were an American expat working for the sheiks, and what we're now learning is that you're something else altogether. If you don't mind my saying, this all seems kind of cloak and dagger."

"I'm a retired Army officer. I have my own company, and I also work for a local emirate company. Sometimes the two companies collaborate on projects, and in other instances, like this one, they don't. Trident has a lot of capabilities, as you'll see, but the work it does in UAE for the US government is sensitive, and I'm not at liberty to discuss it."

"What's your background in the Army, Pat? You were very evasive when we talked about our biographies earlier," Jim asked.

"I'm from South Boston. I was commissioned through ROTC as an infantry officer. I retired after twenty; I had a good run. My last assignment was in D.C. with the Army staff. I formed Trident the same month I retired."

"Where did you serve?" asked Jim.

"My first unit was the Ninth Infantry Division at Fort Lewis. Later I moved across the airfield and served in the Second Ranger Battalion. I commanded a company from the First Armored Division during Desert Storm, and after that, all of my experience was with the Rangers and USSOCOM except that final job in D.C."

Bob asked, "What did you do at USSOCOM?"

"I had a lot of jobs. I was there for more than a decade. My last job was as a Joint Special Operations Task Force Commander in Iraq."

"Which one?" asked Jim.

"All my rotations were with the numbered units."

"Now I get it. You're a ninja, and if you tell us what you used to do, you have to kill us," Bob said.

"Nothing like that. I had to sign a lot of nondisclosure forms when I retired, and since I have no desire to ever see a prison cell, I work hard to avoid the subject."

"Fair enough," said Jim.

"Is there's nothing else. I'd like to excuse myself for ten minutes, and when I come back, we'll have a discussion on the way forward."

I left the conference room and went to the lobby and ordered a cappuccino. While on the elevator, I texted Major General Dana Peterson, the deputy CENTCOM commander, and asked him to call Jim Granger. CENTCOM was headquartered in Tampa, but the deputy had a forward headquarters located in Camp Arifjan in Kuwait. For all intents and purposes, Fleer worked for Major General Peterson, and a phone call from the general should be all Jim needed as far as a reference was concerned. I needed an immediate response from Fleer because the situation was changing rapidly, and the window to claim the equipment was quickly closing. My guess was that we'd have six months for recovery before the Iraqi government was strong enough to put a stop to it.

The agreement I had made with Mike Guthrie was that the dispensation of everything recovered would be decided by Mike. He'd already given the approval to allocate two tank battalions of forty-four M1A1s and one heavy artillery battalion of eighteen M109A5s to the Peshmerga. In addition to the spare parts, the ammunition for the tanks and artillery would also come out of the APS-5 stockpiles. I wasn't going to drop that purchase order until after a few spare parts orders had gone through. I'd already contracted the mechanics and the trainers through a smaller military services company in the United States.

As I reviewed the meeting in my head, I felt two of the three were on board. Ambassador Tobin was clearly in favor; he was, in my estimation, purely a power-and-money kind of guy. I'd known I had him the first time I caught him eying my Cartier watch. Jim Granger was also going to provide full support; he would talk to General Peterson and then proceed forward out of a sense of duty.

Bob was the person who I thought might have some reservations. Bob was too smart not to realize I was withholding information on the true purpose of the requirement. I'm sure that if I could tell him the true purpose was to arm the Peshmerga with a tank brigade while bypassing the congressional approval process, he'd be okay with it. Unfortunately, I didn't have the authority to read Bob in on the CIA's plan. The funny thing was, I was sure the US Congress would approve the effort without too much dissent. The trouble would come from other nations, who would learn of the plan during open congressional hearings. That was why the guys in Langley had decided it was better for Russia and Turkey to learn the Peshmerga had this capability after it was too late to do anything about it.

When I went back into the conference room, Jim was on the phone with Major General Peterson, and Bob was also on the phone, talking to someone at the Fleer office in Kuwait. He had the purchase order in his hand. As I entered, Ambassador Tobin greeted me as though we were old friends. Both Jim and Bob quickly wrapped up their phone calls.

Jim was the first to speak. "It looks like we're in business. Bob will get back to you with the details on the terms and conditions as soon as possible, and I'll get the corporate office to expedite the due diligence process. Unless there's a red flag, we should begin to flow supplies to you within the week."

"That's great news. I really appreciate you gentlemen making the trip to Dubai on such short notice and the quick response to this requirement."

Bob said he would need a day to validate the pricing, but the T&Cs in the purchase order were fine. He would get me the banking information for the wire transfers, and once everything was agreed, he would send me a pro forma invoice for payment.

The three men escorted me to the lobby and said their goodbyes. It had been a productive day in Dubai, and I was looking forward to getting back to Abu Dhabi.

The way I saw it, the war against ISIS couldn't last more than another year. At that point, I planned on talking to Mike Guthrie about exiting the scene. Once I had everything wrapped up with Mike, my plan was to transfer my responsibilities at Falcon to Saed Al-Hananiah, my highly competent protégé, and begin retirement. I'd recently built a small beach complex in the Bahamas, and I was anxious to get to it.

Chapter 12

Riyadh, Kingdom of Saudi Arabia

Sheik Meshal greeted Sheik Rasheed from United Arab Emirates and Prince Bandar from Saudi Arabia. The three were attending a Peninsular Shield strategic conference on Yemen that included all the GCC allies participating in the combat actions against the Houthis and their Iranian backers in Yemen. This meeting was held at Prince Bandar's palace in Riyadh. The three had spent the afternoon at the Peninsular Shield operation center with the other coalition leaders receiving updates on the Yemen combat operations. In 2015, with the backing of a UN resolution, the coalition had intervened in the Yemeni civil war in an attempt to return President Hadi to office after he'd been deposed by the Iranian-backed Houthis. Almost a third of the country still remained in Houthi hands, including the major city of Sanaa. Coalition bombing was killing 113 civilians per day, Saudi casualties were in the thousands, and UAE had already lost more than eighty soldiers to the conflict. Despite the GCC declaration that ground operations had ceased after the June peace talks, the reality was that once the peace talks had ended, the fighting had intensified. The three were discussing their willingness to do what was necessary to deny a further Persian expansion into the Arabian Peninsula when the subject shifted to ISIS.

Sheik Meshal, as the ISIS project leader, explained the situation. "The turning point for the Assad regime is the battle for Aleppo. With renewed support from Iran and Russia, the Syrian government has been on the offense for the past thirty days and has made the recapture of Aleppo a major objective. The reason Syria can concentrate on the anti-

Assad rebel forces in Aleppo is because the pressure they were getting from Daesh has all but ceased. The Kurds are defeating Daesh. Daesh has lost more than a quarter of its territory. Once the Syrian government seizes Aleppo, the ISIS-held territories in the northeast of Syria, including Raqqa, will be between the twin vises of the Syrian government and the Kurds. Our plan to use Daesh to destroy the Iranian puppet, Assad, and then allowing the Western coalition to destroy Daesh is failing. The Western-backed Kurds are having too much success against Daesh in northern Iraq and Syria."

Sheik Rasheed from the UAE asked, "How can we get the Daesh forces to press the attack against Assad's forces?"

Sheik Meshal answered, "We must first relieve the pressure Daesh is receiving from the Kurds."

"How do you suggest we do that?" asked Sheik Rasheed.

Prince Bandar jumped in. "We've made overtures to President Erdogan in Turkey, and he's responded with targeted attacks against Kurdish military forces along the border. This has helped, but it's not enough. I suggest our next step should be to reduce the flow of weapons and ammunition to the Kurdish forces. Most of that supply flow is coming from the US and is traveling through UAE; together, we need to make every effort to disrupt it."

Sheik Meshal added, "A combination of forcing the Kurds to defend against the Turkish incursions from the north and slowing the weapons flow will reduce Kurdish pressure on Daesh, which, *inshallah*, should free Daesh to concentrate on Assad's forces. I'll take the lead on disrupting the Peshmerga supply chain."

Chapter 13

Abu Dhabi, UAE

I woke up at four in the morning in the owner's cabin of the *Sam Houston*. I turned on the TV. With the help of Apple TV, a satellite link and an MLB.TV subscription, I tuned into the fourth inning of the Red Sox game. The owner's cabin was plush by any standard. It had a queen bed, a bathroom with bathtub and shower, a sitting area, and a work desk. My attention was focused on the big-screen TV mounted on the wall opposite the bed. Between the six and seventh innings, with the Sox leading 4–3 against Tampa, I went to wake up the crew and make coffee.

As dawn broke, I was disconnecting the power cable and water from the dock station. Once everything was disconnected and stowed, I did a walk-around of the boat, going through a mental list of preoperational checks. I was still new enough to yachting that I used checklists. My first stop was the engine room.

The twin Caterpillar C18 1150-horsepower engines were still shiny and clean and capable of powering the seventy-thousand-pound yacht up to thirty-five knots. I had the boat modified to store an additional two thousand gallons of diesel fuel by placing collapsible tanks in the unused crew quarters. With the modification, the boat had a cruising range of nineteen hundred miles, which meant that if I planned my refueling stops correctly, I could circle the planet. The composite boat had a CE-A rating and that fact along with the fuel range made it a blue water boat.

After the walk-through, I untied the lines and made my way up the stairs to the flybridge. The boat could be controlled from either the helm station on the flybridge or from the one in the wheelhouse on the main deck. The bow and stern thrusters made it possible for the boat to move in any direction using a joystick control. Maneuvering the boat from the slip out onto the open water through the tight confines of the marina was easy. The boat had two gyro stabilizers, which kept the decks level and flat under most conditions. All of the Raymarine controls on the flybridge and in the wheelhouse were fully digital. It had a state-of-the-art navigation system, radar, and depth finder that were fully automated. It was almost impossible to crash, even for a rookie mariner such as myself. I was still infatuated with my boat. At heart, I'm still a poor kid from the Old Colony projects in South Boston. Now that I'd finally achieved some financial independence, I was ready to ditch my day-to-day job and cruise the world.

My plan for the next two days was to cruise from Abu Dhabi to Sohar, Oman. The fishing in Oman was some of the best in the world, and September was the beginning of the peak season. Our route is pretty simple. It's 150 miles due north, off the west coast of Arabia and then through the Strait of Hormuz, followed by another leg 150 miles due south down the eastern coast of the Peninsula. The trip would take ten hours, which would give us a few hours of fishing on the first day. We'd fish again Sunday morning and then head back in the afternoon, getting back into Abu Dhabi late Sunday night.

It was a beautiful day for a boat trip. I was in shorts and a t-shirt. Jenny Lyn was in a pair of black shorts, a loose white t-shirt with BEBE stenciled on the front, and flip-flops. She was in the salon, avoiding the sun like a vampire because she was terrified of darkening her skin. Mia, whose clothing style was every mother's worst nightmare, was wearing jean shorts cut off so high that the pockets were four inches below the denim, a loose pink tank top, braless of course, and no shoes. I was sitting behind the controls at the flybridge helm station with the wind at my face, cruising at twenty-eight knots with mild seas. I was feeling rather good about life. I needed to do this more often.

At around ten, the traffic became heavy as we neared the Strait of Hormuz and the sea lanes narrowed. At its narrowest, the strait is thirty miles wide, with Iran to the north and the tip of Arabia to the south. Most of the oil from the Middle East passes through this strait.

I tried to maintain twenty-eight knots as we threaded the *Sam Houston* around the giant slow-moving oil tankers. I was keeping track of all the ships around us using the MARPA (mini-automatic radar plotting aid) on the radar display. It has a feature that allows me to tag every hazard and every craft, displaying range, heading, and speed for each. Because of the amount of traffic and clutter, I had the radar dialed down to display a range of only ten miles.

Once the *Sam Houston* passed the peak of Ras Musandam, I steered the boat south and west out of the major sea lane and away from all other traffic and set the autopilot on a heading due south toward the UAE coastal city of Fujairah.

I was about to turn the controls over to Jenny Lyn when I heard a chirp on the radar alarm. I glanced down at the screen and saw three boat icons approaching from behind. They were ten miles back and closing fast in a column formation. The system tagged each boat at a speed of forty-five knots. I throttled the twin engines up to full and turned the boat westward to get closer to Omani waters. I was guessing it was a harassing patrol from the Iranian Navy, and my movement close to the Oman coast would hopefully be enough for them to leave me alone.

The icon on the radar screen changed heading to an intercept course, which for the first time caused me to worry. I divided my time over the next few minutes between watching the radar and checking the nav system to see how close we were to Oman. Several minutes later, we were three miles from the Omani shoreline with the fast boats still pursuing us. I reached under the console and grabbed two of the wireless headsets we used when we were docking and handed one to Jenny Lyn. I told her to put it on and to close to within a mile of the shore and then head south.

I slid past Jenny Lyn and ran down both sets of stairs to the owner's cabin, unlocking the hidden storage area under my bed. I yanked out a heavy black nylon bag that was two yards long and weighed over a hundred pounds. I put my arm through one of the straps and slid it onto my back and then I headed back upstairs. The bag made a loud thump when it hit the stern deck.

I was breathing hard as I fumbled with the zipper with my sweaty fingers. Once I got it open, I reached in and found a pair of Steiner 7x50 Marine Commander XP binoculars. I braced my elbows on the dining table at the back of the aft deck before bringing the lead chase boat into focus.

"What's the distance to the closest boat?" I asked Jenny Lyn over my radio set. I was trying to find a flag or other identifier on the lead boat, but even with the binoculars, it was too difficult to make out any details.

Instead of Jenny Lyn, it was Mia who replied in a nervous voice, "Four thousand, five hundred meters, speed is fifty-three knots."

That was close enough for me. I reached back into the bag and slid out a case containing a Barrett M107 semiautomatic .50-caliber sniper rifle. I extracted the weapon from its soft case, extended the bipod, and set the weapon on the shelf behind the bench chair on the other side of the table. I set four ten-round magazines of GD Sniper Elite red-tipped armor-piercing incendiary rounds on the table next to the butt-stock, then I sat down and brought the rifle to my shoulder. I flipped off the protective caps from the Leopold Mark IV scope and slid a magazine into the well and chambered a round. Looking through the sixteen-by-forty mildot scope, I was able to positively identify the boats. They were Iranian fast-attack boats, flying the Iranian flag.

The boats were about forty feet long. I could see twelve rocket launcher tubes across the front of the wheelhouse. In the bow there was a heavy machine gun with a man standing behind it.

"Mia, what's range?" I asked.

"Range is two thousand, four hundred for the lead boat. There's two more behind it."

"Count down every five hundred meters."

"Okay."

We were in sight of the shoreline, but it didn't look like the Omani Navy was going to come to the rescue. I was still not completely sure if this was the Iranians playing games and harassing us or if it was something more, so I held my fire.

"Two thousand," Mia said.

I kept my cheek to the stock and reached on top of the Leopold scope and dialed in a range of twelve hundred meters. I put my finger on the windage knob to make an adjustment but thought better of it and left it at zero. I kept the weapon trained on the DShk gunner of the lead boat.

"Fifteen hundred," Mia said.

I watched the muzzle flash of the DShk 12.7mm machine gun as it opened fire. Before the sound even reached me, I pulled the trigger. The snap of the rounds zipping high over the port side reached my ears while I watched the gunner's head turn into a red mist.

Moving at fifty knots along the water, even in mild seas makes for a rough ride. We were moving at thirty-five knots in a much bigger boat and had the advantage of two Seakeeper gyrostabilizer systems. We had a big advantage when it came to accuracy.

I rapid-fired the remaining nine rounds into the wheelhouse and hull of the first boat, then I changed magazines and turned my attention to the machine gunner in the second boat. The gunner was wildly returning fire in long twenty round bursts. I could hear the impacts behind me. It took me three rounds before one of my bullets sent the machine gunner sprawling backward.

I ignored the boat this time and shifted fire to the machine gunner in the third boat, which was coming evenly abreast of the second boat. I got lucky and dropped the third boat's gunner with a single chest shot. Once again, I emptied the remainder of the magazine into the wheelhouse and hull of boat three and watched it erupt in flames. The only boat still pursuing us at that point was the second. I slid another magazine into the well, but before I could engage, the boat did a one-hundred-and-eighty-degree turn. Boat two was quickly out of range, while the first and third boats were burning.

"Reduce speed to ten knots," I said to Mia.

I got up from behind the Barret and went back to my bag. This time I pulled out a two-foot-long rectangular box. I extended the attached legs and set the box at a forty-five-degree angle upward. I removed the cap on the top and reached for the ground control station inside the bag. The AeroVironment Switchblade is a kamikaze UAV that has a range of ten kilometers and the explosive equivalent of a 40mm high-explosive grenade.

I powered up the ground controller and launched the UAV. Within two minutes, the UAV was over the second boat. Through the video feed, I could see sailors pulling a survivor from one of the other boats onto the deck. I pressed the safe-to-arm button on the controller and began the attack. The Switchblade dived down at a forty-five-degree angle from five hundred feet above the water. As the Switchblade descended, I could see on my controller screen the picture from the video camera in the nose of the UAV. A sailor on the deck looked up and pointed directly at the camera.

I aimed the suicide drone at the rear of the vessel, where I knew it would find the fuel tank. The picture on the controller went black, and seconds later, I heard an explosion. Looking up at the horizon, I saw three columns of black smoke. After tossing the disposable UAV launcher overboard, I stowed the rifle and UAV controller and put everything back into the bag, returning it to its original hiding space.

Once back on the main deck, I found Mia in the wheelhouse. She was ashen faced, sitting behind the controls.

"Where's Jenny Lyn?" I asked.

"I don't know," replied Mia.

"Can you find her and make sure she's all right? I'm going to put us back on course," I said.

I put the autopilot on a heading toward Fujairah and set the speed to eighteen knots. I was just about to do a walk-around tour of the yacht to check for damage when I heard a scream.

I found Mia in the narrow walkway between the cabin and the port rail on the main deck. When I reached her, she was kneeling over Jenny Lyn's lifeless body. There was no use going for the first-aid kit. Jenny Lyn's tiny frame had been hit in the upper torso with a 12.7mm bullet, and most of her chest was missing. I knelt down beside Jenny Lyn and, just to be sure, checked for a pulse. I closed her lifeless eyes and brushed the hair away from her face. I looked over at Mia, who was holding on to the side of the yacht, trembling, with tears running down her face. I couldn't remember ever feeling so bad about anything. I carried Jenny Lyn's body to the stern deck and covered her with a blanket.

The trip to the marina in Fujairah took over an hour. I spent some of that time on my laptop. Mia was silent the entire time. I called the marina and was unable to get a slip because they were full, so I anchored a few hundred meters offshore. Once we were anchored, I asked Mia to pack.

Mia finally spoke. "Are we going to jail? What's going to happen?"

"Going to jail is not a worry; your safety is. Being near me right now is dangerous. A driver will be here soon. I've booked an Emirates flight leaving today from Dubai to Manila. I'll transfer enough money into your account to allow you to remain in the Philippines for a long time, forever if need be." While I talked, I was printing the boarding pass from my laptop.

"What about Jenny Lyn?" asked Mia.

"I'll make sure her body gets back to her home in the Philippines, and I'll take care of her family. I'm sorry. I had no idea this was going to happen. Finish packing, and don't forget your passport. The driver will be here shortly. I'll prep the tender and take you to the dock once he arrives. You'll go directly to Terminal 3. Stay in the business class lounge until they call your flight. Don't leave the Philippines unless I call you and tell you it's safe."

I went to the stern of the boat and removed the cover from the Williams Turbojet 325 tender that was perched on the hydraulic platform at the tail end of the boat. I felt a stabbing pain as I glanced up at the gray blanket covering Jenny Lyn's body. While I waited for Mia to bring up her luggage, I called Mike Guthrie on my cell. It was a little after one in the afternoon in UAE, which meant on the East Coast, it was five in the morning. Mike picked up on the third ring, I don't think he ever slept.

"I have a serious situation, and I need your help. Somebody is trying to kill me."

"What makes you think that?" asked Mike.

"About two hours ago, just off the coast of Limah, Oman, my boat was attacked by three fast-attack boats. No warning or anything. They chased me down and engaged with fifty-caliber machine-gun fire."

"Iranians?" asked Mike.

"I think so. That's the flag they were flying, and I don't know anyone else who has those boats. All three were destroyed, and I don't know if there were any survivors. I'm now anchored off the port of Fujairah. Jenny Lyn was killed in the attack. Her body is on board, and I'm in the process of sending Mia back to Philippines. I'm assuming I'm the target, but I have no idea why. I need your help to clean this up."

After listening quietly, Mike replied, "Find someplace safe and sit tight. I'll check back in with you in four hours, and we'll discuss next steps."

I received a text when the limo arrived. I went downstairs to help Mia with her bags and walked into her cabin as she was closing her last suitcase. The color had returned to her face, and she looked steady.

Mia turned to me. "What should I do?"

"You'll be safe in the Philippines. Just go back to your village and keep a low profile."

I used the hydraulic control to lower the tender into the water. Before starting the engine, I asked Mia to give me her phone and then tossed it into the water.

As soon as I returned from dropping off Mia, I stowed the tender. I made sure the automatic identification system was in its standard position, which was off, meaning we weren't sending our location out to the world via satellite. I cut the master power and began a sweep of the boat using a multispectral signal detector. It was nagging at me that someone had been able to find and ambush me so easily.

I couldn't find any listening devices or trackers. I refueled the boat at the Fujairah Marina and set a heading of eight knots south toward Muscat.

Once the autopilot kicked in, I grabbed a Sam Adams from the fridge and reclined on the bench chair on the flydeck. I've been in more than a few firefights, and I've seen some bad things, but the sight of poor innocent Jenny Lyn laying on the deck wasn't ever going to leave me.

The realization that I was responsible for getting her killed was just starting to set in. Getting caught by surprise and endangering civilians was unforgivable. The problem is, I had no idea I was involved in anything that would draw such a reaction from anyone, especially the Iranians. I don't have anything to do with the Iranians.

I spent the rest of the afternoon drinking beer and trying to sort out why the Iranians would want to kill me. If someone wanted me dead, why not just shoot me on the way to the office? Why be so dramatic and sloppy about it?

As the sun set, I turned on the running lights and anchored the boat. Two miles out from the Omani shoreline, the water was too deep to anchor, but the boat's positioning system automatically kept me in position without any drift using the jets. When my iridium satphone chimed, I picked it up.

"Hey, Mike."

"Cleanup crew has you in sight. They're in a fishing trawler. Keep an eye out."

An hour later, the men from the fishing trawler departed with Jenny Lyn's body. I was more morose than ever when I returned to my perch on the flydeck. No sooner had I sat down when the iridium phone chimed again. It was Mike.

"Sorry it took so long to get back to you. We have a lot of people working to figure this out, and I just came from a meeting with the 7th floor on the subject."

"Any idea why the Iranians want me dead?"

"It was definitely the Iranians who attacked you. We have satellite imagery showing the fast craft leaving their base in Iran, pursuing you, and finally being destroyed by fire from your vessel. From the imagery, it looked like you hit them with a fifty-caliber sniper rifle and some kind of guided rocket. Kudos on that. None of our people can understand why the Iranians would put a hit on you. The spooks at Fort Meade have been given a tasker but they'll need a couple of days to do a meta search. If they don't find anything, we're at a dead end."

"I understand. I'll return through the strait tomorrow. I swept the boat and couldn't find any tracking or RFID devices. I don't expect another incident. After what happened today, they won't be sending any fast boats after me. I doubt they expected me to be armed. Next time they attack it'll probably be a long-range missile shot, and there's nothing I can do about that."

"Why not just leave your boat in Fujairah? It's not a great idea to pass through the strait a second time."

"I have an appointment on Monday with Dr. Schneeberger. She's going to evaluate my tendency toward risky behavior, and I want to have something to talk about."

Chapter 14

Kuwait City, Kuwait

Abdul-Rahman waited outside Sheik Meshal's office at the Kuwait National Guard headquarters. His olive-green dress uniform was perfectly tailored, his broad chest resplendent with badges and ribbons, and the crease in his trousers was razor-sharp. The waiting area was covered with photographs of the aging sheik, sporting his black Peter Sellers mustache, with various foreign leaders. In addition to Abdul-Rahman's counterterrorism battalion, there were eight other units in the KNG, including two mechanized battalions and two riot-control battalions.

Kuwait was threatened at its borders by the Iranian-backed Shia, and it was threatened internally by a large Shia population as well as an active local Sunni protest movement. The KNG counterterrorist battalion and the two riot-control battalions were very active.

Ever since the Americans had recaptured Kuwait from Saddam Hussein's Republican Guards in 1991, the external defense of the country had largely been outsourced to the US military. The United States kept a heavy brigade in Kuwait on a rotational basis, along with an Air Force fighter squadron, and the Navy's Fifth Fleet was always parked nearby in Bahrain. Kuwait's internal security issues were primarily the responsibility of the Ministry of the Interior and the Kuwait National Guard. Kuwait did have a regular army, but they were more of a show pony than a warhorse. During the Iraqi invasion, the only casualties incurred from anyone who actually fought back were from the KNG; the regular military ran for the hills.

When Abdul-Rahman was finally summoned into the KNG deputy chairman's office, he was not asked to sit. He remained standing at a position of attention across the desk of His Highness Sheik Meshal Al-Sabah.

Skipping the ritual greeting, Sheik Meshal got right to the point. "I've entrusted you with a very important task. One that must be completed successfully and quickly. What can you tell me about your progress?"

Remaining at attention, Abdul-Rahman replied, "Your Highness, you made it very clear that any action to kill the American arms dealer cannot be traced back to us for political reasons. I used a contact in Lebanon who, through a Hezbollah agent, provided a message to Iranian intelligence about a person supplying weapons to the Iranian Kurds. I also provided information on when the American would be passing through the Strait of Hormuz in a motor yacht."

Sheik Meshal cut in, "How did you know when and where the American was going to sail?"

Abdul-Rahman replied, "We received the information from our counterparts in the UAE; they keep a very close eye on him and his associates."

"What have our friends in the UAE been able to tell us? Did the Iranians act?"

Abdul-Rahman paused and looked at his feet before responding. This was the part he'd been dreading. "Cee Dee, the Iranians were given notice of when the American sailed from Abu Dhabi. The Iranians ambushed the American's motor yacht with three fast-attack craft armed with rockets and heavy machine guns. The American pleasure yacht destroyed all three Iranian boats. Nine Iranian sailors were killed, none survived, and the American escaped unharmed."

Sheik Meshal's eyes bulged, and his cheeks were red. "That's not acceptable. We have to kill the American. What will you do next?"

"The Iranians are no longer an option. Nobody will know that we were behind the attack, but we can't use them again. Another organization we can use that won't point back to us is Daesh. Our friends in the UAE are still able to keep track of the American. He often travels to Iraq and sometimes Syria with air shipments of weapons and equipment. We'll attack him the next time he accompanies a shipment."

Sheik Meshal stood up and walked around his desk. Abdul-Rahman was visibly nervous. He'd never seen the sheik so intense, and he stood even more rigidly at the position of attention.

Sheik Meshal put his hands on the shoulders of Abdul-Rahman and said, "I have given my word to the Council that we will get this done. I want you to personally lead this next attack. Do not fail. Make sure you have everything you need and take every precaution to ensure the attack is not traced back to us."

Chapter 15

Al Dhafra Air Force Base, UAE

I watched the forklift raise the pallet and then motor toward the ramp of the waiting C-130. This was the last pallet, and Bill Sachse, the loadmaster, and Dmitri Migos were rushing to secure it with A7A straps so they could stay on schedule. Today's load was small-arms ammunition, grenades, and mortars. The six pallets were double-stacked and covered the entire cargo bay in the fuselage, leaving a space just narrow enough to walk through on either side. The two pilots, Joe Ferguson and Joe Kilpatrick, had already completed the walk-around and were going through the preflight checklist in the cockpit.

The joking banter between Migos and Sachse was nonstop. Migos had left the Army from the Fifth Special Forces Group at Fort Campbell. Muey Muey Migos—a name he claims to have been given by a Venezuelan *Sports Illustrated* swimsuit model because he was so much more than the average man—was an extremely funny character. He'd left the Army after serving twelve years, most of them as a member of a Special Forces ODA team. Migos had studied Arabic at the Defense Language Institute in Monterey, California, and had an 18B military occupation specialty, which was a Special Forces weapons specialist. Migos was five-eight and 220 pounds of muscle. He had huge biceps, Popeye forearms, curly black hair, and a bushy unibrow that accented a constantly grinning face. Migos almost never stopped talking.

His loadmaster and workmate, Bill Sachse, was the polar opposite. Sachse was tall and thin. He had close-cropped gray hair and wore wire-rimmed eyeglasses. Sachse was as quiet as Migos was loud. He was a procedural fanatic; the term *anal retentive* would not begin to describe the methodical and laconic Sachse. Every part of the aircraft behind the cockpit was Sachse's domain, and he kept it immaculate.

I stepped onto the back ramp of the C-130 and sat on a web-mesh jump seat in the very back of the aircraft. A headset was already plugged in next to the seat, and I put it on before connecting the seat belt and shoulder-restraining harness. Migos kept up a steady banter with the two pilots on the intercom, Joe and Joe, as they began to taxi toward the runway. It had been three weeks since the attack in the Strait of Hormuz, and I still had no idea why the Iranians had targeted me.

With the loss of Jenny Lyn and Mia, keeping the boat up had become a sad and lonely chore. Earlier in the week, I notified Ahmed, the Falcon CEO, that I was leaving the company. Ahmed had committed to continuing the relationship between Falcon and Trident with me still managing the deals and Falcon continuing to run the end user certificates. My plan was to extricate myself from the CIA arms dealer business. The coalition gains had been steady, and I was optimistic that the conflict could be over and I could be out in six months.

Today's delivery was going to the Peshmerga brigade leading the fight to retake Mosul. The fifty-five-hundred-man element located outside of Mosul was being supported from Erbil, the next major city twenty miles to the east. ISIS had lost almost a third of their previous gains in recent months, but they still inhabited an area close to the size of West Virginia. The Erbil International Airport was in excellent condition. It had an undamaged runway and robust ground support. Earlier in the week, we'd used the airport to make a delivery of 122mm rockets and 152mm artillery rounds from Ukraine, supplied by Andre. The artillery ammunition had gone to the Peshmerga artillery forces, who were pounding Mosul in preparation for the final ground assault. The area of Erbil was very safe at this point, so today's flight was going to be a milk run.

The nylon seats on a C-130 are very uncomfortable. Four hours into the flight, I was lying flat on top of a pallet, resting my head on my jacket, when Migos tapped me on the boot.

"Boss, we're twenty minutes out."

I moved off the pallet, put my headset back on, took a seat, and strapped in next to Migos and Bill Sachse in the far back of the aircraft, nearest to the tail ramp. In Iraq and most war zones, aircraft didn't make the long, gradual approaches commercial travelers were accustomed to. The safest procedure is to maintain altitude as long as possible to avoid ground fire and then corkscrew down to the runway.

As we began the approach, I could hear the pilots talking to an Erbil air traffic controller, who spoke excellent English. Minutes into the landing, an alarm sounded over the intercom, and I heard one of the Joes announce in a calm voice, "Missile lock. Evading."

The plane banked and shuddered from the staccato discharge of the IR and chaff countermeasures firing from launchers on the fuselage and wings. The engine noise roared as the aircraft went to full power and started to climb. I felt a second discharge of flares going off, followed by an explosion that shook the aircraft. On the intercom, one of the Joes reported to the air traffic controller that we'd been hit and were making an emergency landing. Without any windows within my view, I couldn't see anything that was going on outside.

All of a sudden, the aircraft dove straight down and began to spin. Gradually, it stopped spinning and started to level, that's when Joe Kilpatrick, in his best Chuck Yeager voice, announced, "Brace for impact."

I instinctively tried to bring my chest down to my knees and grab my legs in a crash position, but when I tried, I realized I was in a shoulder harness. The plane hit the ground hard, then it bounced up, and hit the ground again before sliding nose-first for several seconds. Finally, it came to a sudden violent stop that lifted the tail of the aircraft up into the air before crashing down one final time.

Migos, Sachse and I were seated in the very rear of the airplane. We were facing toward the center with our backs to the fuselage. The final impact was back-wrenching, but our harnesses helped a lot. I was shaken, but not hurt. Over my headset, I heard Sachse request a crew check. Migos said he was up and then I reported the same. There was no response from the cockpit. I released my seat belt. Sachse opened the side exit door, and the cargo hold was instantly filled with heat and smoke from the burning wings. I ran to the ceiling storage above the ramp area and released the go-bags. Migos and I each grabbed two before jumping out the side exit door. The fuselage was lying flat on the desert sand. There was not a drop from the door, because the landing gear had been crushed. Once on the ground, the three of us ran away from the fire engulfing the wings.

One hundred fifty yards from the rear of the aircraft, my legs were burning from the sprint. I found a depression on the desert floor and jumped in along with Sachse and Migos. Seconds later a huge explosion, followed by a blazing hot concussion wave, swept over us. For a few seconds, the air was excruciatingly hot and there was no oxygen to be found. Gradually, the desert returned to what felt like a cool ninety-five degrees, and we were able to breathe again.

Without speaking, the three of us strapped a go-bag onto our shoulders, connected the waist straps, and walked out of the sandy depression to survey the damage to the aircraft. I was shocked to see the devastation created by the combination of the aircraft's fuel and the cargo's explosives. I sent Migos to search around the aircraft counterclockwise while I went the other way with Sachse to survey the smoldering remains and hopefully find the pilots. Eventually we all met up in the vicinity of the cockpit, which was crushed flat against a sand dune, it was plainly obvious that neither pilot had survived.

"Gear up, it looks like we're going to be hoofing it to Erbil," I told Migos and Sachse.

I donned my body armor and helmet, attached a drop-leg holster, and loaded my pistol and carbine. I used the GPS and got a fix on our location. We were only three miles west of Erbil International.

"I'm gonna call the American advisory team working with the Peshmerga brigade and request evac," Migos said as he pulled out a cell phone.

"They saw the explosion. They're sending a vehicle convoy to get us," he said a few minutes later.

While we were waiting, I sent Migos back to retrieve the fourth go-bag.

"What just happened?" I asked Sachse after Migos left. Sachse is a retired Air Force master sergeant with twenty-plus years of experience in the MC-130, often in hostile environs. I thought Sachse would have the best idea of what had just transpired.

Sachse replied in his slow Kentucky drawl, "Sir, I figure at about six thousand feet, we got locked on and engaged by a MANPAD. The countermeasures worked against the first missile, but we were engaged by at least two more and that was just too much for our defenses.

"Thing is, those couldn't be regular MANPADs. We had the latest electronic and IR countermeasures on that airplane. The BIRDIE IR is a gen-four system, and only the very latest Stinger missiles, like the FIM-92J, can defeat that system.

"What doesn't make sense is that besides us, only our most trusted NATO allies have advanced Stingers. If the US supplied them to the Kurds, we'd know about it. Besides us and maybe the Brits, nobody else in this country should have 'em.'"

Sachse's explanation of the engagement was making me paranoid. When Migos got back, I told both Migos and Sachse that we were going to make this a tactical linkup. I picked out some high ground for them to overwatch the linkup. It was about three hundred yards from the crash site. I told them to have their weapons ready to engage in case something went wrong.

I put out an orange VS-17 panel on a piece of burned-out debris close to where the cockpit was destroyed to mark the linkup point, and I stood nearby. I released the retention strap on my holster and made sure my pistol had a round chambered. I kept my M4 carbine slung over my shoulder, not wanting to appear hostile to the friendlies I hoped were coming to pick us up.

Half an hour later, I got a call over the radio from Migos. "Rooster tails from a three-vehicle convoy are heading our way."

I followed the dust trails until the vehicles came into view. The road they were on must have turned in the wrong direction because the vehicles turned off the road and headed cross country, toward our location. The smoke from the burning Hercules made finding us easy. I stood near the bright orange VS-17 panel with my weapon on my shoulder and watched the vehicles approach. When they got to within a quarter of a mile, I could see the vehicles were American HMMWVs with .50-caliber machine guns mounted on top. The vehicles approached in column. When they got to within seventy-five yards, they stopped.

I walked forward to the lead vehicle. A bandanna-wearing .50-caliber gunner in the cupola followed me with his weapon. Suddenly, his head exploded, and from the direction of our overwatch position I heard the report of a rifle discharge. I dove for cover behind the small sandy knoll to my right, where I'd stashed my gear. The gunners in the two trail HMMWVs were spraying machine-gun fire in the general area of Migos and Sachse.

I dug into my go-bag and pulled out a M72 LAW (light antitank weapon). I extended it, removed the safety, popped off the top cover, and launched the rocket at the closest HMMWV just as a replacement gunner was emerging into the cupola. The 66mm rocket-propelled charge detonated on impact, and the HMMWV exploded in a fireball. Meanwhile, the gunners from the second and third HMMWVs were slumped forward against their weapons, shot by Migos and Sachse. I pulled an M67 frag grenade from a pouch on my plate carrier. Baseball is a lifetime passion of mine, and I have a pretty good arm. As soon as I had the grenade in my hand, I flicked off the safety and pulled the pin. While holding down the spoon with my right thumb, I raced toward the second HMMWV.

With my rifle in my left hand and the grenade in my right, I got to within twenty yards and tossed the grenade, then dove forward, flat onto the ground. It was a perfect throw, and two seconds after the grenade fell through the cupola hatch, it exploded into a ball of flame. The third and remaining HMMWV was still gunner-less and was getting pinged by bullets from Migos and Sachse. After the second HMMWV exploded, the third did a fast turnaround and headed back toward the road.

The route brought the vehicle within a hundred yards of Migos and Sachse. They were ready, and both fired M72 rockets at nearly the same time. The first went high, the second connected with the hood of the HMMWV, and the front end of the vehicle burst into flame. A door on the disabled HMMWV opened and a figure emerged. The man was quickly cut down by a rifle shot from the overwatch position. When a second figure staggered out of the burning HMMWV, I yelled into my radio for Migos and Sachse to stop firing—we needed a prisoner.

I dropped my rifle, helmet and plate carrier into the sand and ran after the lone figure who was scurrying away. He was running with an awkward limping gait. It took only a few minutes for me to close within fifty yards of the struggling man. I was breathing hard and in a full sweat as I got close.

The man was obviously badly wounded and started to slow even more. When I got to within twenty yards, I stopped and drew my pistol from the drop-leg holster on my right thigh. I steadied myself in a firing position, took aim, and fired three rounds into the legs of the fleeing assailant. The man tumbled forward, face first into the desert sand. With my pistol still drawn, I cautiously approached. The man was wearing a coyote-brown body armor vest over a set of desert camouflage fatigues, and I couldn't see his hands. When I was ten yards from the prostrate figure, the man suddenly rolled to his left revealing a pistol in his right hand. I pulled the trigger twice, hitting him in the face and killing him instantly.

I searched the body and found absolutely nothing—no cell phone, wallet, or identification of any kind. The dead man was well groomed, short, and physically fit. He was a tough guy, running hurt and fighting to the end. I was curious about him; his build, sterile uniform, and be- havior had the markings of a professional, which was not an ISIS trait. I thought of taking a photo of the face, but there wasn't enough left to identify.

With nothing else to do, I walked back and retrieved my gear; Migos and Sachse were already there.

"How did you guys know they were hostile?" I asked.

"Easy, boss. I was talking to Captain Fowler from the SF team, and he told me they were going to pick us up in two Land Cruisers."

"Don't you think that's something you should've shared with me on the radio while I was standing out in the open, big, dumb, and igno- rant, to greet them?" I said.

"No time, boss, I just had to go with it."

"What's the status on the pickup? We may have to escape and evade before more hostiles show up," I said.

"I think I see them now. Stay cool. We have a ride out of here," replied Migos.

While they were waiting for the vehicles to arrive, I took out my cell and called Mike Guthrie.

"I just lost two of my guys. I was strap-hanging on a delivery into Erbil, and the bad guys shot us out of the sky with missiles. It was another ambush, only this time from the air."

"This is escalating. Anything else?" Mike asked.

"The plane had the latest countermeasures, Sachse says it had to be the latest US ordnance that was used against us, an advanced Stinger. Both of my pilots were killed. I'm still at the site, three miles west of Erbil International. While we were waiting for extraction, we were attacked again, this time by three armored HMMWVs. We destroyed all three, and we were unable to capture a prisoner."

"How long ago was this?"

"Just a few minutes ago."

"With everything going on in Mosul, we have a lot of assets in the area. I'll get a team to investigate the site," said Mike.

"Okay, and I have another request. I'm going to need some help recovering the remains of my pilots. I'll have to notify the families, and it'll be a little bit easier on them if I can at least return the remains."

"What are you going to do about the plane?" asked Mike.

"I'm going to have to lease one for a while until I can replace it. The cargo will be replaced as soon as we can get it reloaded from Ukraine. They have huge stockpiles of the stuff. It's not going to disrupt the business, but this is getting personal," I said.

"I'll be in touch just as soon as I know something," said Mike.

Once at Erbil International, I arranged a charter back to Abu Dhabi. The timing of the boat attack and air attack was too precise. Some actor in the UAE had to be providing information to the ambushers. I was definitely under surveillance by someone who meant me harm. Once I got back to Abu Dhabi, it wouldn't take long for the bad guys to learn they'd failed once again.

While seated at the Erbil airport food court, eating a Big Mac, Migos asked, "What happens next?"

"When we get back, I'll call both wives, I'll attend the funerals, and make sure they get the death gratuity all of you have been promised. I don't know what else I can do. You're both encouraged to attend the funerals. As for work, after a couple of weeks, you'll rotate with the other crew until I can replace the aircraft. This was a catastrophe today, no doubt, but the work continues, and if you still want it, you still have a part to play."

The taciturn Sachse responded, "I'm in," to which Migos replied, "Well, I better stay on and look after Grandpa. Without me, I don't know what would happen to him. Probably find him wandering around in the desert, babbling incoherently, lost, wearing one of those old people nightgowns." The joke brought a grin from Sachse and chuckle from me.

"Speaking of old, boss, you're not too bad to have around in a fight," Migos said.

"Thanks, Migos. Coming from you, that means a lot."

Chapter 16

Alexandria, Virginia

I was in the gunfighter's seat in the back of the narrow dining room of the Warehouse Bar & Grill located on King Street in Old Town Alexandria. The Old Town tourist area is lined with small upscale restaurants and antique shops. The quaint restaurant is an unlikely spot for a clandestine meeting between a senior CIA agent and his asset, which, knowing Mike, was probably the reason he chose it.

I arrived fifteen minutes early and the maître d' was able to seat me without delay as the restaurant was still mostly empty. I was enjoying a glass of Jeff Gordon 2012 that was chilled and surprisingly good. The waitress, who'd introduced herself as Carley, was a vivacious ponytailed blonde with a pretty face and a flirty demeanor. If her behavior was contrived to increase tips, it was definitely going to work.

The dinner rush hadn't yet arrived, which gave Carley and me time to chat. Turned out she was working on a master's degree in international affairs at Georgetown. Spending as much time as I do in the Middle East, where the women are so horribly repressed, the openness and confidence of the American female is refreshing. It's a shame they always break my heart.

Mike arrived and slipped into the seat across from me. Without prompting, the attentive Carley poured him a glass of wine. Mike took a sip and nodded his approval. He was still dressed in a suit and tie while I was wearing jeans and a loose black turtleneck. Carley came back and took our orders. I ordered the she-crab soup and the halibut, and Mike went with the crab cakes and a filet mignon. It was an excellent meal. We spent the time talking sports and the Army. I was enjoying the ambience and the conversation.

After the table was cleared, I shifted the conversation to the matter at hand.

"What do we know about the people who killed my pilots?" I asked.

"We found the launch containers and traced the serial numbers on the Stinger missiles. That led us to a German unit in Mazari Sharif, Afghanistan, who reported them captured in 2015. The trail went cold after that."

"Did you learn anything from the vehicles, or the personnel we took out?"

"The vehicles were delivered to the Iraqi government by us in 2009 and captured by ISIS in 2012. We weren't able to identify all of the people, but those we did identify were a mixture of Tunisians, Iraqis, and Kuwaiti jihadis."

"What about that guy who was trying to get away? He had some training," I said.

"He did. His name was Abdul-Rahman Al Ghaneem. He was US-trained Special Forces, a major in the Kuwait National Guard before he ran away and joined ISIS. He was high level in the caliphate. Our intel suggests he was one of the top guys, working directly for Baghdadi."

"Am I being hunted?"

"We think so. I've dedicated a team of analysts whose only task is to get to the bottom of these two attacks. They have a few leads and are developing a working theory on the reason behind the attacks."

"Are both attacks from the same source, or is it just a coincidence that Iran and ISIS decided to off me at roughly the same time?"

"You don't have that many enemies. We're operating on the assumption that it's a single threat. Someone with the ability to utilize the Iranians and the ISIS fighters as proxies."

"Maybe I need a Dale Carnegie class on winning friends and influencing people."

"You don't need any help in the influencing people department. The task force we've dedicated to the case is calling themselves the double-O section. Those guys and gals have been poring over your every movement, past and present. You're becoming a bit of a cult figure."

"No kidding. Why is that?"

"Despite what many people think, Langley's a boring place filled with people who lead very conventional lives. The way you live and the things you do are much more in line with how the office staff see the life of a covert agent."

"Covert agent? I thought I was hired help."

"You're a NOC, Pat. Completely off the books, one of our more valuable assets."

"Wow, I made the big time. That must be why everybody wants to kill me," I said.

"Dr. Schneeberger didn't help matters. You spent a week on the couch being shrunk by the coldest fish in the pond, and our highly trained professional psychiatrist returned to base acting like a blushing bride. She was gushing about you; I kid you not"

"I have a lot of unreconciled emotional issues that women, especially shrinks like Stephanie, find compelling."

"No doubt. So, do you want to hear about our working theory?" asked Mike.

The perky waitress stepped forward and poured the last of the wine. I signaled for a second bottle. She smiled and walked away. It was turning into a pleasant evening. It was reassuring that Mike was looking out for me, and if the body language from Carley the waitress was any indication, my string of bad luck was coming to an end.

"Can you fill me in on what your team has come up with?"

"There's no way either the attack on your yacht or the attack on your plane could've been coordinated without the help from someone inside the UAE government. In both cases, they had to know when you were departing, your route, and your destination. This is all information that's closely held, especially the C-130 delivery schedule. The most likely source was UAE intelligence."

"You think UAE intelligence is after me?"

"Not necessarily the organization. It could be that someone inside UAE intel with access to your movements and communications is supplying that info to your hunter."

The waitress returned with a second bottle of white wine and fresh glasses.

"I'm not sure how we should follow up on that. What else do you have?" I asked.

"We used fingerprints to identify Ghaneem, the Kuwaiti who was killed trying to escape. He was a very bad guy. He was the officer above Jihadi John and the rest of the savages who filmed all of those executions during the ISIS heyday. Ghaneem's a graduate of the Q course and the Marine Corps Staff College. We've been requesting more information about him from the Kuwait government, but they're stonewalling."

"This is getting interesting."

"The Trident operation is supported by the UAE government at the highest levels, so there's no way the UAE government is trying to kill you. That said, the likely connections between the UAE and Kuwaiti government can't be overlooked. Our working theory is that there's a rogue element within UAE and Kuwait that wants to put Trident out of business by killing you."

"That doesn't make sense. The Iranians would never work with either UAE or Kuwait, and I was definitely attacked by the Iranians."

"The Navy intercepts just about every radio call in the Persian Gulf and records most Iranian military traffic. From what little we were able to capture, we think those fast boats were sent by the IRG to intercept a drug runner. The UAE has a large Iranian population in Dubai, mostly in the Deira area. They're involved in all sorts of smuggling and contraband. In order to fight the cross smuggling that goes both ways, the two governments have back channels for communications. We believe a message was sent to the Iranians flagging you as a drug smuggler and that's why you were attacked."

"Can you prove that?"

"No, we don't have the message traffic from UAE to Iran, only the internal radio comms within the IRG that indicate they were going after a smuggler."

"Why would someone in UAE or Kuwait want to shut down Trident and our support to the Peshmerga?"

"There are three possible motivations. It could be anti-Kurd, it could be pro-ISIS, or it could be something more complicated."

"If I have to guess I'll go with more complicated. In the Middle East, the most complicated answer is usually the right one. It's the corollary to Occam's razor. What's next?"

"We have your back. Carry on the same as before but stay off the cargo delivery runs and remain hypervigilant."

I nodded my head and finished my glass of wine. I watched Carley as she carried a tray to a nearby table.

"Notice I said vigilant and not vigilante. I've seen your temper in action. Let's not have a repeat of Afghanistan," Mike said.

"Once we figure out the culprit, or culprits, I won't go off half-cocked. Whoever had the stroke to pull off those last two attacks is a heavy hitter, so we're going to have to be very careful." Which was my way of saying, *Hey, if you know who did this, you can share it with me. I won't do anything stupid without your approval.*

"Once we figure this out, I promise I'll bring you in, we'll settle this together."

"That's good with me. I don't want to disappoint my vicarious team members in the double-O section. They expect me to fight my own battles."

Mike chuckled at that. We hung around for another hour and finished the second bottle of wine while swapping stories. I asked for the check and tucked inside the folder was a piece of paper with Carley's cell number. It was a little after ten, and the restaurant closed at eleven. I gave her my credit card and asked if she was free to go out later. Mike looked at me after Carley left and shook his head.

"Seriously? She's half your age."

"The poor thing is desperate. This is D.C. She told me earlier that I'm the first guy she's met in this town who wasn't either gay or married. Besides, I'm smitten."

"The only way a girl with those looks is going out with you is if she's being paid by the opposition. In the trade, we call this a honey trap."

In my most matter-of-fact, authoritarian tone, I replied, "I don't want to lecture you on tradecraft, but I've already taken precautions. Before you got here, I hacked the employee records and verified she's been employed at this restaurant for two years. She has a perfect performance record and I've already confirmed she has no homework tonight. This a cleared operation, and everything is a go."

Mike laughed at that. "Tradecraft? Where did you learn that word? I hate to break it to you, but you're a knuckle dragger—what we in the business call a shooter. Your exploits may moisten the analysts' panties back at Langley, but when done right, an agent's job is supposed to be boring. Your skill set is something entirely different from that of an intelligence operative."

"Don't worry. I'll be safe. I'll use protection, I promise."

"Seriously, Pat, I'm not kidding. Don't be too cavalier about things. Someone serious is trying to take you out and you don't have the right kind of training to handle every situation."

Mike could see from my expression that I wasn't too thrilled at his remark. He continued, "If you think you do, take this test. Look around the room for a moment and see if you can pick out the two members of my personal security detail."

I took a few minutes and inspected every table of the half-empty restaurant.

"It's the nondescript middle-aged couple closest to the door." I figured that was the best tactical option. Because the table covered the entire dining room, and allowed them to control the ingress and egress, and the couple was nondescript, as a security detail should be.

"Too obvious," said Mike. "Nobody would take that spot." He tapped a message into his phone and two people at different tables in the dining room stood up and then sat down.

"Why does someone in your position need a PSD in your own hometown anyway?"

"My staff does event-based threat assessments. Being anywhere near you at this moment is considered very high risk."

"Jesus, what a buzzkill you are."

As we stood up to leave, Carley came over with a big smile, jacket on, carrying her purse. She announced that her boss had let her off early. I grinned as the three of us walked to the door. Mike shook my hand and hopped into his government car along with his security detail. Carley and I walked arm in arm out into the crisp fall night.

Chapter 17

Eleuthera, Bahamas

I walked through the sliding doors to the sun deck on the second floor. I was holding a small cream-colored towel that was spotted with blood to my chin. The towel was wrapped around some ice cubes and was chilly against my face. I sank into a deck chair comforted by the fact that the blurriness in my vision was gone. I could see the two outbuildings straddling the infinity pool and the line of swaying palms that bordered the beach. It was difficult to see the water through the palms, but the roar of the surf was an unmistakable reminder of the ferocity of ocean.

Eleuthera is an Out Island, located fifty miles east of Nassau, Bahamas. It's little more than a sand dune that's one hundred and ten miles long and less than one mile wide in most places. It's mostly deserted with a year-round population of only eight thousand. Eleuthera is famous for its pink beaches and native vibe. It isn't commercialized and crowded like Nassau and so many of the other islands of the Caribbean.

I inspected my makeshift ice pack and rotated it to an unused spot. The bleeding had almost stopped. It was hurricane season. Tropical Storm Nicole passed over the island yesterday, and was still generating huge swells. Today's waves were over twenty feet. I'd gone out on my Xanadu Chase big wave board this morning with the dawn patrol.

Surfing is addictive. Not only is it a great workout, but there's a Zen quality to it that's hard to explain. Fighting through the surf to get out from the shore, picking the right wave, charging and dropping into a big swell, and then riding into the curl is an intoxicating experience. It takes a lot of effort, especially if you don't do it very often, but it's great fun when the conditions are right.

If I hadn't been exhausted, bleeding and possibly concussed, I'd probably still be in the water. Like all adrenaline junkies, being crushed by a breaking wave, nearly drowning while tumbling through the washing machine, and taking a shot to the jaw from my own board wasn't what I'd remember from this morning's experience.

The home on Banks Road in Governor's Harbor is a long-term project. When I'm done with the guns and ammo business it's where I plan on retiring. It's more a complex than a home. In addition to the main house it has two outbuildings. One is a pool house with an attached chapel and the other is a four-bedroom guesthouse with two apartment suites. One of the apartments is the home of Father Tellez and his sister. Father Tellez has been a friend since we served together in Germany, before the First Gulf War. He's originally from Columbia, and he served as an Army Chaplain until he retired a few years ago.

The second apartment is the home of Maria and Jonah, the Filipino couple who maintain the property and double as household staff. Both are devout Catholics who attend daily Mass with Father Tellez in our private chapel along with a handful of neighborhood faithful. Jonah and Maria are wonderful people. I met them while working at Falcon and offered to bring them to the Bahamas. It's been less than a year and they're already starting to bring over relatives. Which I imagine means they like it here.

I placed the damp towel on the glass top of the wicker table next to me and picked up my cell. Yesterday, while I was on the private charter from Dulles to the tiny Governor's Harbor Airport, I had an idea. Which is why I decided to run it by Mike.

"I've had an epiphany," I said.

"I'm not sure if that's the right word to describe whatever happened between you and that waitress."

"No, it's about what you said about my not being cut out for the cloak and dagger. I'm a fighter. Hiding and waiting for the answer from a bunch of Ivy League analysts at Langley isn't playing to my strengths."

"What do you have in mind?" Mike said.

"I'm going to spend a few more days taking care of business in the Bahamas, and then I'm going back to Abu Dhabi. I'm going to talk to the people who are surveilling me and figure out who supplied my travel plans to the attackers."

"How do you plan on doing that? Intel agencies aren't typically very cooperative about such things."

"I have some cachet with the UAE government, you told me that yourself. I think they'll help me if I ask."

"We're highly confident the info on your movements made it to your attackers through the Emirati's. You probably do have enough *wasta* to get them to do a mole hunt, but even if they identify the culprit, don't expect them to give you any information, that's not how things work."

"Yeah, I know, but I'm pretty sure I can get access to the mole if they find him."

"If there's a mole, and you get access, then what?"

"Then I'll follow the mole's contacts up the chain until I find whoever killed my guys."

"Don't get your hopes up, but it's worth a try. If you need any help opening doors, just let me know."

"So that's a green light, then?"

"Yes, it is. Do it."

I ended the call, got up from my chair and went back into the house. This was only the second time I'd visited the house and the first time it wasn't finished. Years ago, I moved the Trident Headquarters to the Bahamas when I started working for the CIA. The lawyers told me it would offer more liability and tax protection. I only started building the house because there was a minimum investment needed to obtain government approval. The investment in the office and property put me over the limit. The package Trident obtained from the Bahamas included citizenship and resident visas for my staff. Now that I had a place to stay on the island, I was starting to really like it.

My home office covers the entire top floor. It's about the only space in the house I spend any time in. The office has two picture windows. One window faces the dark waters of the Atlantic to the east and that the other faces the Caribbean side of the island to the west. Technically it's not the Caribbean, it's the Bight of Eleuthera, but that's how Eleuthera advertises itself and how people know it, as an island splitting the Atlantic and Caribbean. The waters to the West are bright turquois and placid while on the Atlantic side they're much darker and turbid.

The view out the western window overlooks Banks Road, which is the only route to the house. Beyond Banks Road is Edwin's Turtle Lake Marine Preserve, and in the far distance, the Grand Bahama Reef.

In Eleuthera, the sun rises over the Atlantic side and sets over the Caribbean side. My office is paneled with light wood and has a rich blue carpet and contemporary wooden furniture matching the paneling. It's more of an office suite because it has a work area, a large sitting area with a leather couch, love seat, and recliner, a bathroom and even a small bedroom.

After a couple hours of paperwork, I headed out. On my way out the door, I donned a pair of Ray-Bans and climbed into my blue Tahoe. First stop was the Trident office, which is a converted house off Queen Street, the main drag in downtown Governor's Harbor. When I moved the Trident headquarters from North Carolina, Jessica agreed to relocate and run things. Jessica and two local Bahamian women manage the Trident financial and administrative operations from the office on Queen Street.

The building had originally been a two-story residence when it was built in the late nineteenth century. It was a grand home commissioned by a wealthy trader and constructed in the style of the West Indies, with exterior stone walls covered with conch-pink stucco. White wooden storm shutters surrounded the windows, and four white pillars stretched from the ground to the roof in the front. Jessica had completely renovated and modernized the house since we'd bought it.

Governor's Harbor has a daily ferry to Nassau and a small airport that makes travel very convenient. A flight to Fort Lauderdale is only 250 miles. Another benefit of the office location is that it's only a two-minute walk to the First Caribbean Bank.

Jessica got up and gave me a big hug when I walked into her second-floor office. She took me around to meet the two clerks who'd been hired since my last visit. The four of us sat downstairs in a common area that was set up very much like a living room. I used the time to get to know the local women. They seemed very nice, and the chemistry between the three ladies appeared to be very good.

After the meeting, Jessica and I left the building and strolled up Buccaneer Hill to the Buccaneer Club for lunch. We sat outside in the shade surrounded by a garden of bougainvillea, hibiscus, and coconut palms. The small fenced in seating area has a rooster that runs around loose.

It was a little after two and I hadn't eaten all day. When the large Bahamian waitress came over, I ordered the conch soup and grilled grouper. Jessica ordered the curried crawfish and shrimp fried rice. Jessica is an evangelical Baptist and doesn't drink. We both ordered iced teas. We spent some time catching up on family news. Jessica's husband's latest business enterprise is captaining a fishing boat. I knew better than to ask how the business was doing.

The loss and replacement of the C-130J was an unexpected expense that had Jessica a little concerned.

"You need to take it easy with the checkbook for a while," Jessica said.

"I will. Do we have enough coming in to cover things?"

"Yes, just barely, so no new toys," Jessica scolded.

"I'll be on my best behavior. I promise."

Jessica smiled. "I know you will. How did you get that bump on your chin?"

"Surfing. My board hit me."

"You just look for ways to get into trouble, don't you?"

"Falling off a surfboard isn't trouble. It's a distraction to keep my mind off the real trouble."

"This is the first time I've ever heard you admit to being worried. You're either evolving or you're in over your head, which is it?"

"I'm definitely in the deep end, but I can handle it. If you have some difficulty getting ahold of me for the next little while, don't panic, it's just me solving the problem."

"The same problem that killed Joe Ferguson and Joe Kilpatrick?" Jessica said.

"Yes, that's the one."

"You be careful," she said.

"I'm always careful, you know that."

Jessica reached across the table and touched the bruise on my chin.

"You're not always careful. Call me if you need anything, anytime."

When I got back to the house, I found Father Tellez in the kitchen with Maria. The father is a big hugger and he caught me right away. He led me outside, and we sat on the second-floor deck. It had been long time since I'd seen him and I gave the padre an appraisal. At sixty-one, the Colombian priest looked at least ten years younger. His face had barely a wrinkle. His hair was medium-length and still jet black. He had Central American features with brown eyes, a thick nose, wide expressive mouth and a square jawline. A former member of the Colombian national football team, Father Tellez had grown soft over the years, and he now sported a small belly. He had a warm face and a gentle manner of speaking. One of the mannerisms I've always found endearing is his habit of ending sentences with the word *really*. When we met in the kitchen, for example, he said with a thick Spanish accent, "Pat, it is so good to see you…really."

Maria brought out coffee and the macaroons the father loved. The time I spend with the father should be billed as the meeting between the sinner and the saint. I've always been open with him and he knows just about everything there was to know about me. I don't keep secrets from the padre; I've never seen any point in it. He seems to know things without ever being told. There are some things I've heard about Father Tellez and some that I've seen firsthand that make me think he has a connection with the big guy like no one else on Earth.

"How long are you going to stay?" Father asked.

"I'm leaving tomorrow night."

"Back to Abu Dhabi?"

"Yeah, back to the desert."

"There's a storm coming."

"It's hurricane season, what do you expect. But don't worry, this place was built to withstand anything."

"That's not what I meant. When you return to the Middle East, you're heading into a storm."

"How can you know that?" I asked.

"I can see it on your face. I knew you when you were on active duty. Seen you many times with that look. That's what I see. You're heading into a fight and you shouldn't be. You did your service. Whatever is going on over there is not your fight."

"I don't know if it's my fight or not. All I know is that someone is after me, and they're killing the people around me. I don't see where I have much choice."

Eventually the conversation shifted to family and the foundation. Once I started to build excess cash, I created a charity and made Father Tellez the head of it. His job was to figure out where to donate. It was the perfect role for him, although there always seemed to be more worthy causes than cash.

After the Father left, I told Maria she should go too. She asked if I wanted something for dinner, but I declined. Later, after the sun set, I walked over to Tippy's Restaurant. Tippy's is the quintessential Caribbean beach bar. Even on a Sunday night during hurricane season, the place drew a crowd. It had an open-air design with a series of partially enclosed wooden thatched-roof gazebos located on top of the pink sands of the most beautiful beach on the planet. Off-season, there was no band, but the crowd was always lively.

I sat at the bar and ordered a Sandy's beer. Because it's so close to my house, I ate at Tippy's a lot. A well-publicized review in the *New York Times* put Tippy's on the map and created enough buzz that people drove from the far corners of the island to visit. The food might be over-rated slightly, and the prices were silly. But the view was spectacular, the bar staff outstanding, and if I felt like having a few beers, all I had to do was walk five hundred yards back down the beach to get home.

The bar is open on all four sides, and I had a full view of the ocean from my seat. There was no moonlight, and it was too dark to see anything except the bioluminescence of the surf crashing onto the shore. Diane the waitress came over and delivered my beer, pouring the Sandy's lager bottle into a tall glass. Diane was dressed in cutoff jeans and a yellow Tippy's t-shirt. She's a smiley long-haired brunette with a tall athletic build and green eyes. From my seat, I couldn't read the menu, which is posted on a chalkboard on the other side of the bar, so I asked Diane for a recommendation. She suggested the lobster and shrimp pasta, and I nodded in agreement.

"I saw you out on the water this morning. I was in early for lunch prep, the storm swells looked gnarly."

"Why are you still here? That's a long day," I said.

"One of the other girls called in sick, so I'm working a double."

"The conditions are supposed to be the same tomorrow. You should join me. I could use some pointers."

"Okay. Do you mind if I bring a friend?"

"Not at all," I said as I touched the bruise on my scabbed jaw. "You've seen my skills. The more lifeguards the better."

I finished my dinner, which turned out to be an awesome recommendation and walked back to the house. Surfing was a welcome distraction from the morbid thoughts I was having about Jenny Lyn and our two pilots. I preferred to focus on the tide, wind, and other items that determined surf quality. My plan was to be in the water at first light. Hopefully, Diane would show with her friend. She was a legitimate expert, and anyone she'd bring would likely be of the same caliber. That, in my opinion, is the best way to learn anything. I've always been a pretty decent athlete, but since I've never had the time to dedicate to the sport, my technique is basic. It would be nice to get some pointers from an expert like Diane.

The next morning, I was out on the water alone at seven o'clock. An hour and a half later, Diane and her companion joined me beyond the break. Diane introduced her friend as Finley. Like Diane, he looked to be in his mid-twenties, and just from watching him effortlessly glide through the impact zone, he was in a different league than me. Both Diane and Finley had seen my last run from the beach, and when they finally reached me, they gestured approvingly. It made me laugh at myself, because I genuinely craved the approval of those two twenty-somethings.

After reaching a point of exhaustion by the late morning, I invited the hard-bodied übertalented surfers to lunch. To my surprise, they packed it in early and joined me, although it may have been because the conditions were shifting due to the tide. Maria prepared an enormous meal of barbecued pork ribs, chicken, and steaks, and we drank beer and told stories until I had to wrap things up because I had a flight to catch. Finley is quite a character; he's a web designer from California who relocated to Governor's Harbor two years ago. Finley has an excellent sense of humor, and his impressions of the island tourists had me in stitches.

I took a private charter from Governor's Harbor to Miami and then flew Emirates direct to Dubai. After the exertions earlier in the day, I slept like a rock during most of the flight. If I learned nothing else during my time in the Army, I'd learned to take advantage of the downtime while traveling.

I woke up and ordered breakfast. I had to wait until the cabin stewardess was done being chewed out by a flabby Arab guy over the limited yogurt selection. Beyond learning to sleep on anything that moved, the Army also taught me to appreciate how good I had it these days. I can't imagine what would make someone get so worked up over yogurt.

As I reclined in first class, the abusive jerk triggered memories about the discomfort of military airborne operations and my one mass tactical combat jump with the Rangers. I was subconsciously preparing myself for a fight. I was going to approach this problem with the same grim determination I had as a soldier. Like the fat Arab guy throwing the tantrum, my enemy was most likely a soft bully who'd never taken a punch. That's my biggest advantage. I've been getting knocked around my whole life, and I have a very high pain tolerance.

Chapter 18

Abu Dhabi, UAE

I woke up in my cabin aboard the *Sam Houston* and put on my workout clothes. I made myself a cup of coffee in the galley and then walked through the salon to the aft deck and sat on the couch. The weather was dry and warm, which is the best part about October in the UAE.

After returning from the gym, my first stop was the Falcon office. While I'm no longer the COO, I'm still Falcon's biggest customer. I made my rounds, greeting the administrative staff and the few sales guys who were hanging around. I went over some routine shipping and finance details with the accounting and admin teams. Around noon, the CEO, Ahmed Al Junaibi, arrived, and we met in his office.

Ahmed was happy to see me. He had the tea boy bring the *qahwah*, and we enjoyed a small cup of the strong Arabic coffee before getting down to business. The finance manager brought in four sets of contracts that we'd prepared together. Each set consisted of a purchase contract between a supplier and Falcon and a purchase contract between Falcon and Trident. I asked Ahmed to review and sign the contracts. Each was already countersigned by either the supplier or by Trident. It was an easy profit that Ahmed made because of Trident, and he was appreciative enough that he signed on the spot with only a cursory review. When Ahmed was done, I left one set of originals with him and kept the other.

Before leaving, I asked the CEO if Obaid, the company chairman, was in town. I could tell he was curious why I was asking, because he knows I rarely communicate with the chairman. I told him it was a personal matter and that I intended to ask a favor of him.

Ahmed made the call for me and requested a meeting. Obaid told Ahmed to have me meet him at his farm right away. During the hour-and-a-half trip on the Al Ain Highway, I rethought my plan. I'd been confident when I was in the Bahamas that the Emiratis would offer up the traitor, who'd been an accomplice to the murder of Jenny Lyn and my two pilots. Now that I was back in UAE, I began to doubt they'd offer up one of their own just because he'd betrayed an Ameriki. There's an old Arab saying: *Me against my brothers. Me and my brothers against my cousins. Me and my brothers and my cousins against the world.* Instead of expecting the UAE to hand over the traitor, I decided on the fly to encourage the UAE government to flush the traitor out and then snatch him away when they least expected it.

Obaid owns a huge farm near Al Ain, a city adjacent to the Oman border of UAE. During the pre-oil days, many in Abu Dhabi would retreat from the coast to the cooler climes of Al Ain. The hundred-mile trip to the date-palm oasis of Al Ain used to take three days by camel.

I was navigating to a pin that Obaid sent me via WhatsApp. I came to a gate and told the guard I was visiting the General. He waved me through. The road to the main house wasn't paved, it was a winding trail bordered by palm trees. I looked around for the camel herd that Obaid had once mentioned but saw no sign of it. Two miles later, I pulled up at the farmhouse, it was a big spread.

Obaid's house is a rambling single-story stone structure. As I approached the front door, a male servant opened it and gestured for me to enter. I was escorted into a large room about the size of a tennis court that had chairs and accompanying coffee tables lining three of the walls. The floor was white marble tile. The room was lit by five huge crystal chandeliers and had no exterior windows. It was a traditional *majlis*, very common to the area. General Obaid was seated alone at the far end of the room on an elevated dais.

General Obaid is a short muscular man who, since retiring from the military several years back, had begun to sport a belly. He has a large hawkish nose and longish black hair and a short well-groomed beard without a hint of gray. A volatile personality, prone to emotional outbursts, he has a reputation as a keen intellect. Obaid's a member of one of the most prominent families of Al Ain; his family has been closely aligned with the ruling family all the way back to the days when the tribes had defended the Al Ain oasis from interlopers with swords. What I've always liked about him is his uncharacteristic candor, he's one of the few Arabs I've ever met who says what he means and means what he says.

After all the courtesies were dispensed with, I laid out the situation for him as clearly as I could. I described the attack on my boat and the Stinger attack on my C-130. Obaid listened quietly without any interruption. When I was finished, he went right to the point.

"Who wants you dead?" he asked.

"I don't know. All I know is that neither the attack on the water nor the attack in the air could've been accomplished without detailed information on my travel plans. I was the only person who was aware of the plans for both trips, and I didn't attack myself."

"Maybe you have more than one leaker, one for the boat, one for the plane?" he said.

"Only three people had knowledge of the boat trip schedule—myself and my two crewmates—one of whom was killed. With all the traffic in the strait, the Iranians couldn't have intercepted us without accurate information on our departure time and route."

"What about the air cargo mission?" he said.

"That had more people in the know, but they were all cleared, and most were on the aircraft when it was attacked."

"Like I said, it could be two sources."

"The timing on the C-130 attack had to be even more precise. Beyond the people in the aircraft, the only other people who knew the flight details were the US military and the Agency. I don't see any motive for them to destroy the supplies they paid for, and I'm just a cargo hauler doing something both the UAE and USA want done."

"Who do you suspect?" asked Obaid.

"Someone in the UAE intel service that's surveilling me. Because I'm an expat, and because of the business I'm in, I'm under constant surveillance by the UAE government. I think someone who had access to the information collected on me by the UAE government surveillance program provided the info to the bad guys who used it to attack me."

"The UAE would never tip either the Iranians or Daesh. We're on very hostile terms with both. UAE isn't the only government that surveils you, is it?" he said.

"You have me on that point. But the UAE does it the most consistently and the most thoroughly. I really have no idea why someone wants me eliminated. But I'm almost positive the only element that had the information to plan both attacks was UAE SSI."

The general poured himself some Moroccan tea from a gold tea set in front of him. "When you called me, you said you were visiting to ask a favor of me. What is it you ask?"

"Sir, I want to request His Highness initiate an investigation of the UAE intelligence personnel who have access to my files. I'd like for him to identify the person who accessed my file on these dates." I handed the general an index card with two time windows on it.

"Why these dates?"

"Each of those time frames represent the windows from when each trip was planned to when each trip began. As you can see, neither window is more than two days long; the search should be quick and simple. We're talking about electronic files. I was in the secret government world for a while. I know every time someone opens an intelligence file, it leaves a record of who opened it and a timestamp of when it was opened. It should be a simple matter to identify the person who opened my file inside those time windows. Whoever that person is, that should be the mole."

I drove away from General Obaid's farm convinced I'd started the chain reaction I wanted. General Obaid would raise the matter to the parent group chairman of Falcon, Sheik Abdullah. The group chairman is the brother of the crown prince. Within the hierarchy, he's number three, behind the crown prince and the president. In addition to serving as chairman of the largest company in the UAE, Sheik Abdullah is also the minister of national security, which means that all the intelligence directorates report to him, including the agency responsible for electronic surveillance. I'm positive General Obaid will attend the Sheik's majlis this evening and forward my request.

Because of my former work at Falcon, I have a working relationship with the national security personnel. For the most part, they're selected based on family loyalty and education. I've seen enough of them to have a decent idea of their capabilities. As a rule, the agents are good citizens, loyal, hardworking, and well educated. These are men who've grown up in palaces and never experienced deprivation of any kind. They're at the top of a very rigid caste system, and they've been bossing the lesser classes around since they were old enough to form words and tell their nannies what to do. I don't expect any of them to hold up well under pressure.

It was mid-morning the next day when I stopped in at Al Dhafra Air Force Base and checked on the team. When I reached the company hangar, I found the plane parked inside and the whole team hanging around the break area. I went around to each of the guys, checked on how they were doing. It's hard on everyone when you lose people, like we did with Joe and Joe. Eventually, I broke away and went into the airplane. I'm sure the guys watched me walk up the ramp and return with a go-bag on my shoulder. This was something that has never happened before. There was never any reason to move the go-bags. I could feel the eyes on me.

With the bag on my shoulder I returned to the entrance of the break area, which is sectioned off from the hangar with a waist high chain link fence. I said one word loud enough for all to hear—"Budweiser"—and then turned around and went straight to my truck. The OPSKED "Budweiser" is our code word for "Move to the alternate air base." The alternate base is a leased hangar at a civilian airport in Paphos, Cyprus. It meant for all future shipments, the paperwork would continue to go through Falcon in Abu Dhabi, but until further notice, transshipping would be done through Cyprus.

I hurried to my truck, not wanting to answer any questions. I knew the team would immediately get to work. They had a lot to do: filing flight plans, conducting the preflight, getting approval from security command to depart UAE, and generally taking all actions necessary to get out of UAE airspace as soon as possible.

I tossed my bag in the back of the truck and covered it with a blanket. I figured it would take at most an hour before the Trident Team was safely away from the reach of the UAE government. My replacement Herc and crew weren't due to arrive for another week. I'd get the word to them through Jessica.

My next stop was the Al Dar building which is located near the airport. The building is a giant twenty-five story disc. It's an office building that houses a number of corporate offices as well as a handful of government agencies. Most countries hide their versions of the US National

Security Agency in places like Fort Meade, but for some reason the SIA is headquartered in one of the most conspicuous buildings in the world. The building also hosts the company they contract to do most of their IT work, it's named Dark Matter and has an equally Marvel Comics feel about them.

I've been to the Al Dar building dozens of time, because it's the Abu Dhabi headquarters for several of the larger global defense companies. From a surveillance perspective it's a dream, because it has only one access road. I found a spot in the above ground parking area with a view to the main entrance and access road and waited.

For the next five hours, I observed dozens of vehicles drive to the building. I had a couple of false alarms, but none completely fit the profile I was looking for. I was filching through the go-bag for night vision when three white Nissan Patrol SUVs with black-tinted windows exited the highway and turned onto the access road. That was the confirmation I was waiting for. I hopped on the Al Salam highway and headed toward downtown Abu Dhabi.

The National Intelligence office is in one of the busiest sections of downtown Abu Dhabi. The complex covers an entire city block and is surrounded by an intimidating twelve-foot brick wall with triple-strand concertina on the top and hundreds of surveillance cameras spaced every five meters on top of the wall. The front gate has triple-layer security with an armed guard and a hydraulic metal barrier that descends to allow traffic to pass. I've been through the main gate a few times in the past, but never inside the main building. All commercial business with civilians is transacted in a sterile building next to the main office.

It was already dark when I found a parking spot on Al Falah Road. While at Falcon that morning, I'd borrowed a REBS collapsible ladder from the samples inventory. It's a three-foot-long tube that telescopes out to a length of ten feet. As it extends, ladder steps branch out into place. The top of the ladder has a big hook that can be used to secure it to a ledge.

The flaw in the security is too much security. The height of the wall and number of cameras are intimidating, but no human can effectively monitor the hundreds of cameras surrounding the perimeter wall. AI computer systems can do it, but I'm betting they have only a few guys staring at banks of constantly flipping video screens. I was travelling light in covert mode. Beyond the tube ladder in my hand, I had a SkeetIR thermal monocular in the cargo pocket of my Beyond tactical pants and a SIG P226 with an extra mag and an OSS suppressor in my other cargo pocket. A set of flex cuffs were stuffed inside my belt.

I made the quarter mile walk from my truck without attracting any attention. It was early evening and there was a fair amount of road traffic, but no other pedestrians. I approached the southern wall on the opposite side of the entrance wall and extended the ladder between two cameras, compressing the concertina wire on top. I scurried up the ladder and then while standing with my feet on the wire, I flipped the ladder around and climbed down. The ladder collapsed smoothly as I hurried to a nearby grove of trees. I advanced to the edge of the tree line and then set up an observation point.

At a little past midnight, a convoy of vehicles pulled up to the front gate. The driver of the first vehicle rolled his window down and the metal barrier descended.

When the convoy reached the main building, the first and third vehicles kept going, and the second stopped at the main entryway. I stayed in the shadows and creeped my way to the back of the SUV. The driver and passenger doors opened. I was crouched behind the tailgate as the two men preoccupied themselves with assisting their prisoner out of the truck.

When I stepped around the truck, the prisoner was standing with his hands cuffed behind his back. Each of the other two men had a hold of an arm and all three were facing the entrance way to the building. I pounced and hit the intel officer on the far right with an openhanded strike to the back of the head. The strike knocked him down face first and made a thunderous clap. The intel officer holding the prisoner's left arm spun his head in my direction and freed his right hand from the prisoner. I hit with a left jab to the nose and a right uppercut to the jaw that sent him to the ground. I grabbed the prisoner by the neck, pushed him into the backseat of the still-running truck. I closed the door and got into the driver's seat. The security guard couldn't see through the darkly tinted window of the Nissan, he just automatically lowered the metal barrier as I approached.

The prisoner was still lying flat along the backseat of the Nissan as I pulled up behind my Explorer. The prisoner was stick thin with a wispy beard. He was wearing a white kandura without the headdress. His eyes were filled with terror as I pulled him from the Nissan and dragged him into the backseat of the Explorer.

My right hand was throbbing as I steered the Explorer along the Corniche Road to the Marina. The intel officers were just doing their job and I didn't want to kill them. I pulled into the Intercontinental Hotel parking lot and found a spot close to the *Sam Houston.* I opened the tail gate and strapped the heavy go-bag around my shoulders, then I opened the rear side door to get the prisoner.

No sooner did I have the door open than the prisoner began to scream, he sounded like a young girl on a roller coaster. I dragged him out by his feet and lifted him to a standing position with my right hand tight around his throat. The prisoner stopped screaming. I put him in a headlock and dragged the 140-pound kid onto the boat. Once I got up the stairs to the aft deck, I tripped him onto the ground and flex-cuffed his legs. He flopped around like a fish as he was dragged through the salon doors across the hardwood floor forward to the wheelhouse. I secured him to the captain's chair and left him to untie the *Houston* and get ready to cast off.

He stared at me with a pleading look when I cranked up the engines and set a course due north into the darkness and isolation of the Gulf of Arabia.

I killed the engines once the nav system showed we were twenty miles offshore. The radar didn't show any boats nearby and the nearest oil rig was beyond line of sight. I untied the prisoner and dragged back to the stern and out the salon doors and onto the aft deck. I sat him down on the back couch. Despite our having been together for about two hours, we'd yet to speak a word to each other.

I broke the ice.

"There are two possibilities for how this night is going to work out for you. The first possibility is, you tell me what I want to know, and I'll return you to Abu Dhabi alive. The second is, you don't honestly answer my questions, and you die a painful death after I find out what I need to know."

He seemed perplexed by my words until I snapped his head back with a quick left jab. I went back inside the salon to retrieve my video camera. I set the video camera up on a tripod and turned on the deck lights. The prisoner watched me with horror. He still had a trickle of blood flowing out of his nose when I pulled a deck chair over and sat down in front of him.

"What do you want from me?" the man pleaded.

"Start with your name and then tell me your story."

The prisoner didn't say anything. I got up and went into the galley and returned with a large knife.

"Let's start with your name and where you work," I said with cold determination in my eyes.

"My name is Mansour Al Sadiki. I work for SIA as a senior analyst."

"Why were you arrested by National Intelligence?"

"I was detained by mistake; I've done nothing wrong. Before I had a chance to explain, you kidnapped me," Mansour said in an offended tone.

I wasn't in the mood for a verbal duel. I got up and went to the rail and retrieved a tie-down line. I wrapped it around Mansour's skinny waist, tied it off and then picked him up over my head and tossed him overboard. With the cuffs on his hands and flex-cuffs on his feet, Mansour sank like a rock. After fifteen seconds, I grabbed the line and walked down the stairs to the hydraulic platform and began to pull him in. Soon he was laying on his stomach, with his soaking white dress up to his waist gasping for air.

"Are you ready to cooperate, or do you want to go for another swim?" I asked.

Mansour nodded, and so I pulled him back upstairs and put him back in the chair.

"Why were you arrested?"

"I accessed files I was not supposed to access."

"What was in the files?"

"They were your files, audio and data files from you and your associates."

"Who am I?"

"You're Pat Walsh."

"Who were my associates?"

"I don't remember the names. They were people who work for you."

"Who told you to access my files?"

He didn't answer right away. I waited patiently. After a minute without a response, I grabbed Mansour under the armpits and tossed him back into the ocean backward. This time I waited thirty seconds before reeling him in.

"Are you ready to continue?" I asked.

"His Highness Sheik Rasheed asked me to copy your file and forward it on two occasions, and that's all I did. I didn't do anything wrong. I can't say no to a Highness." He whimpered.

"If you had said no to a Highness, three people would still be alive right now. You killed two men and an innocent woman," I said.

I spent the next hour probing the details of how Sheik Rasheed had communicated with Mansour and how he'd accessed and relayed the information. When I was satisfied Mansour had divulged all he knew on the subject, I set course for Sir Banyas Island. The Anantara Beach resort is the only building on the island. I brought the *Houston* as close to the hotel's beachfront as I dared, put a life preserver in his cuffed hands, cut the flex ties binding his ankles and pushed him backward into the water.

I wasn't sure how long it was going to take for the authorities to pick up Mansour and discover what he'd revealed to me, but I knew I had to hurry if I was going to maintain the element of surprise. I steered the boat back to the city. Abu Dhabi has a lot of coastal islands, and the going was slow as I threaded my way through them in the dark. The *Houston* has an advanced radar and a FLIR camera, but it's what's below the surface that had me worried. I had no way of being sure the data in the yacht's navigation system was current with the endless reclamation work being done in Abu Dhabi. My next destination was Al Hudayriat Island, which is a deserted man-made island that's less than a thousand yards from the most expensive gated community in the world, Al Muzoon.

Al Muzoon island is another reclamation project, it's connected to Abu Dhabi by a long narrow land bridge with a heavily guarded gate. The island is one half a mile wide and three miles long and the only residents are members of the royal family and a few billionaires. The residences are palatial, each with hundreds of rooms. I've never been on the island. I was relying on the information provided by Mansour who as a member of Sheik Rasheed's majlis was a frequent visitor to his palace.

I anchored the *Houston* in ten feet of water on the Gulf facing side of Al Hudayriat Island. It was three in the morning; the water was calm and the moon was full. I was kitted up for what lay ahead, wearing black sportive climbing shoes, a climbing harness, and a fanny pack. Inside the pack was my pistol, a diving knife, a taser, tape and some additional climbing gear.

I pushed the tender off the hydraulic lift, hopped in and started the small outboard. The moonlight was good enough to allow me to find the narrow canal bisecting Al Hudayriat Island. As I exited the canal, I spotted Sheik Rasheed's palace, it was hard not to, as it was directly in front of me. I tied the eleven-foot tender onto one of the rocks that bordered the shoreline. The moment of truth was rapidly approaching, I was about to find out if I'd made a mistake letting Mansour live.

I disembarked and scrambled over the seawall. A few yards in, I encountered a four-foot-high wall that surrounded the property. I crouched behind the wall and listened for signs of movement on the other side. I was confident Mansour had already made contact with the authorities, but I knew they would only interrogate him in person and given his location and the time of night, I expected that to take hours.

My plan was based on speed and a lax security. The UAE government and its royal family are loved by its residents—not just the one million or so citizens, but also the other eight million expatriates who live in UAE. It's not an uncommon site to see the ruler of UAE having a cup of coffee with a small security detail. I was expecting minimal security at Sheik Rasheed's palace, in fact, I was counting on it.

I hopped over the fence and sprinted across the grass to the main building. The ornately designed stone walls made for an abundance of handholds and footholds. The climb upward to the third floor was easy. There was only one balcony on the third floor, so I had no trouble finding the right one. I peered onto the balcony before climbing higher and then stepping down onto the balcony rail. I lowered myself to the balcony floor and creeped to the door. I turned the doorknob and walked straight in.

The bedroom was enormous, and in the dark, if it weren't for the snoring, it would've been impossible to find the bed. As I drew close, the shapes of two sleeping bodies came into view. I rotated the fanny pack around my waist and withdrew the strips of duct tape I'd pre-cut and hung two pieces around my wrist. I removed the Taser and kept it in my right hand. I made it to the side of the bed without alerting anyone, then I reached down and yanked the covers off. I jammed the Taser against the midsection of the bigger shape and pulled the trigger. While the Taser was still shocking the sheik, I covered the mouth of the startled woman with my left hand, who looked like she was about to scream.

I dropped the Taser and taped the woman's mouth and flex-cuffed her hands and feet. Then I taped the sheik's mouth and flex tied his wrists. With a piece of tubular nylon, I made a figure eight and put an arm through each loop. I reached around my back and connected the two loops with a carabiner. I used another tubular nylon piece to make a field-expedient harness around the sheik's waist and clipped a carabiner onto the front. Then I flex tied his ankles.

I stood the sheik up and took a knee in front of him, allowing him to rest on my back. Reaching behind, I connected the carabiner on my back to the carabiner in front of the sheik's climbing harness, then I used another piece of tubular nylon to cinch the sheik tight to me in a piggyback position. I used my last nylon tube to wrap around a column on the balcony and connected it with a carabiner. I clipped the byte at the midpoint of my climbing rope onto the carabiner and threaded it into my figure eight descender.

The sheik was overweight, and I struggled to get over the balcony rail with him on my back. I abseiled slowly to the ground and headed off back to the tender at a slow trot. I staggered across the perfectly manicured lawn, crawled over the wall and then down to the rocky ledge where I left the tender. After I untied it, I brought the tender over broadside and rolled into it with the sheik underneath me. I felt like an upside-down turtle.

I cut the figure eight off me, moved over to the outboard and started up the engine. The sheik was flopping around on the tender floor like a fish. I navigated back toward Al Hudayriat Island and found the small canal opening. Before long I was back at the *Houston*. I dropped the hydraulic lift below the waterline, moved the tender on top and then raised it and the sheik above the water line.

The sheik struggled mightily as I positioned him for a fireman's carry and climbed the stairs with him to the aft deck. I took him through the salon doors and dumped him on the hard wood floor of the galley.

Moving forward to the wheelhouse, I raised the anchor and headed out into international waters. In less than an hour, I was in the shipping lane, heading North to the Strait of Hormuz.

I found an oil tanker heading in the same direction and positioned the boat in the shadow behind it to mask detection by any of UAE's coastal sensors. By early evening, I found myself thirty miles off the coast of Muscat.

I stopped the engines and set the autopositioning system to keep the boat from drifting. I left the helm station and went back to the galley, where I'd dumped the sheik so many hours earlier. He was still on the floor, bound and gagged and by the look of it, had urinated in his gray silk pajamas.

I'd been going nonstop for over a day. I stepped over his prostrate body and walked to the salon and collapsed onto the couch. When I awoke three hours later, I felt recharged. I ate a bowl of cereal and then went down to the master cabin, shaved, showered, and put on fresh clothes. Returning to the main deck, I dragged the prisoner by the ankle cuffs out onto the aft deck. I set the video camera up on the tripod for the second time in as many days.

I wrapped the tie-down line around his girthy waist and tied it off. Except for being on the receiving side when I was in the Army attending SERE, I'm a complete novice on the subject of enhanced interrogation. However, since the improv water treatment worked so well last time, my plan was to rinse and repeat. Besides, the prisoner smelled terribly. I ripped the duct tape off his mouth and before he had time to say a word, I pushed him over the rail. At the sound of the splash, I dashed down to the hydraulic ramp and slowly pulled him in. When I pulled him onto the platform, he was choking and spluttering.

I brought the sheik back up to the couch and played the video of Mansour's confession for him on my camera.

"There's no sense in denying what you've done and no reason for you to suffer unnecessarily. The only reason you're still alive is to explain why you did and who else is involved," I said.

It took another three hours, but after a great deal of resistance and many trips into the water, not to mention grand offers of riches, threats, and pleas for mercy, I finally got on record the information I was after.

It was already dawn when I connected a diver's weight belt to the flex tie binding his ankles. He was too spent to offer even the slightest resistance as I pushed him one last time over the rail and into the depths of the Gulf of Oman.

My next stop was the Sultan Qaboos Port in Muscat. At the entry dock, I raised the Q flag, and walked over to the customs office to officially enter Oman. After undergoing a cursory walk through inspection of the *Houston*, I was cleared. I refueled and headed six miles further down the coast to Marina Al Bustan. I paid a thirty-day docking fee, connected all the hookups, and set up a base of operations for the next phase of the operation.

I gave the *Houston* a thorough cleaning to remove any evidence of my last visitor. While wiping and scrubbing, I began to formulate a plan. Once everything was shipshape, I showered and walked over to the Blue Marlin Restaurant in the main marina building. I hadn't had a decent meal in days and the grilled kingfish and Stella Artois was amazing.

Back on board, I opened my laptop, connected the camera and uploaded the video from both interrogations. From the laptop, I uploaded both files to a Dropbox account, then I sent an email to Mike Guthrie, asking him to download the files.

While I was waiting for a response from Mike, I booked a round-trip flight to Kuwait for later that evening along with a hotel reservation at the Regency Hotel for a week. I chose the Regency because it's only about half a mile from Sheik Meshal's palace on Nassar Al-Mubarak Street. I was at the dining table in the galley, engrossed in map reconnaissance using Google Earth, when I felt someone stepping onto the boat. Looking through the triple glass door from the salon to the aft deck, I saw a man with his hands up at his shoulders facing me palms forward. I went to the door and let him in.

The man was overdressed for a marina. He was wearing a blue suit; he looked to be about thirty-five, with short sandy hair and a heavy muscular build. The first words out of his mouth were, "Mike Guthrie asked me to deliver a message."

I invited him into the salon and gestured toward the couch. I assumed he was with the Agency, most likely working out of the embassy. The man looked athletic. He had a strong face with intelligent gray eyes and a square jaw. Put a flat-top on him, and he could've been on a US Marine Corps recruiting poster.

"What's the message?"

"Mike wants you to remain in place. He'll be here tomorrow morning, and he doesn't want you to leave this boat until he arrives."

"You can tell him that I'll stay in the marina area until he arrives. I'm sure he sent you to keep an eye on me. Did you bring a bag, or are you going to stay in those same clothes until Mike shows?"

The man smiled. He stood up and stuck out his hand. "The name is Walt Berg. I have instructions not to let you out of my sight. I'll try not to be a nuisance."

"No problem, Walt. Let me know if you need anything. There are two empty cabins below. Pick one and make yourself at home. There's food and beer in the fridge. Help yourself to anything you want."

"Thanks," said Walt. "If you don't mind, I need to go back to my car to get some things and make a call."

While Walt was gone, I changed my plane ticket and delayed the trip to Kuwait City by a day. I saved copies of the interrogations onto a USB drive and hid the thumb drive in the engine room, then went into the wine storage in the galley and selected a bottle of Patrimony 2013 Cabernet Sauvignon and decanted it. In the main salon, I activated a switch that elevated the fifty-five-inch TV from the cabinet and turned on a replay of game two of the Cleveland Indians and Chicago Cubs World Series game. Walt joined me and for the next three hours we talked baseball and drank wine. Afterward, I made a salad and grilled steaks on the flydeck for dinner. Walt was good company.

Chapter 19

Muscat, Oman

The weather was sunny and a dry eighty-four degrees, just a beautiful day. Walt and I were walking back from breakfast at the Blue Marlin. It was a pleasant surprise to discover the restaurant served bacon, a rare treat in the Middle East.

As we approached, I noticed someone sitting on the flydeck. By the time we reached the boat, Mike was at the starboard gate to meet us. We shook hands. Walt stayed on the stern deck while Mike and I went into the salon and closed the glass doors for privacy.

"Can I make you some coffee?" I asked.

"Yeah, thanks."

I made a quick coffee for Mike in the Keurig machine and set it down for him on the table in the galley, along with the sugar and cream.

"Where's Sheik Rasheed?" he asked.

"He's dead and gone, under a thousand feet of water."

"What were you thinking? How do you expect the Emiratis to react?"

"I don't expect them to do anything."

"Seriously? You don't expect them to do anything? You attacked the national security office, assaulted two intelligence officers, and kidnapped a third. You broke into a palace and assaulted a sheik's wife, who also happens to be the niece of the UAE president. Oh, and let's not forget you kidnapped and killed the sheika's husband, the seventh most powerful sheik in the country, a member of the UAE National Security Council and half-brother to the president and the crown prince."

"Sounds pretty bad when you put it like that," I said as I made ginger tea on the galley stove. "But let me ask you this. Has anyone from the UAE leadership mentioned anything about this situation to the United States through official or unofficial channels?"

"So far, no," said Mike.

"The only reason I let Mansour, the intel guy, go was so he could tell his story to the government. When the leadership learns that Sheik Rasheed was responsible for the attacks against me and the deaths of two Americans, they're going to cover everything up. You just watch, that's what they do, they hide mistakes. Sheik Rasheed was working against UAE interests. He was running rogue, and he paid a price. The UAE will conduct an in-depth investigation, and they'll eventually uncover most of the information that was in the confession I sent you."

"How sure are you about that?"

"I'm positive. I've been working with these guys long enough to be sure. Mistakes are always hidden, as are the people who make them. I'll bet Mansour spends the next decade in jail, and Sheik Rasheed reportedly dies of a heart attack and is buried with honors at a state funeral once they confirm he's dead."

"After I received your video files, I briefed the deputy director of clandestine operations, and he hit the roof. Then I had to brief the director. He watched the interrogation of Sheik Rasheed twice. The first time, I thought he was going to have a coronary. He wants your head on a spike. I finally convinced both the DDC and director that it would be in everyone's best interest for me to come out here and bring you in."

"Let me get this straight," I said. "The director of the CIA watches a film where Sheik Rasheed confesses to funding and supporting ISIS, along with his two accomplices Sheik Meshal from Kuwait and Prince Bandar from KSA. In the video, he confesses that he practically co-founded the organization with Baghdadi, nurturing it from its early days to the height of its power. ISIS, an organization that has killed hundreds of thousands of innocents, tortured and enslaved tens of thousands of Christians and Yazidis, and done some of the worst things in the history of man. And the head of US intelligence's first thought when he sees all this is to punish me. That's tragic, what a political hack. The next step isn't to bring me in and yell at me. The next step is to kill Sheik Meshal and Prince Bandar."

Mike finished his coffee. He looked tired. He had bags under his eyes, and it was obvious he was managing a good deal of stress. "If you're so confident the Emiratis are going to do nothing, why did you move your operations to Cyprus?"

"I expect some personal harassment, but nothing officially against the US. They're going to want revenge against me for killing one of their own even if they know he deserved it. While they would never do anything in the open that could be misconstrued as an endorsement of Sheik Rasheed's actions, they'll do something to show that they're beyond touch. The last thing we need is for the personnel and aircraft we rely on for delivery operations to be locked down in UAE because of some paperwork error motivated by payback."

Mike nodded. I knew there was a team in Langley dissecting my every move and thought for the last few days. Most of what I was saying to Mike had no doubt already been predicted by the geeks.

"Let's say you're right, and the crown prince and Sheik Abdullah choose to bury the unfortunate business with Sheik Rasheed. What're you planning on doing next?"

I took my teacup and saucer and sat across the table from Mike on the bench chair.

"Let's remember that Sheik Abdullah owns Falcon, and makes a good profit from our operations. What we're doing not only supports the security needs of UAE, it also benefits these guys financially. Even so, they'll do an investigation, and when they do, they'll find a money trail to ISIS from Sheik Rasheed. They may also find a connection to Sheik Meshal and Prince Bandar.

"It may take them weeks or months, but I think we should assume they'll learn these things. And when they do, they won't use the info to seek justice. They'll use the info for political advantage, which means Meshal and Bandar will skate. We have a small window of time to act. My plan is to travel to Kuwait tonight and take out Sheik Meshal before the disappearance of Sheik Rasheed raises alarm. I doubt anyone but the Emiratis know Sheik Rasheed was taken. By the time I go after Prince Bandar, he's going to know I'm coming for him, so he's going to be the hardest target. But first things first."

"A bunch of guys back at Langley are scratching their heads at what you've been up to—the audacity. It's incredibly bold stuff—impressive and slightly psychotic, but also lucky as hell. The complacency and lax security that made your moves possible in UAE won't exist in Kuwait, believe me."

"I do believe you, but I don't need to conduct a high-risk snatch and grab. Rasheed told me all I need to know. I'm done talking. I don't need to get close. I just need a clear shot."

"This is crazy, but I'm going to try to get a green light on this. Joe Ferguson and Joe Kilpatrick were our guys too."

Mike went outside and got on the telephone with his higher-ups. I could see him pacing with his phone to his ear off and on for over an hour. I imagined, he was shadowboxing with the political appointees and bureaucrats. Finally, he returned to the salon.

"What's the verdict?" I asked him.

"You're okay to travel to Kuwait."

"That was fast."

"The video you sent is very damning. These people created ISIS. Everybody wants you to take them. The problem is we have laws against this sort of thing."

"How'd you get approval then?"

"Officially, I have no idea where you're going or what you plan to do. You're a private citizen with a contract that supports the Department of Defense."

"Meaning?"

"You're on your own. I won't stop you, but I can't help you either. If you get caught, we'll deny everything."

"That's fine by me."

"It's not fine by me, but it's the best I could do, and orders are orders."

I landed at Kuwait International at seven thirty that night. The airport, like most of the infrastructure in Kuwait, was badly in need of modernization. I waited in line at the visa desk for forty-five minutes and then another forty-five minutes in customs clearance and passport control. I was dressed in smart casual, as they call it in the Middle East, wearing a blue sports jacket, white oxford shirt, and tan slacks. I took a taxi to the Regency, which was on the water and in the Salmiya neighborhood where Sheik Meshal's palace is located.

By the time I checked into my room, it was past nine. I walked up the street that parallels the water and ordered a hamburger at a Johnny Rockets restaurant. I'd already changed into jeans, a black polo shirt, and a pair of running shoes. I was unarmed. It wasn't possible to fly with a weapon, and the Agency wasn't going to provide me one in country. Sheik Meshal's palace was only a ten-minute walk from the hotel, and I thought I'd do a preliminary reconnaissance before calling it a night.

The walk around the sheik's place took thirty minutes. The building covered a city block and was bordered by a public sidewalk. Across the street from the palace was a park with children's swing sets, trails, and palm trees. The other three sides of the building were across the street from residences. The streets and sidewalks surrounding the palace had open access. In front of each entryway was a small guard station manned by Kuwait National Guard soldiers.

The palace was a fortress. From the sidewalk, I was close enough to see the refraction in the windows which was a sure indicator they were bulletproof. The weather was pleasant, but none of the windows were open, which was another sure sign. The building had no balconies. The palace was a perfect rectangle, as though the architect was inspired by a simple brick. The two shorter sides of the rectangle each had a pedestrian doorway. There was a large retractable garage door on one of the longer sides, the one along Nasser Al-Mubarak Street, which is a main thoroughfare.

I walked back to the hotel, but once there I couldn't sleep. My mind struggled identifying a viable plan of attack. Unlike the sheik's palace in UAE, where I was given a quality description of the objective from Mansour, I had no idea where to find the sheik inside the palace and no hint at the security layout within the massive building. More troubling was my lack of access to any weapons or tactical gear. Making a forced entry was going to be nearly impossible.

I woke the next morning feeling less than refreshed. I dressed in the same jeans, black t-shirt, and running shoes and went downstairs to the breakfast buffet. After a small breakfast, I rented a Nissan Xterra SUV at the kiosk inside the hotel. My first stop was the Rumaithiya Co-op, located less than three hundred yards from the sheik's palace. The malls in Kuwait open late in the morning, but every neighborhood has a co-op with a grocery store, bakery, coffee shop, hardware store, and pharmacy.

I went to the pharmacy and the hardware store and eventually found a Motorola battery-powered video baby monitor that was suitable for my needs. Inside my SUV, I put the monitor into operation. With the camera in my hand, I walked down Nassar Al-Mubarak Street toward the palace. I dropped down to tie my shoe and placed the video camera at the base of a tree across the street from the guard shack and garage door. Nassar Al-Mubarak is a two-lane road, divided by a small grass island and trees.

I headed back to the co-op and went into the Starbucks. The baby monitor has a four-inch screen. The Starbucks was four hundred yards from the camera, which is barely within range of the walkie-talkie-like radio link. With fresh batteries, the signal was good enough to pan the camera and receive the video stream.

After two hours and three cappuccinos, I felt like I had a good enough understanding of the morning traffic into the garage which consisted of deliveries and staff. There were two guards manning the shack. Both were armed with rifles and pistols in drop-leg holsters. Some vehicles they let right in, while others they stopped and checked IDs before raising the automatic garage doors. The garage had to be enormous. One of the trucks that entered was a sixteen-foot, three-ton reefer and it made it with room to spare.

Attacking through the garage to hunt down the sheik was a possibility, but without knowing the locations of either the security personnel or the target, it wasn't a good one. My lack of a weapon wasn't insurmountable; I'm pretty sure I could always take one from one of the KNG soldiers inside the shack. I've seen the KNG in action and for the most part, they're little more than walking holsters. I ruled out a suicidal garage entry and decided to look at target options outside the palace.

I spent the rest of the afternoon studying the traffic in and out of the palace. The sheik has four wives and a lot of kids and there were a lot of high-end vehicles coming and going with security personnel inside. It was obvious the sheik maintained a large personal security detail. Most appeared to be Arab, but a few were European.

At six forty-five, after it was dark, I walked back down Nassar Al-Mubarak and retrieved the baby monitor. While I was eating dinner at the hotel, I had a eureka moment. I had the idea to pinpoint the sheik's location based on light patters. Later that night, I walked the perimeter every hour until three o'clock in the morning. The palace was huge, and many of the rooms were never lighted. Arab Monarchs hold court at night. It's a nocturnal society, because of the daytime desert heat. It was easy to pick out the majlis on the first floor and as the night went on the lights shutting off as people went to bed. When a big section of lights went out at the same time on a section of the top floor is when I had my suspected target location.

I continued my surveillance for three days. I augmented the ground surveillance with a small unmanned aerial vehicle I found at the hobby store in the Shark Mall along the Corniche. The helicopter UAV allowed me to surveil the rooftop, which was almost three hundred yards long and one hundred yards wide. The rooftop was unguarded.

The contrast between UAE and Kuwait City was stark. Even in a posh Kuwaiti neighborhood, the streets were dirty and cluttered, and the landscaping was haphazard. In Abu Dhabi, the streets were always clean, and the landscaping was immaculate. The clutter and lack of streetlights made my task easier, but it was difficult not to recognize that Kuwait was an oil-rich nation whose investments were being made abroad and not within. I'd once been told that the invasion of Kuwait by Saddam Hussein had affected the psyches of the Kuwait leaders. I once heard someone quip that Kuwait was the only city in the world where the closer to the airport you got, the higher the home prices. Every resident expected another invasion, and the closer the route to escape, the better.

With the concept of a plan sketched out, I put together a list of equipment and sent it to Jessica for purchase and delivery. I told her to send it to the alternate air base in Paphos and booked myself on the next available flight to Cyprus.

I arrived at the alternate Trident base of operations at two in the afternoon. A Trident C-130 was parked inside the hangar and a couple of the guys were working. Migos was one of the first to greet me. He was obviously very curious about the equipment that had recently arrived, but he knew better than to ask.

A leased Ilyushin Il-76 landed at five o'clock and taxied to the Trident hanger area. I did a preflight briefing with the aircrew and then left them to file the flight plan and eat. The Il-76 is a long range cargo jet. It can handle a cargo of over forty tons and has a range of more than 2,100 miles. With the cargo ramp down and the crew briefed, I went to work loading it up.

The first piece of equipment I prepared for operation was the SkyRunner. It's a four-wheel dune buggy that can fly. It uses ram-air parafoil wing technology and a three-blade propeller to take to the sky. It has a max speed of fifty-three knots and a max range of 120 nautical miles. The biggest limitation is the cargo weight, which maxes out at 317 pounds. The maximum takeoff distance is 450 feet, and the landing distance is 400 feet.

Next to the SkyRunner was a pallet of parachute-rigging gear. I inspected the ATV parachute-rigging kit. The easy part about rigging the SkyRunner is that it's made to hang from a parachute, so the attachment points are already built in and perfectly balanced. The key to success was going to be constructing the compressible landing platform from corrugated cardboard that I needed to absorb the landing shock. I was going to air drop the SkyRunner under a single G-12 chute. Included in the parachute set was my personal rig, which was an MC-6 steerable parachute and accompanying reserve. The final item in the kit was a portable GPS retrans kit that would enable GPS inside an aircraft.

The third set of equipment was a breach kit. The kit came in a large Pelican box. I had requested a Wilcox Patriot Exothermic Breaching System. The system uses fuel rods promoted by pure oxygen and comes on an assault backpack that has two fifteen-minute oxygen tanks and a cutting wand. The exothermic cutting rod makes it possible to cut through one inch of hardened steel like a knife through butter.

The next piece of gear came in a small Tyr Tactical daypack. It was a SIG P226 with a suppressor and green laser light combo inside a drop-leg holster. The bag also contained a small rappelling kit, complete with climbing harness, carabiners, figure eight, and jumar ascenders. I also found a Miko diving suction cup with latch and a handheld radar system from TiaLinx for seeing through walls, called an Eagle-5. I planned on supplementing this kit with some items, like ballistic protection and night vision from a go-bag. The final item was a military free fall NAVAID GPS system.

I spent two hours training on the SkyRunner before refueling the system, packing it up, and turning it over to Sachse the loadmaster to rig for a parachute drop. By eight o'clock, all the equipment was stowed inside the Il-76 with the rigged SkyRunner stored closest to the ramp. It was shackled down with A7A straps on a set of conveyer wheels, which would allow it to easily slide out the door when the time came.

Migos should've gone home hours earlier, but he'd insisted on helping Sachse with rigging everything. He was practically jumping up and down, trying to figure out what I was up to. Finally, he couldn't restrain himself anymore.

"This must be Delta stuff. I spent years at Bragg and never saw anything like this. What're you up to?"

"This is a special delivery that I'm taking into Iraq tonight. If you check the manifest for the leased aircraft, you'll see they'll be landing in Basra." Migos's face looked crestfallen because I wouldn't confide in him.

The Il-76 was wheels up at eight forty-five that night. We left on a five-hour route that would take the aircraft directly over Kuwait City with the final descent beginning at the Iraq-Kuwait border and a landing at one forty-five a.m. in Basra, the largest city in southern Iraq.

I woke up at midnight from my resting place on a bench chair. I donned my equipment and at one fifteen, I could feel the aircraft descend to ten thousand feet after clearing Kuwait International Airport air traffic control. I checked my GPS NAVAID to confirm our location as the ramp was opened by the aircrew. The static line from the cargo parachute and my static line were both attached to the static line retriever. As soon as the aircraft entered Iraqi airspace, the green light went on inside the cavernous blacked-out interior, and the aircrew slid the ATV cargo load out the back ramp.

I waited three seconds and then chased after the ATV. Ten thousand feet is a very high altitude to conduct a static-line drop, and with the unpredictable winds at such a height, it's impossible to know within a grid square exactly where the cargo load was going to land. The desert along the Kuwaiti border is unpopulated and clear of most obstacles, so precision wasn't all that important anyway. My parachute snapped open with a jerk. I grabbed the toggles and steered the chute toward the large green cargo chute five hundred feet below me.

When I saw the cargo chute collapse as the ATV hit the ground, I yanked on the left toggle and turned into the wind. With my feet and knees together, I managed to execute a half-decent parachute landing fall onto the soft desert sand. I yanked on the canopy release assemblies detaching the parachute canopy and jumped up to get to work.

After shedding my parachute harness, I cached one of the three five-gallon jerry cans of fuel that were in the back of the ATV. In the same place, I stuffed the two parachutes into carrier bags and on top of the pile, I cracked an IR Chemlite so I could find them later. I made sure to record the location on the NAVAID. I did a walk-around the dune buggy and was reassured to find that it was still air worthy. The wind was a bit gustier than the forecast. I hopped into the SkyRunner and drove until I found a small dirt trail a few minutes from the landing point.

On the trail, I readied the dune buggy for flight, connecting the airfoil to the two attachment points on the top and distributing the combat load in the driver seat and the small storage area behind the two front seats. I extended the black airfoil behind the dune buggy, pulling it backward until the risers were straight. I updated the NAVAID, making sure my start point was recorded and verifying the waypoints I'd already plugged in for the flight.

The dune buggy controls are very simple. Turns and elevation changes are made with the steering wheel that turns left and right like a conventional wheel, but can also move up and down. Acceleration is done with the gas pedal. The dashboard has an altimeter, airspeed gauge, a GPS and a transponder, which I'd already deactivated for the mission. My little runway was in southern Iraq, located fewer than ten miles northwest of Safwan, which is about fifty miles south of Basra and sixty miles north of Kuwait City.

I gradually accelerated along the trail, dragging the rising airfoil behind me. When I reached thirty miles per hour, the airfoil rose up above me into position and the dune buggy began to lift. Once in the air, I pushed the speed up to forty-five knots. Within minutes I was crossing over the Iraqi border fence into Kuwait. Two miles later, I crossed a second fence, which belonged to Kuwait. I dimmed the controls and dropped my night vision goggles mounted on top of my helmet down onto my eyes. I stayed on a heading of 173 degrees almost due south for fifty-five minutes until I crossed Highway 80, the major north-south highway between Kuwait and Iraq.

I crossed Highway 80 along Mitla Ridge, the part of Highway 80 nicknamed the "highway of death" because during the First Gulf War, a big chunk of Saddam's Republican Guards was caught retreating along the route by the US Air Force. I changed the heading to 145 degrees and stayed on azimuth until I crossed Highway 801 fifteen minutes later and went out over Kuwait Bay.

Once over the water, I set my night vision goggles back up into the store position. The bright lights of Kuwait City were directly to my south, and for the last forty minutes of the flight, I'd have no problem finding my landmarks with the naked eye. The next landmark was the iconic Kuwaiti Tower, which is unmistakable because of its three 150-meter-high white conical spires, with zero, one, and two huge blue balls on them respectively. I remained at an altitude of a hundred feet and kept the ATV to the east, off the coast as I passed the prince's balls, as they were referred to locally.

My next landmark was the Marina Mall. Once I reached the mall, I turned over land and turned hard left, following the coastal road until I flew over the Regency Hotel. At the Regency, I banked ninety degrees right and followed Nassar Al-Mubarak for the final half mile of the trip. I pulled back the steering wheel and brought the altitude up to 150 feet until I crossed the foliage and green expanse of Rumaitha Park. I made sure the third-floor windows of the palace weren't lit before starting my descent.

The SkyRunner touched down fifty yards beyond the leading edge of the roof. I jammed on the brakes, bringing the dune buggy to a stop with another hundred yards to spare. I jumped out and stuffed the airfoil inside the rear stowage and then got in and drove to the edge of the rooftop closest to the park. After turning the dune buggy around, I shut it off and positioned the airfoil behind the SkyRunner, making it ready for takeoff. Then I topped off the fuel tank with the jerry cans.

I put on the climbing harness and donned the Wilcox assault pack with the thermal breacher. I also clipped a nylon bag with the Eagle5-NCL handheld see-through-the-wall sensor. The TiaLinx Eagle 5 is a radar that can detect the movement of a beating heart ten meters behind a concrete wall. I used a grappling hook on the rooftop to position a rope directly over my entry point. I'd spent enough time going over light patterns that I was almost positive that my entry point was the bathroom of the sheik's master bedroom.

The sheik had a *diwaniya* or what people in UAE would call a majlis, which is a traditional Kuwaiti social and business gathering. The sheik held his on Sunday, Tuesday and Friday and they always broke up late into the early-morning hours. My entry point selection was based on the assumption that the sheik would be the last family member awake after those meetings. If my assumption was wrong, I was going to be in for a seriously bad experience.

I jammed a three-eighths fuel rod into the Hellboy handset, set the oxygen flow, and then stuck the rod into the igniter. With the handset in my right hand, I stepped over the ledge and abseiled down to the window ledge. I locked the descender and attached a levered suction cup to the window to use as a handhold. I stepped over to the far right of the ledge and, going from bottom to top, cut through the metal frame of the six-foot-high window in seconds with the torch. I switched sides and did the same on the right side. I shut off the oxygen, and as the window began to fall, I held it up by the suction device and stepped inside the dark room. I intended to gently set down the heavy ballistic glass. Instead, it slipped off the lip and landed on the tile floor with a loud thump. I stood still and listened. After a minute, I resumed.

It was pitch black. I took off the assault pack and clipped it onto the rope to secure it in position inside the window. I put my night vision goggles back into operation and turned on my helmet IR light.

I was in a big bathroom, which was an encouraging sign. I slowly made my way to the entry door. I stowed my goggles and placed the Eagle 5 see-through-sensor against the door. The radar showed only a single red dot, signifying only one heartbeat. The target was approximately twenty-five yards away, in the far-left corner from the bathroom door. I stowed the Eagle, returned my night vision goggles and screwed the silencer onto my SIG before quietly opening the door and creeping into the bedroom.

The room was empty, except for someone sleeping on the bed. I walked straight to the bed and stopped five feet short. All I could see was the back of his head, so I walked around to the opposite side of the bed. I fired a suppressed subsonic round into the sheik's head and two seconds later another into his heart. The sound of the suppressed discharge was little more than a hand clap. I bent down and retrieved the expended shell casings just as the bedroom door opened. A woman was silhouetted in the doorway against the light of the hallway. She looked at me and I looked at her, and then she started to scream. I raised my pistol, and she ran. I bolted to the bathroom to make my exit.

I was hanging outside the window, stepping into the jumar ascenders, when the bathroom door was splintered by submachine gun fire. I fired three 9mm rounds through the door and pumped my arms and legs as fast as I could to climb the rope. While I was scrambling over the rooftop, another burst of submachine gun fire erupted from the hole in the window. I leaned over the roof and fired down, hitting the gunman's arms, which were extended through the window opening.

I tossed my equipment into the back of the SkyRunner as I jumped into the driver's seat. I hit the ignition and then I hit the gas, accelerating along the rooftop. I was able to lift off the building with over a hundred yards to spare and was clear of the building before any security made it onto the roof.

I flew back against a headwind and it took me another hour and forty-five minutes to retrace my route. I spent the entire trip with my head on a swivel, looking for helicopters that never came. When I cleared the border fence between Kuwait and Iraq, the fuel gauge was in the red. I touched down and immediately made my way to the cache and refueled.

The next leg of the flight was a direct line to Basra International fifty miles due north.

It was twilight, predawn when the SkyRunner skipped over the cargo air terminal fence by only ten feet and skidded to a stop between two hangars. I rushed to detach and stow the airfoil and then raced up the ramp on the waiting Il-76. I'd been working with the same Ukrainian cargo service for several years, but this was the first time I'd used them for anything except a cargo run. They'd always kept me informed of the black operations services they offered and I have to say, I've been impressed with the level of professionalism they offer. They asked very few questions and delivered as promised.

While we were descending into Paphos, I asked the loadmaster to drop the ramp. Once the ramp was down, I walked to the end, unholstered the SIG P226, disassembled it, and tossed the pieces out into the depths of the Mediterranean. When the aircraft landed and taxied to the company hangar, I helped with the unloading and wished the crew well as they made short work of refueling and getting on their way back to Ukraine. The hangar was empty, with my guys out on a delivery, so I stowed everything myself and locked up.

Chapter 20

Abu Dhabi, UAE

Mike Guthrie sat back in the leather chair, feigning interest in the daily Abu Dhabi newspaper, the *National*. The small waiting room was well appointed and laid out similar to what you might expect in a New York City law firm, with thick carpet, dark mahogany and brown leather furniture. Instead of pictures of the senior partners on the wall, the walls sported portraits of Sheik Zayed, the founder and first president of UAE, Sheik Khalifa, his son and the current president, Sheik Mohammed Bin Rashid Al Maktoum, the ruler of Dubai and UAE's vice president, and Sheik Mohammed Bin Zayed, the crown prince of Abu Dhabi. The crown prince's brother, Sheik Khalifa, is the president; however, for health reasons, he hasn't made a public appearance in years. Mike was waiting to visit the most powerful man in the UAE.

Mike had been waiting for thirty-five minutes and was anxious to meet with the crown prince of Abu Dhabi. HH Mohammad Bin Zayed Al Nayed (MBZ) had requested the meeting personally during a conversation with the American ambassador at his majlis two nights earlier. Because of the eight-hour time difference and fifteen-hour flight time, Mike's response to the meeting was as swift as it could be. He had met with the sheik on several occasions in the past, but this was his first time meeting him in his private office in the Mahmoud government offices on Airport Road.

The office manager, wearing traditional local dress, opened the door and signaled for Mike to follow. He led him through the hallway, opened the door to the crown prince's office, and ushered Mike in. As Mike approached, the sheik stood up and stepped around his desk, greeting him with a handshake. The crown prince led Mike to a seating area. The office was surprisingly modest for a national leader who also happened to be one of the wealthiest men in the world. The sheik was a tall, fit man, with glasses and a well-trimmed beard that was mostly gray. He had a long thin face, with piercing brown eyes and a high forehead. If the strain of the oil crisis and being engaged in two wars was taking its toll on the crown prince, his face and body language didn't betray it. The man sitting across from Mike exuded energy and a calm confidence.

After the tea was served and the polite inquiries were completed, the crown prince began the discussion. "We've completed the investigation into the death of Sheik Rasheed. The video you provided of his last moments was terribly upsetting. The matter has been closed. I'm satisfied that he and the other members of his cell no longer pose a threat."

"Your Highness, we had a lot of internal discussions about providing you that tape, but ultimately we felt total transparency was essential to putting this matter behind us."

The crown prince smiled and took a sip of his black tea. He made eye contact with Mike. "Transparency is an interesting word choice. As partners, we think it best that when these issues are identified by your people within our borders, we are informed before action is taken, not after. These are matters best handled internally and not by outsiders."

Mike could see a flash of anger behind the mask of calm and warned himself to tread carefully. "Your concern is well received, Your Highness. Pat Walsh operates on a very loose chain. Officially he doesn't work for the US government. He has a lot of independence, and his actions caught us by surprise."

The sheik gave Mike an incredulous look. "Do you mean to say that your man was operating alone?"

"Your Highness, that's exactly the case. Pat's my friend; I've known him a very long time. When he was attacked, and his people were killed, he consulted no one. He sprang into action, and he never informed us of his plan or received permission to execute it."

"I didn't ask you to come here today so you could lie to my face." When he chose to use it, the crown prince had a very expressive face. Mike could clearly see that this conversation was dangerously close to escalating into a conflict.

"Your Highness, if you'll afford me a few minutes, I'll explain. I am about to go well beyond what my superiors wish to reveal, but I believe it's the only way to avoid a misunderstanding between us."

The sheik nodded.

"Your Highness, I recruited Pat in Afghanistan to work as an asset for the CIA. The reason I recruited him was because I served with him for many years in the Army, and I trust him. He's a gifted soldier, but a political novice; that's why he was eventually forced out of the Army. Despite his lack of political sense, he's smart. What truly sets him apart is his fierce loyalty.

"I'll tell you a war story to help explain. In 1986, Pat and I were together in Honduras on the Nicaraguan border, back in the days when we were fighting communism. We worked along the border, conducting counterterrorism operations against the Sandinistas. Most nights we would depart from our patrol base and occupy ambush positions in four- to six-man teams to ambush the enemy fighters smuggling weapons and supplies across the border.

"One night, while I was the lead person on my patrol moving to the ambush point, I walked right into an enemy ambush. I was shot twice in the opening volley and went down like a ton of bricks in the middle of the trail. The remainder of my team had to fall back to take cover and return fire.

"It was triple-canopy jungle, zero light, and both sides were in a long firefight, with me in the middle. Tracers were going everywhere. Pat was two kilometers away, already in his own ambush position with his team, when he heard the firing and a report on the radio from my team that they were engaged and had a man down.

"Pat left his guys in place and ran in complete darkness toward the sound of the firing, through some of the worst terrain and vegetation in the world. The black palm trees have three-inch needles that completely cover the trunk, and they rip exposed skin to shreds. I've never known anyone who's run through that jungle at night. Pat ran blindly toward the sound of an ambush, and then he ran directly through the enemy fire until he was on top of the ambushers and able to kill every one of them at point-blank range.

"After he killed the last one, he slung his weapon over his back, picked me up, and ran with me in his arms all the way back to the patrol base. That final run was more than three kilometers. The doctor told me later that I'd lost so much blood that if I'd arrived even a few minutes later, I wouldn't have made it.

"Pat didn't give a moment's thought to what he did. He's like a shepherd dog. He's a protector. When the wolf attacks, he responds and attacks right back. The men who directed the attack on his boat crew and the attack on his plane crew probably had no idea of the fury they were unleashing. Sheik Rasheed, Sheik Meshal, and Prince Bandar attacked his people. They killed three members of his team, and he's not the kind of person to let that go unpunished."

The crown prince was a military man. One of his roles was deputy supreme commander of the armed forces, and Mike could see he understood the mentality of people like Pat.

"Pat's a force. We can both agree on that. Still, you know him so well. How could you not have predicted his response and given me a warning?" he asked Mike.

"Your Highness, the first attack against Pat was from the Iranian Navy, the second attack was from the Iraqi Daesh. At most we suspected someone was surveilling Pat from within the UAE. We had no idea it was an element from your own national security and a member of the royal family. If we had, we would've notified you immediately. Pat struck too quickly; it was lightning speed. First, he baited the intel guys to search for and arrest the mole, then he snatched the mole, and within hours, he captured, interrogated, and killed the target. We found out about the details of the operation the same way you did. We were sent a copy of the interrogation videos."

Sheik Mohammed studied Mike. "I believe you. The rescue of our two SOC operators is proof to me that Pat is the man you describe. Still, he should've come to me. I would've solved the problem."

Mike placed his right hand over his heart and said, "*Shakrun*, Cee Dee."

The crown prince said, "Now tell me about this business in Kuwait."

Mike replied, "Two nights ago, Sheik Meshal was executed while sleeping in his bed. The intruder entered the bedroom through an exterior window, shot the sheik dead, and managed to escape the same way. The intruder, as I am sure you've guessed, was Pat."

"Did you help him?" asked the crown prince.

"Your Highness, we're only days from a presidential election. The party in office is trumpeting the defeat of ISIS in Mosul. There is absolutely no interest in risky foreign policy ventures at the moment."

"After the death of Sheik Rasheed, Meshal must've known what was coming. It's hard to believe that your man was able to do it without your assistance."

"Your Highness, it was done without our help, and I have to tell you—I know how it was done, and it was truly one of the most creative missions I've ever seen."

The sheik grew intrigued. "Tell me what you can."

Mike then described the mission in detail. When he was done, he explained that after the Agency had learned of the sheik's death, they had been able to use satellite footage to piece together the operation. He also mentioned that while they didn't object to the outcome, they had been prohibited from any involvement.

The sheik just smiled, understanding Mike's message.

"Tell your man to return to Abu Dhabi. I wish to sit with him. Daesh is failing in Mosul, but the fighters are blending in with the population, and if they're funded, they'll continue to be a problem. Millions have died, and while the butchers holding the knives must be killed, those who are providing the funds must be stopped and brought to justice. Bring your friend Pat to me."

Chapter 21

Paphos, Cyprus

The small office I kept in the hangar was an austere affair. The only office equipment was a desk, chair and a lamp. I spent the morning on my laptop updating the tedious contracts, purchase orders, proposals, and invoices that are the daily reality of the business. The aircrews had returned the previous night, both Hercs were parked, one inside the hangar, the other on the outside. There was a cargo 777 parked in Trident's secured area with a complement of contracted security standing guard. Today's task was going to be transloading the cargo from the 777 over to the two C-130s for delivery to Iraq tomorrow.

Looking at the airway bill and commercial invoice, I saw that the load consisted of four thousand AT-4 rockets and eight explosive ordnance disposal kits. The Peshmerga must be gearing up to clear the areas they've captured of IEDs. The four thousand 84mm bunker busting/antitank rockets was puzzling, but those decisions aren't mine to make.

The aircrews drifted in at ten o'clock, and I spent a few minutes with each of the guys as they went about their daily chores. It was clear from their faces that jumping to the alternate base and assisting with the mission prep for the Kuwait job had them curious about what I was up to. Nobody brought up the subject and I didn't volunteer anything.

The equipment and munitions being cross-loaded from the cargo 777 belonged to Falcon. The equipment wouldn't have shipped from USA unless Falcon and the UAE Government signed off on the export paperwork. I was a little surprised and took it as a good sign that Falcon and the UAE government were still fulfilling their part of our arrangement.

At three o'clock, I said my goodbyes and had Migos take me around to the airport passenger terminal. I passed through security and passport control and caught a private charter I'd booked to Muscat. I arrived at the Marina Al Bustan with a couple of hours of light remaining in the day. It was good to be back on the *Sam Houston*. I used the remaining sunlight to pull the covering and clean the accumulated dirt and sand off the decks. Once inside, I did a complete sweep of all the interior compartments with my bug detector, just in case.

With my chores completed, I was walking through the salon doors on my way to dinner when I noticed Walt Berg standing at the entrance gate on the starboard side.

"I was on my way to dinner. Care to join me?" I said, while shaking his hand.

"I can't. I'm just here to deliver a message," he said.

"What's up?"

"Mike's in the region. He'll be here tomorrow morning. He wants me to make sure you're around."

"What time?"

"I don't know yet."

"Ask him to come early. I'm planning on fishing for mahi-mahi tomorrow and I'd like to be off by ten."

"I'll let him know."

Companionless, I caught an Uber and went to the Muscat Intercontinental Hotel inside the city. It'd been an intense couple of weeks and I felt like blowing off some steam. Once inside the lobby, I headed into Trader Vic's and took a seat at the bar. I've always been a big fan of the Polynesian-themed tiki concept and I'm a big fan of rum drinks.

It was a Thursday night, the first night of the weekend in Oman, and the place was packed with Western expats. The exterior windows had a nice view of the ocean, and a three-piece Cuban band was playing on a stage set between the bar and the dining room. On the small dance floor, adjacent to the stage, a group of salsa aficionado couples were showcasing their practiced moves.

The bartender was a Filipino man garbed in the requisite Trader Vic's floral Hawaiian shirt. I ordered a Mai Tai, because it was Trader Vic's and I felt it was a tribute to American innovation. Having missed lunch, because I thought the charter was going to provide it, I moved to a table and ordered ginger scallops, fried rice and spring rolls.

Like most hotel bars in the Middle East, Traders was filled with Western Expats. Because of restrictive licensing requirements, the number of bars in places like Muscat are limited, and unlike in the United States, where night spots tend to cater to narrow target audiences, in places like Muscat and particularly in Trader Vic's, the range of people is vast. Young and old, male and female, rich and not so rich, and a veritable United Nations of races and nationalities.

After dinner and a few drinks, I was befriended by a group of British schoolteachers. I was a respectable salsa dancer. Having taken my Filipina boat crew dancing at least once a week for the past couple years, I'd learned a few things. I moved to a table with three girls, and the food, drinks, and laughter flowed for several hours of escapist fun.

The next morning at around eight, I sensed someone on the deck above. I put on a white terry-cloth robe and walked up the stairs to the main deck, where I found Mike standing outside the salon doors.

"I wasn't expecting you until a little later. Come on in and have a coffee," I said.

Mike walked in through the triple glass doors and headed to the galley table. I made two cups of coffee and joined Mike in the breakfast nook.

"It's good you came early. I have a situation, and could use your help," I said.

Mike looked over with concern on his face. "What do you need?" he asked.

"It's not a small ask. I need you to put all of your CIA training and intel contacts to use and find something out for me," I said.

Mike's expression became even more serious.

"Last night I went out for dinner. Later, at the bar, I met a woman, and we had a great night. She's amazing. Totally gorgeous, Mike. I'm talking about extraordinary talents. Gifted, even—a former ballet dancer."

Mike's curiosity was piqued. "So, what's the problem?"

"I can't remember her name."

"What do you mean, you can't remember her name? Do you have Alzheimer's or something?"

"I don't know. Maybe I do. There were three of them, and they told me their names, but it was loud, I had a few drinks, and I couldn't keep track, so I just numbered them by looks. Right now, number one is downstairs in my stateroom, and I have no freaking idea what her name is."

Mike began to laugh. Softly at first, but the mirth grew the more he processed the absurdity of the request, until he had tears in his eyes.

I got up and made two more fresh cups of coffee.

"You know, Pat, the Iranians are about to go nuclear any day now. They're testing long-range missiles. Aleppo is under siege, and thousands are dying daily. Mosul is surrounded and the offensive is stalled. A million and a half people are anxiously awaiting liberation. But you've given me a new priority. You want the head of CIA clandestine activities in the Middle East to spy out the name of your latest conquest."

That made both of us laugh. "Yeah, if you think you're up to it."

As we were laughing and enjoying our coffee, a woman who could have been Emma Watson's clone emerged from the ladder that led down to the lower deck. Dressed in a Chinese silk bathrobe borrowed from the stateroom, the girl whose name I couldn't remember approached the galley table where we were sitting. I stood up and said, "Good morning."

Mike intercepted her on her way to the table and stuck out his hand. "Hi, I'm Mike Guthrie. I'm a friend of Pat's."

With a dazzling smile, the composed young woman replied in a refined British accent, "A pleasure to meet you. My name is Sarah Winslow."

That caused a secret grin as I got up to make another coffee. I asked Sarah to join us fishing, but she declined. I called a limo service to take her home, and gave her the twenty-five cent tour of the *Sam Houston* while we were waiting for it to arrive.

Hours later, the *Sam Houston* was positioned ten miles off the coast of Al Salfa, midway between Muscat and the Yemen border, approximately thirty miles south of where we'd started from at the marina. It was a pleasant sunny day with light winds and a gentle sea. Mike and I were sitting in a pair of attachable fighting chairs on the hydraulic ramp at the tail of the stern. We each had a fishing pole in a holder in front of us. We started out trawling for mahi-mahi but for the past two hours we'd been having better luck dropping our lines deep and catching yellowfin tuna. Mike had already caught five, and I had two. Mike landed the biggest fish, which weighed in at twelve pounds.

Tuna are fighters, and reeling them in was a workout. Mike was having the time of his life. We avoided business talk and kept the conversation to small talk. At around three, we decided to get out of the sun and began the prep to get back to the marina. I moved the ice cooler with the fish up to the aft deck and stowed the chairs. On the way through the galley, I grabbed two more bottles of Sam Adams and joined Mike in the wheelhouse.

I started the engines and set the speed to a comfortable twenty-two knots. The Azimut 64 Flybridge is a soft ride. The gyrostabilizers made for a smooth ride, and the engines were as quiet as a luxury car. The ride back was smooth and relaxing.

With his attention looking through the huge windshield at the empty expanse of ocean, Mike asked, "Have you given any thought to your next move?"

"I have a plan," I said.

"If it's anything like the last one, I can't wait to hear it," said Mike.

"It got the job done. It was an execution, nothing to be proud of," I said.

"You shouldn't feel bad about it. That guy practically created ISIS. You know, when we pulled out of Iraq in 2012, there were almost a million and a half Christians. Today, the number is barely over two hundred thousand, and that number didn't change because they emigrated. With some of the other populations, the numbers are even worse, like the Yazidis. It's been a genocide, pure and simple. Now that ISIS is on the run, the fighters and leaders are melting away. If we let the big shots continue to fund them, then those fighters who're escaping are going to continue the battle in other, perhaps even more deadly, ways, closer to home. You did the right thing."

"Why don't I get the feeling that's the opinion of the people you work for?" I said.

"That's just Washington. If the people I work for wanted you to stop, then you would've been stopped. There's a political reason why they want this hush-hush. Believe me, you have total support from those who matter."

"That's good to know, because this next job is going to be difficult, and as a humble asset working without any official cover or official support, my probability of success isn't all that great."

"I thought you said you had a plan."

"I do have a plan, just not a good one. It's a fifty-fifty play at best."

"That's no-go criteria. You need to do better," said Mike.

"I'm trying," I said.

"Hey, you don't want to disappoint your fan club back in Langley. Once we had the incident report, we used satellite imagery to follow your departure in Paphos to Kuwait and back. We have the entire mission on film, start to finish. That was clever stuff."

"Beyond the fawning adoration of the geek squad, do you think we can get something constructive out of that task force you set up? This next job is a ballbuster. I need the benefit of your intel, the imagery, the SIGINT, the HUMINT, everything. There are too many unknowns," I said.

"I'm helping as much as I can. That's why your Trident operation continues unabated, and why we've allowed the special mission-related purchases you're making to go through. But that's it. I can't actively assist," said Mike.

"Why the heck not? Didn't you just say these guys are genocidal maniacs?"

"This is silly season. The presidential election is Tuesday. If you get killed or captured, nobody in the State Department or the White House wants to explain to either our Kuwaiti or Saudi friends why one of our own is picking off royal family members in their respective governments."

"What about the Emirates?" I asked.

"That's a different story. The folks running the UAE are cut from a different cloth. They don't like that you took matters into your own hands, but they don't disagree with your actions."

"You're kidding me, how do you know that?" I asked before finishing the last of my beer.

"I met with MBZ myself, and that's what he told me. And I believe him. By the way, he wants to meet with you."

"What does he want?" I asked.

"I think he wants to offer assistance—the same assistance that you're requesting from the USA."

"That's pretty ballsy of him and I'll take what I can get. I still don't understand why the USA won't step up to the plate," I said.

"It's a huge political risk. Let me try to explain who we're talking about. Prince Bandar is the tenth son of King Abdul-Aziz, the first monarch of Saudi Arabia. Unlike his fellow princes, the guy wasn't born with a silver spoon in his mouth. His mother was a Moroccan servant. His mother, Bazza, must've been something, because when Bandar was in his teens, she managed to get the king to acknowledge Bandar as a son and receive him as a prince instead of as the impoverished peasant he had grown up as. As a bastard, he was a minor prince, and so he wasn't gifted the big pay package of the major princes. King Abdul-Aziz had thirty thousand descendants with the title of prince. The government pays the major leaguers in the first ring in dollars—about two hundred and fifty thousand per month. The guys the farthest from the power, the minor leaguers in the last ring, get about three thousand a month. Bandar is a minor leaguer."

"How does a guy like that become the Saudi ambassador to the US?" I asked.

"He's a clever guy, a true Machiavellian. He formed an alliance with the house of Wahhabi to gain influence with the house of Saud."

"That still doesn't explain why the United States is protecting him."

"Prince Bandar was the ambassador to the USA from the 1990s until 2005. He's extremely close to the Bush family, and he's a major friend and donor to the Clintons. Even though fifteen of the nineteen hijackers in the 9/11 attacks were Saudis, and there were numerous contacts and a financial paper trail leading back to Prince Bandar, the day after the attacks, when every other plane in the USA was grounded, the president personally gave authorization to allow Prince Bandar to fly back to Saudi Arabia. This guy and his compatriot Wahhabis have been funding every anti-Western and anti-Jewish terrorist group for decades."

"So then why is the US so reluctant to go after him?" I said.

"He's a bad guy, but he's not an extremist. For a Saudi, he's considered a centrist. He's not as progressive as the king and his court, who control the government, and he's not as extreme as the Wahhabi imams who control the people. He's in the middle. He's the go-between, and he's parlayed that role to immense wealth and power. Officially, the US considers him to be a pragmatist, a scrapper who's clawed his way up the ladder. He represents the compromises the Saudi royal family must make with extremists to placate the masses and retain control. In some ways, he's pro-American. He just sold his house in Aspen for forty million dollars, he mixes easily with the Hollywood and Silicon Valley crowd, and the American politicians on both sides of the aisle love the guy. Remember where he came from—he's a bastard, and his mother was an African slave. His actions are driven by ambition, not principle or religion." After he finished, Mike got up and went to the galley and then returned with two fresh beers.

"You're telling me this guy is financing the worst people on this planet to maintain support from the radical extremist Wahhabis, and the Saudi government won't stop him because they need the support of the Wahhabis to govern?"

"The Saudis not only won't stop him, they'll defend him. This won't be like Kuwait. They know who you are. If you try to fly into Riyadh to do a recon, you're going to get arrested at the airport and then publicly executed," Mike said.

We sat in silence for a long while and drank our beer and felt the vibrations of the sleek hull carving away the miles. The sun was starting to set on the port side, and the orange-and-purple light against the blue sea horizon was captivating.

"Our government won't help you, because they can't afford to lose the Saudis over this. You need to look at this from the Saudi perspective. The US made a commitment to defend Saudi Arabia in exchange for an uninterrupted supply of oil back in the 1970s after the oil embargo. In 2012, we withdrew all of our forces out of Iraq and left the ground to the Saudis' biggest enemies, the Iranians. This cabal of Rasheed, Meshal and Bandar did what they did to provide a counter to the Iranian influence in Iraq and Syria. Bandar views himself as a patriot. He has support not just from the Wahhabis, but also from the members of the Saudi government, who believe the US betrayed them when we turned their northern neighbor Iraq over to their worst enemy."

I walked back to the fridge in the galley and returned with two more open bottles. I gave one to Mike and sat back down behind the wheel.

"I don't really care about the realpolitik of it all. Prince Bandar is going to die; I owe that to Jenny Lyn and to my guys. His death may not stop Saudi funding of genocide and terrorism, but I'll do my best to make sure Bandar's demise sends a message."

We were coming up on the marina so we moved up to the flydeck. It's a lot easier to dock from the helm station because it has a 360-degree view of the yacht. Once we had the *Houston* tied down, I handed off the cooler with the tuna to a pair of Bangladeshi laborers who worked at the marina. Tonight's special at the Blue Marlin was going to be today's catch, blackened tuna, and I was looking forward to it.

Chapter 22

Abu Dhabi, UAE

The *Houston* looked good back at its home port at the Intercontinental Marina in Abu Dhabi. Although it felt like an eternity, it'd only been a couple of weeks since my hasty departure. Mike had assured me that the UAE police weren't going to arrest me, and that helped to manage my apprehension at returning to the scene of the crime. With a ton of nervous energy and a day before my big meeting with the crown prince, I got right to work restocking, refueling and readying the *Houston* for whatever lay ahead.

That night, I went next door to the Belgium Café for dinner. I'm a huge fan of the exotic beer menu they have. I ordered a bottle of Delirium Tremens, which is both a medical condition, sometimes referred to as the DTs and the single best beer in the world. To eat, I defaulted to my go-to, which are the pork spareribs flavored with Leffe blond beer. The Belgian Café is like the Church of Beer.

The next morning, I woke up early and went for a run along the Corniche. The weather was perfect; at seven o'clock it was seventy degrees, dry, and cool. The Corniche running and bike trail is a beautifully maintained tree-lined ten-kilometer route that extends the full length of the beach. In the Fall, the weather in Abu Dhabi cools and the City comes alive with events. Formula One, Yacht Racing, Airplane Racing, a major Triathlon and music festival are all held back to back in the same season. The Formula One Grand Prix is the biggest event of the year and with it comes a lot of festivities including a concert series that has a wide range of acts, from current superstars to the lesser-knowns and has-beens.

My running route was littered with posters of this year's headliner, Rihanna. It's hard to believe she's a headliner in a Muslim country, but given the unease I felt about my upcoming meeting, I was reassured by the posters, because they were further evidence that UAE is not your typical Islamic republic.

After a quick breakfast, I put on a suit, found where I'd parked the Explorer, and left for the Falcon office. I arrived a little after eight and spent some time with the admin staff. I could tell by the warmth of the reception that none of my recent exploits had reached the Falcon team, and for that I was grateful. The next two hours were spent with Shihab, the finance manager, reconciling the accounts between our two companies. Shihab thinks I'm the greatest, because Jessica pays Trident's bills on time, which is a phenomenon Falcon has never experienced from the UAE Government. One of the invoices Shihab handed me was for a product shipped by Airbus-UK and recently transferred by Falcon to my hangar in Al Dhafra Air Force Base.

The UAE has a nascent space program. They've already launched a couple of commercial satellites and have ambitions one day to put a man on Mars. One of the first revelations from the conflict in Yemen was a shortage of satellite surveillance systems. Inadequate geospatial capability meant a lot of the targeting and battle assessment imagery had to be gathered by fighter jets, which are expensive to run and have limited loitering time. I discovered a quick-fix solution for the problem a while ago when I was still working for Falcon. Initially, we tried to get the UAE Air Force to buy the system, but they had a tight budget and didn't want to pay for an unproven system. I couldn't get Falcon to buy it either, which was to be expected. I was convinced it was a great idea and without any other takers, I decided that Trident would buy it and lease it out to the UAE Air Force.

I dropped five million dollars on the first aircraft, plus an additional one point five million for a ground control team. I offered to provide the service to the UAE Air Force for free for three months with the option to lease it long-term after the trial period. I was positive they'd agree to a lease. Fighter jets with intel payloads cost over twenty grand per flight hour, so the system paid for itself.

My quick fix is the Airbus Zephyr HAPS (high-altitude pseudo-satellite) and the reason for the invoice was because it had just been delivered. Sitting in the Trident hangar at Al Dhafra AFB, I had an aircraft and a ground control team capable of launching a UAV with an operating altitude of seventy-five thousand feet and the ability to fly nonstop for ninety days. The payload on the fully solar-powered aircraft with twenty-five-meter wingspan weighed twenty kilograms and included an amazing optical and IR package with a ten-centimeter resolution, which was as good as the best intelligence satellite systems. The UAV has the ability to stream real-time video or provide still shots. The Zephyr has a maximum speed of only forty knots, but the key feature is that it runs on electricity. Air-breathing engines found on most military fast jets aren't designed to operate above fifty to fifty-five thousand feet. The lack of oxygen at altitude causes the jet turbines to flame out. My new solar-powered electrically driven Zephyr has no such problem. And because there's not usually an air defense threat above fifty-five thousand feet, the Zephyr has carte blanche to roam freely over the Middle East.

If Sheik MBZ decides not to send me to the gallows after our meeting this afternoon, my plan is to launch my new toy to Riyadh and find my quarry, posthaste.

I drove the Explorer off the main avenue onto a service road that was tucked behind a row of tall trees. Two miles down the road I came to a checkpoint and was asked to step out of my vehicle while it was thoroughly inspected. Once through the gate, I was directed down a mangrove-lined trail, until I was stopped at another security gate. I was waved through and directed to park on a concrete pad next to a sprawling two story building. A soldier wearing a Presidential Guard unit patch intercepted me before I was out of the SUV and ushered me down a walkway to the entrance of the main palace building. I didn't have much time to gawk, but it was a stunning view, the huge expanse of green lawn leading into the lush green mangrove trees with the Gulf visible between breaks in the mangroves.

My escort took me into a sitting area and told me to wait. He closed the door, leaving me in a small room that was modestly decorated with floral patterns and gold accents. No servants came and asked me if I wanted anything to drink, which struck me as unusual and made me wonder if Mike hadn't misread the situation. After a forty-five-minute wait, a short heavyset guy in a white kandura entered and asked me to follow him. When I passed through the double doors into the sheik's office I was dazzled by the expansiveness and elaborate décor. The waiting area they'd warehoused me in was definitely not the VIP waiting room. I was guessing that I was in the ceremonial office, the room designed to intimidate, and it was making an impression.

The sheik remained seated behind an enormous ornate lacquered desk as I approached. The assistant gestured for me to take one of the two seats directly in front of the desk. The office had seating along the wall for at least thirty. I saw two local gentlemen sitting along the wall I didn't recognize and one I did: Major General Tenaji, the crown prince's military aide. Once I sat down, there was an uncomfortable silence for what seemed like several minutes.

Finally, I broke the silence. "Your Highness, thank you for inviting me."

"I'm a little surprised you came, considering your recent crimes," said the crown prince who was leaning forward on his desk with his hands clasped in front of him.

"Your Highness, I know the work I do in Iraq has your support. When my men were killed, I naturally assumed the persons responsible were defying your will and didn't enjoy your protection."

His brow furrowed, and I saw even more intensity in his eyes.

"You should've brought this situation to me to decide and you to learn what actions do and do not meet my approval. We have laws in this country. You should not have taken matters into your own hands," he said with his index finger pointed straight at me across his mammoth desk.

"I was careful to avoid collateral damage. I apologize if I've caused offense."

"What about Sheik Meshal? Were you also responsible for his death?"

"Yes."

"That was a very complex operation. It's difficult to accept that you were working alone," said the crown prince.

"You'll have to accept my word on it. Although I think you know the current American leadership well enough to believe they'd never help me."

For the first time, I detected a flicker of civility from the crown prince. "Why did you return to the UAE?" he asked.

"I met with Mike Guthrie over the weekend, and he told me you requested a meeting."

"You had no concerns?" said the crown prince.

I touched my heart with the palm of my right hand and spoke. "Your Highness, I know you could easily imprison me if you so desired. I think you also understand my motivations were not to harm the UAE or you or anyone who was not involved in the killing of my people. They were the exact opposite. I've lived in the UAE for a long time. I have many friends in this country, and I have a great respect for you. I took a risk coming here because I thought as a military man, you would understand."

"What are your intentions regarding Prince Bandar?"

"I'm going to kill him."

A look of surprise showed on his face. I don't think the sheik was expecting me to be so direct.

"Does the US government know of your plans?" asked the sheik.

"No, I don't think they do—at least not at the top level."

"How do you think the United States will respond after he's killed?"

"If he dies the way Sheik Meshal did, the Saudi government will protest, and the US government will hunt me down and lock me up. However, if he dies after making a full confession on video, where he outlines in detail his involvement in starting and supporting Daesh and the killing of American citizens in Iraq, I don't think anyone will come to his defense."

"Your plan is to capture him, force a confession, and then kill him?" asked the crown prince. "That's a very difficult task."

"It is."

"Are you here to ask for assistance?"

"Sir, no, I'm not. Unlike in UAE and Kuwait, where I'm positive Rasheed and Meshal were operating outside of the wishes and support of their governments, I'm not sure that's the case with Bandar. If things go wrong and I'm captured, I'll talk. Everybody talks eventually, and I don't want a trail leading back to you or anyone else in the UAE. This is a personal matter, and I intend to settle it on a personal level."

"I know the king of Saudi Arabia very well, and I'm certain he doesn't support Bandar's actions, but I respect your consideration," replied the sheik.

The crown prince pressed a button on his desk and a servant arrived with Arabic coffee. The sheik changed the subject, and we talked for about forty-five minutes on a wide range of topics, from military training to fishing. The crown prince was a truly impressive guy. I came into the meeting with a great respect for the man, and my assessment had only increased. The only other point of substance mentioned during the discussion was an invitation by the crown prince for me to return Trident operations to Al Dhafra Air Force Base, an invitation I accepted.

As I returned to my SUV and began the drive off the palace grounds, I felt elated with the same sense of relief I feel after surviving a firefight. The outcome of the meeting was better than even my most optimistic expectations. I would've loved to accept his direct assistance, but the political ramifications were too risky. Being able to operate out of Al Dhafra Air Force Base and stage out of UAE was as much as I could ask for. Now I just needed to figure out how to find and capture Bandar.

I arrived at Al Dhafra Air Force Base later that afternoon. There were a couple of cars parked outside the Trident Hangar. The main hangar door was closed, so I entered through a regular-sized door on the side. Inside, I found the team of Airbus engineers fully engaged and my brand new Zephyr HAPS fully assembled and on display in the center of the floor.

I found the lead engineer and introduced myself. Holger was a German with a no-nonsense attitude and a strong accent that made his English difficult to understand. The gist of it was that the aircraft would be available for launch within the next forty-eight hours. Part of the system was a twenty-foot container that had an external plug connected to the hangar's power. The container was a ground control station (GCS). Communication from the GCS to the UAV was via satellite. The Airbus crew had mounted a satellite dish outside in a trailer. The fragile aircraft consisted mostly of a twenty-five-meter-wide solar-panel-covered wing with two wing-mounted electric propellers and a fuselage that was little more than an aluminum tube. The tail wing spanned a good ten meters, and it too was covered with solar panels. The payload was housed in the bottom center of the wing with the batteries. Beneath the Zephyr HAPS was a thin-framed carriage on wheels that was used to keep it stable and off the ground when not in flight.

The plan was to launch the Zephyr as soon as it was ready. The Airbus crew would be responsible for positioning the aircraft seventy-five thousand feet above Riyadh and for recovering the aircraft once the battery power reached the bingo level. We were approaching the shortest days of the year and the deficit between the solar charge and energy consumption was going to limit the time on station to only seventy to seventy-five days instead of the advertised ninety days.

The flight profile was simple. The aircraft would remain in UAE airspace until it reached seventy thousand feet, and then it would pass into Saudi Arabia. Once on station over Riyadh, the Zephyr would be placed in a racetrack pattern circling the city, and payload control would transfer to another control station located in Edinburgh, Scotland. The control in Edinburgh would be performed by a company I'd already contracted to conduct imagery analysis, named GSS. GSS is a private company affiliated with the University of Edinburgh. It's a trailblazer in the application of artificial intelligence and satellite imagery.

Most of the applications for this cutting-edge technology are commercial. The convergence of computing power, machine learning, and satellite imagery have been called a perfect storm that's just now becoming possible because of recent advances in technology. The questions that can be answered using geospatial data and AI software are limitless and will benefit a wide variety of fields, including agriculture, mining, meteorology, environmental science, and defense.

The problem I plan to give to David Forrest, the CEO of GSS, is at the limit of what's possible with the technology. I'm going to give him a picture of Prince Bandar and ask him to find Bandar in Riyadh using the Zephyr imagery and the GSS capabilities.

I know David is going to want some background on the prince, including details about his position in the hierarchy, wealth, and looks. My information on Bandar is paper thin. His looks are going to be the biggest enabler, because Prince Bandar has a unique visage. He looks like a five-foot-ten-inch Ewok. A dead ringer for the rotund lovable bearlike creatures from *Star Wars*—same bushy gray beard, same fat face, nose, and eyes, same portly body, and even the same undersized limbs. He's unmistakable.

Before the current situation, I'd already contracted with GSS and we'd already discussed the need to do a demonstration for the UAE. I was going to make finding Bandar the finding a needle in a haystack mission that we'd planned on doing. Professor Forrest is a math genius, a quant jock who double-hatted as the head of the computer science department at the University of Edinburgh. He's a heavyset, affable man with the stereotypical absentminded professor dishevelment. Because the UK armed forces these days is only slightly larger than the New York City Police Department and because of a lack of funding, sensitive UK intelligence programs are sometimes forced to be combined with commercial and academic applications to survive. If a program like GSS's existed in the United States, and it probably did, it would be so heavily funded and so secret, I'd probably never even know of its existence. Professor Forrest wasn't able to separate GSS from the university because the system relied on the university's supercomputer.

After conferring with the Airbus personnel, it was agreed that tomorrow they'd do final systems checks, and if no faults were detected, they would launch early the next morning. Satisfied with the progress, I returned to the Intercontinental Marina and the *Sam Houston*.

Back on my perch on the flydeck that afternoon, I broke out a bottle of 95 Far Niente Cabernet to celebrate that after my meeting with MBZ I was still converting oxygen into carbon dioxide. The first person I called was David Forrest to give him the go ahead to start work on the demo. I sent him what little I had on Bandar. Then I called Jessica and gave instructions for the movement of operations from Cyprus back to Abu Dhabi. Even at seven in the morning Bahama time, she was her usual upbeat self. The company cash situation had improved since our last meeting and that's the kind of thing that makes Jessica happy. I told her I'd be sending an email with a list of sample equipment I needed shipped and that I'd greenlighted the contract with GSS.

Chapter 23

Edinburgh, Scotland

Twenty days after the Zephyr launched from Al Dhafra, I received a call from Professor Forrest, informing me that Prince Bandar had been found. I caught the next flight to Scotland. Winter was at the doorstep, and I decided to walk from my hotel to the GSS offices on Southbridge Street. It was a brisk thirty-five-degree morning as I made my way across the Princess Gardens. Old Town Edinburgh is dotted with medieval fortresses on hilltops, gray-stoned behemoths complete with towers and battlements. I arrived outside the brick three-story office and was buzzed in by security.

Professor Forrest met me in what I'd guess is a traditional Victorian sitting room on the first floor. The system was still experimental, and I could sense a triumphant air from the professor over this latest success. The description he gave was very technical and detailed and I had trouble following most of it. But, I did catch a few things. He explained that it wasn't possible to keep up with every move made by the software powered by the Cray supercomputer. It was only possible to identify some of the breadcrumbs left by the system in the process of discovering the whereabouts of the target. The professor explained how the initial profile, including the images, had been fed into the software. The computer software had then used the video images from the Zephyr HAPS and information publicly available on the internet to formulate a search.

After tea, the professor pulled out a pipe and began a long ceremonial process of cleaning it, filling it with tobacco, and lighting it. Having spent the previous thirty minutes explaining what the system did, he next went into the how. The thirty-minute dissertation on pattern analysis, spectral sparsification, and algorithms was so completely beyond my comprehension that I found my thoughts drifting to lunch. Finally, the good doctor displayed an iPad with an image of Prince Bandar sitting back on a chair in a garden, looking up toward the sky.

Finally, something I understood. "This is amazing. Your system is miraculous," I said upon seeing the iPad image.

The beaming professor replied, "This was a particularly difficult search. The prince hasn't left this villa, which is not his, by the way, for a long time."

"How do you know that? I thought you just detected him."

"We did, but once we found him, it was an easy task to walk the data backward. Except for having lunch most days outside in his garden, this man never leaves his house."

"Can I get a summary of your analysis, especially his location and movements?"

"Of course. Would you care to see the real-time feed?"

One of the offices was set up as an operations center, with a line of tables with keyboards and small flat-screen displays. There were two large-screen displays on the wall. The fifty-inch flat-screen wall displays showed the real-time video streams from the Zephyr in both IR and regular camera view as well as the position of the aircraft. GSS couldn't control the flight of the aircraft, but they received all the same flight data as the GCS in Al Dhafra Air Force Base. Through the same internet link, they could control the sensors, which included the camera pan and tilt and zoom. These were functions that were controlled by the GSS software, but it was possible to place the camera controls on manual and control them using a computer keypad.

I spent the next six hours in the operations center. Two hours into the study session, I watched on video as Prince Bandar walked outside his enormous villa and had lunch in a traditional English garden, replete with fountains, flowers and hedge borders. Using the Zephyr feeds, I found the external guard locations, the number of personnel on his personal security detail, the number and types of vehicles that drove through the mansion gate each day. I was also able to obtain the same information on the prince's neighbors. At four thirty, I left with a dozen USB drives filled with videos, plus my own handwritten notes.

Once back in Abu Dhabi the preparations began for the second phase of the operation. Being allowed to stage out of the UAE gave me a huge advantage. Saudi Arabia borders Yemen, Oman, UAE, Bahrain, Qatar, Kuwait, and Jordan. Adding to those huge land borders, it has an enormous coastline. Securing the borders is a daunting task for the Saudis and they do what any reasonable country would do, they take risk in some areas so they can reinforce others. UAE is by far their friendliest neighbor, which is why it's the least protected. I picked out a border-breach point based more on the UAE's security forces than the Saudis'. The spot I chose is in a place referred to as the Empty Quarter. From past experience, I know it to be an extremely inhospitable place to travel, with soft sand, high dunes, and very little water, which as an upside translates into very few people.

Packed up and mission ready, I left the marina parking lot at five in the afternoon in a dark gray Jeep Wrangler Rubicon. It was a six-cylinder, 250-horsepower model with a hard top. The Rubicon is one of the best desert off-road vehicles ever made. In the back I had four five-gallon jerry cans of fuel and a Pelican box with my tactical gear. The only items kept in the front seat were a pair of bolt cutters, night vision goggles, and a GPS.

I drove west on Highway 11, the main road going from Abu Dhabi to Saudi Arabia. The road follows the coast. After two hours, it was dark and I was surrounded by desolation. The only features were the occasional sand dune. I turned onto Highway 15, and headed due south and paralleled the Saudi border. After moving thirty miles on Highway 15, I turned right off the highway and headed into the desert cross-country. I shut the headlights off, put the vehicle in four wheel drive, strapped on the night vision goggles and started the forty-mile open-desert night drive to the border fence.

The desert floor was flat and I saw the fence before the waypoint alarm on my GPS alerted me to it. Once I reached the fence, I used a pair of bolt cutters to make a Jeep-size opening in the chain-link fence. Once through it was another twenty miles off-road moving due west before reaching Saudi Highway 95, and from there, it was four hundred miles of open highway to Riyadh. Before I got onto the highway, I switched license plates. As part of my pre-mission prep, I'd snagged a set of plates from a Lexus 470 I'd found in the Abu Dhabi Jumeirah Hotel parking lot.

I drove all night, stopping for breakfast at a pancake house in Al Safarat, west of Riyadh. After breakfast, I drove to a nearby abandoned construction site. Low oil prices had idled most construction projects in the kingdom making it a good place for a nap. A few hours later, I followed the GPS through the insane Saudi afternoon traffic into a very upscale Riyadh neighborhood. Although I'm sure it was nothing compared to his palace, Prince Bandar's hiding place was a very striking villa.

I pulled up to the entrance gate at the home of Prince Bandar's neighbor. In seconds, I was in and out of the Wrangler with a pair of bolt cutters in my hand. I drove up the stone driveway to the villa that my satellite reconnaissance had confirmed was unoccupied. I'd studied seven days of overhead video of the villa, and during that time, the only activity had been an occasional labor crew. The owner most likely spent his time in Europe, as did many of the Saudis who could afford it. I swung the Jeep off the driveway and headed around to the back of the house and parked.

The time was twelve forty-five. My review of the tapes showed that Prince Bandar never took his lunch before one o'clock. With no time to spare, I ran over to the back of the Jeep, popped open the Pelican case and pulled out five objects. The first two objects were twelve-foot telestep ladders. The two-foot-long collapsed black ladders were strong when extended—rated to 320 pounds. I was confident the ladders could handle the four-hundred-pound load I was going to put on them. I also retrieved a set of flex-ties and a rifle. The rifle was a Daniel Defense ISR 300 blackout with a Trijicon ACOG sight. The integrated suppression system, when used with subsonic ammunition, was very quiet, making a sound not much louder than a spitting sound. The final item was a Prox Dynamics PDR-100 Black Hornet Nano UAV. The controller and video display on the PDR-100 looked like a game controller and a mini iPad. The five fully charged Nano day helicopters were four inches long and one inch wide, and each had a twenty-five-minute battery life.

I took the Nano UAVs and the rifle back inside the Jeep and powered up the Prox controller and one of the Nano UAVs. I rolled down the window and extended my hand outside with the UAV in my open palm. With my right hand on the controller, I launched it up into the air. Separating the two estates was a ten-foot wall with a line of cypress trees that were all above twenty feet tall and made for an effective privacy screen. I guided the Nano UAV above the top of the trees, where I could look down into the garden area and the house beyond. The PDR-100 is used by many of the world's elite special forces units. It's not a simple remote-controlled helicopter. The aircraft has a navigation system and a GPS position location system, making it possible to navigate even when it's out of sight. Once in position, the camera in the nose of the helicopter can be directed, and the helicopter can be placed into a stationary hover.

When the first Nano UAV was down to ten percent battery life, I retrieved it and launched a second. Five minutes into the second flight, the screen on the controller showed a maid setting up the lunch table. Several minutes later, the prince came outside. He had a two-man security detail outside with him. The first remained close to the door leading into the villa, and the second took up a forward position on the outside of a small garden gate that separated the garden from the rest of the estate grounds.

After recovering the second bird, I launched a third. When the prince sat at the table, I sprang into action. I slung the carbine over my shoulder, grabbed the ladders I'd left behind the Jeep, and headed to the wall nearest to where the prince was sitting on the other side. I silently telescoped the first ladder and laid it against the wall, and then I opened the second and placed it next to the first. I returned to the Jeep and resumed viewing the Nano UAV video screen. As soon as the maid served the prince and departed the garden, I recovered the Nano UAV and went into action.

I climbed the ladder hand over hand, as stealthily as I could with my rifle slung over my back. Once on top, I carefully lifted and raised the second ladder and lowered it on the other side of the wall, but concealed behind the trunk of a cypress tree. I straddled the two ladders then climbed down on Prince Bandar's side of the wall.

Sandwiched between the wall and the cypress tree, I raised my suppressed blackout 300 and stepped through the cypress branches and out into the sunlight. My first bullet hit the bearded sentry standing at the villa door in the forehead. I pivoted right and fired two quick rounds at the guard manning the garden gate. The guard was already in motion, moving back into the garden with his pistol half raised when my first round hit him in the chest. Before he could fall, I fired a second round, double-tapping him in the face.

The prince was ten feet away and getting up to bolt. I rushed the Ewok doppelgänger before he could move away from the table and stunned the prince with an openhanded blow to the forehead, knocking him to the ground. He fell over the back of the chair onto his back. I flex-cuffed the prostrate man's ankles and wrists, placed a strip of duct tape on his mouth, and stood him up. I bent down and lifted the heavyset prince onto my left shoulder and slung the carbine onto the right. After wading back through the cypress, I climbed the first ladder which was straining from the four-hundred-pound load. I stepped over the wall to the second, retrieved the ladder from Bandar's side and dropped it onto my own.

My legs were on fire from exertion during the decent as the ladder rungs flexed with each step. When my feet finally reached soft ground, my legs were ready to give out. I wove the final thirty feet to the Jeep with the heavy prince still on my shoulders and dumped him into the back.

Before shutting the tailgate, I grabbed the suppressed SIG and headed for the driver's seat. The rear windows of the Jeep were darkly tinted, and I didn't expect anyone would be able to see the prince. But I kept the pistol close to my seat, just in case I was stopped.

I set the GPS and headed to my first waypoint, driving out of the neighborhood at a regular speed. Five hours later, without incident, I was turning off Highway 95 at the spot where the cross-country leg of the journey began. I drove five miles into the empty desert and parked the vehicle in a shallow depression.

I dragged the wide-eyed prince out from the Jeep. His back hit the sand with a thud. I set up two collapsible nylon sports chairs, with one in front of the headlights, because it was going be dark soon. It was late in the afternoon, and the shadows were long. I dragged and lifted the prince onto one of the chairs and went back to the Jeep to retrieve my camcorder and tripod. I set the camera up to face Prince Bandar and then placed the other chair next to the camera, where I knew I wouldn't be visible in the shot. After ripping the tape from the prince's mouth, I turned on the camera.

The look of fury in the prince's eyes was not what I wanted to see. I opened a liter bottle of Evian water and took a drink, then set it in the built-in cupholder on the armrest. The prince was being aggressive making demands and insisting on answers. That made me mad. I got up from my chair, went over to the driver's window of the Jeep, and retrieved the suppressed 9mm pistol from where I'd left it. Once he saw the pistol and most likely the expression on my face, the prince stopped talking. I sat down again, and with the pistol in my right hand and the prince five feet across from me, I began.

"State your full name for the audience," I said.

"Prince Bandar Bin Sultan Al Saud."

"Explain your role in the terrorist attacks on September 11, 2001," I said.

"I had no role. That's a false accusation—a rumor. I never met with any of the hijackers."

While he was still stammering, I shot him in the right knee. The subsonic 9mm round exploded loudly against the bone and splattered so much blood that a few drops made it all the way to me and speckled my pants. The prince let out a shriek and immediately blacked out. He regained consciousness a minute later and screamed nonstop until he was hoarse. I fed the prince some water and returned to my seat.

"You can cooperate, or this can be long and painful. That choice is entirely yours. Now, answer the question."

The prince was a pathetic sight and it was easy to feel sorry for him. I had to remind myself that he was responsible for killing Jenny Lyn, Joe Kilpatrick and Joe Ferguson. Even though it was a line I'd already crossed, torturing the prince was filling me with self-loathing. But unfortunately for him, the confession from Sheik Rasheed wasn't enough. I knew if I didn't provide the US government with proof that they could show the Saudis that Bandar was a bad guy who'd only gotten what he'd deserved, then retribution would be coming my way.

The 9/11 question was a tactic, although I was a little curious. I'd never been sure about the swirling allegations that Saudi Arabia had been involved in the 9/11 attacks. I figured that once Bandar had resisted the more serious charge, then getting him to admit to less horrific crimes would be easy. As it turned out, all it took was a single bullet to the kneecap.

Once Bandar started talking, I couldn't shut him up. He was a treasure trove of information. I would've liked more time to pursue the reference he made at the end about having American protection, but he was spent; most likely because of the shock and blood loss, the prince was no longer coherent. It was time to go. I loaded up the camcorder and before stepping back into the Jeep, I took careful aim and shot the prince three times in the heart.

I found the gap in the fence easily with the help of the GPS and my night vision goggles. The illumination from the moon was excellent. I moved with haste over the forty miles of open desert before I reached Highway 15 and switched on the headlights. Before getting on the highway, I removed the Saudi license plates and buried them in the sand before replacing them with the legal UAE pair.

It was four in the morning when I returned to the *Houston*. The first thing I did was connect the camcorder to my laptop and download Prince Bandar's confession. The video was 124 minutes long. I labeled the file "Bandar" and saved it to a different file-share account than the last one I'd used. After the last time, Mike gave me him a file-sharing site that was better protected. I sent an email to Mike, notifying him that a file had been shared with him.

I was tempted to send a copy to a reputable news network and would have if I actually knew anyone in the news business. Prince Bandar's confession was blockbuster stuff. He was worse than I'd ever imagined. He'd passed information and funds to Mohammed Atta, the Egyptian leader of the 9/11 attackers. He'd admitted to communicating with and providing financial support to several other 9/11 terror cell members. He denied knowledge of the scope and timing of the attack, and I believed him. The information on the funding and support of ISIS was even more damning. Where the confession information became truly thermonuclear was where Bandar described the complicity of the Saudi Leadership. It turns out, I'd been right all along. Meshal and Rasheed were operating against their respective governments; Bandar, on the other hand, was doing his government's bidding.

I made a cup of coffee and sat behind my laptop in the galley dining area. Looking out the window, I could see the early-morning sun shimmering on the water and reflecting off the bright white presidential palace. The Sea Palace was a spectacular sight, even more so with the orange glow of an emerging sun.

I backed up my laptop to a portable hard drive and then went downstairs and hid the hard drive in my hideaway in the engine room, a waterproof box the size of a small jewelry case that I keep at the bottom of a full five-gallon oil can. Inside I have a spare passport, a hundred one-ounce Canadian Maple Leaf gold coins, and now an iPhone-sized hard drive. I was exhausted but decided to stay awake in case Mike got back to me right away.

I was on the flybridge drinking a second coffee when a black Suburban with diplomatic plates drove into the marina parking lot and parked in the space nearest to the *Houston*. Two men exited the vehicle. One of the men looked to be around fifty, the other in his early thirties. I went downstairs and met them as they reached the rear gangway. Without asking permission, the older man walked up the gangplank and stepped on board. Flashing his credentials, he introduced himself as Harold Wasserman from the US embassy.

"We're here to pick up the video you just sent."

"Can I see your ID again?" I asked. The credentials were US State Department. Which would make sense if he was with the CIA. I returned them and ushered him into the salon. I went to the galley and retrieved the camcorder, returning to the still-standing Harold Wasserman and showing him the memory card inside the camcorder.

I gave the memory card and the camera to the younger guy, who'd not been introduced.

Wasserman asked, "Is this everything?"

"Yes, it is."

"What about the computer? If you uploaded it using a laptop, we're going to need that too."

"That's not going to be possible."

"I'm going to have to insist," he said.

Wasserman and his sidekick were wearing loose polo shirts over khaki pants. If they were carrying weapons, they were in concealed holsters in their waistbands under the shirts, which would make them slow to the draw. I'd purposely given the camera to the younger guy, who would safeguard it at all costs. In a fight, the young guy might've been a challenge. Harold, on the other hand, was a cupcake.

"You have what you came for. You can leave now," I said.

Senior government bureaucrats don't take orders well, especially in front of subordinates. I could see Harold wanted to force the issue, but fortunately he had the good sense to realize it would be a painful mistake. The two government agents did an about face and left the boat without saying another word.

I went downstairs to the owner's stateroom and went to sleep. I didn't wake up until three in the afternoon and went upstairs to the salon, where I poured myself a double Macallan 18 and turned on the TV. It was Thanksgiving, and I had nothing to do and no place to be. Holidays can be the worst. They're when the disaster that is my personal life hurts the most. My sudden melancholy might be worsened by post mission letdown, or perhaps even a sense of guilt from executing three men. I wasn't sure. None of the three had put up much of a fight, but they had all deserved what they got. Either way, the matter was finished, and I was glad to have it behind me. Bandar had alluded to Americans who would protect him at the end of his interrogation, but that was all I could understand, and at that point, he'd lost his faculties.

I got dressed at nine and walked half a mile down the street to the Hilton for dinner. It was a Thursday night, and the bars and clubs would be filled to capacity by eleven. Fortunately, it was early enough to walk in and get a table. The Hilton is on the water on the Corniche. It's a landmark and one of the oldest hotels in Abu Dhabi. Despite many newer and far more upscale hotels, it retains a loyal following. I walked through the front lobby to the very back and threaded my way through Hemingway's Pub, to the Jazz Bar. The Jazz Bar isn't really a jazz bar but it is an aspiring upscale nightclub with rotating live acts from South Africa that are usually very good. The Jazz Bar has a full menu, and because it's part of one of the better hotels in the city, it offers a decent wine list.

For a brief moment, the thought of eating and drinking alone in a nightclub on Thanksgiving made me feel even sorrier for myself, but then the waitress arrived with the wine list. I didn't recognize anything on the list, which is unusual, so I picked out a bottle of Chateau Gruaud-Larose Saint-Julien based solely on the price.

The band played its first set at nine thirty. First sets tend to be slower music, and the black female singer did a decent impression of Sade's "Smooth Operator." She even looked the part. At eleven thirty, still feeling morose after a bottle of very good wine and an uninspiring steak, I paid the tab and walked back to the marina.

Taking a route along the access road to the Intercontinental I took a shortcut between the Fish Market Restaurant and the Bayshore Beach Club. As I threaded through the parked cars, I noticed the lights on in my boat. I stopped and watched and then wound my way between the cars until reaching within thirty yards of the yacht. Moving around inside the salon area, I saw a flashlight. The parking lot doesn't have any lights except for those on the surrounding buildings. I stayed in the shadows, trying to find a lookout. To my left, about 150 yards in the direction of the hotel, I spotted a man watching the entryway to the parking lot. He had his back to me.

I approached slowly from behind. When I got to within five feet, he must've sensed my approach, because he turned his head and started to spin his body. I hit him with a right cross to the jaw, and he was down and out. I did a quick search of the body and found a small ICOM radio with an earpiece and a Glock 9mm.

With the Glock in my right hand, I approached the yacht. The tinted glass made it difficult to see inside. I moved fast to the edge of the dock and stepped cautiously through the gateway. When I reached the open salon door, I could see a person lying flat on the floor, holding a small flashlight in his right hand while feeling under the couch with his left.

I crept forward silently until I reached the man, who was still lying flat on his belly and unable to turn his head back to see me. With the Glock pressed against his neck, I told him to slide back gently and put his hands on his head. I took a step back and was looking for something to restrain the man when I felt a blow to the back of my head, and the lights went out.

The next morning, I woke up face down on the hardwood floor of the salon. The back of my head and one side of my face were caked with blood. There was a small puddle that was congealing where my head had lain. After a couple of attempts, I brought myself up to a kneeling position and tried to clear away the nausea and dizziness. I stumbled downstairs and took a shower.

The cut on the back of my head could've used stitches. I made a mess of things trying to make a butterfly bandage through my hair but finally managed to close the wound while working with the mirrors in the bathroom. I must've had a bad concussion, my balance was off, and the wooziness wouldn't go away. I swabbed up the blood on the salon floor and did a brief inventory before running out of gas and heading to my quarters to sleep. The only items I noticed missing were electronics. My laptop, phone, and iPad were all gone.

The next time I woke, it was Saturday morning, a full day later. The nausea was gone, but the dampening fog-like effect from the concussion persisted. I wasn't sharp, but I could discern footfalls on the deck above. *Here we go again*, I thought. I went looking for a weapon and chastised myself for not thinking of it much earlier.

"Pat, are you down there?" I heard Mike's voice yell.

"Yeah, I'm coming up."

I dressed in gym shorts and a t-shirt and put on a red Davidson College baseball cap to hide my sloppy bandage. When I reached the top of the stairs, I saw Mike, already with a cup of coffee, sitting at the galley nook.

"You look rough. Let me guess—there's a pair of dominatrix twins downstairs, and last night you forgot your safe word."

I shook my head. "I should be so lucky. Nothing like that. I had a rough Thanksgiving."

Instead of sitting in the galley, I went over to the big U-shaped couch in the salon and laid on my back in the middle. Mike came over and sat down on the other chair.

Ignoring my degraded condition, Mike asked to do a debrief. I got up and took two Tylenol Extra Strength and then returned to the couch with a large bottle of sparkling water and a glass, which I set on the cocktail table. Mike placed a digital recording device on the table next to the water, and for the next three hours, I told my story, beginning with the launch of the Zephyr and ending with my waking up in a puddle of blood, face down on the salon floor.

When I was finished, Mike made some observations but didn't offer any conclusions. He kept the recorder on, because his intent was to send his observations back to Langley for analysis.

"Professor Forrest and GSS likely have MI6 associations. British involvement is a possibility," he said. "During your interrogation of Bandar, you never pressed him on American connections. He implied several times in his responses that he was under US protection, but you never followed up. At the end of the interrogation, he said America and then became incoherent.

"Harold Wasserman is not CIA. He works for the State Department Diplomatic Security Service, and he's assigned to the UAE embassy. Nobody from CIA asked State to retrieve the hard copies from you. Nobody from State should've been aware of what you were doing, much less known of the existence of the Bandar video confession. Last time, I picked the hard copies up myself. Why would it be different this time?" he asked, stopping his musing and looking to me for an answer.

"That was my mistake. The video was so much more explosive than the Sheik Rasheed confession, I assumed it would be treated differently, and I didn't expect anyone from the embassy to brandish CIA credentials. State Department seemed right."

"The guys who jumped you were Americans, top-level operators, I imagine. Even after a bottle of wine, you're not an easy target. Wasserman was tasked by someone, probably at State, to collect any copies you might have had. That team might have been connected to him and given the task of finishing the job."

I sat up on the couch for the first time in hours and poured another glass of water. I hadn't eaten in two days, and my energy level was reaching a critical low.

"It looks as though the State Department and CIA are at cross purposes on this thing. I was in too much of a hurry with Bandar. I regret not pursuing an American connection to his activities, but that idea is so far-fetched, it's hard for me to take seriously. I figured Bandar was just deflecting. Plus, I can't see the motivation for US involvement."

Mike walked to the fridge in the galley and retrieved a Sam Adams. With an open bottle in hand, he sat back down across from me. "As revolting a thought as it may be, the United States defense spending following the attacks on September eleventh exceeded six trillion dollars."

I nodded. "Yeah, I can definitely see how a conspiracy theorist could put these facts together. I punched Bandar's ticket, so he's done talking.

Whoever was responsible for attacking me must know there's nothing incriminating about them on the Bandar confession. They're safe. Bandar didn't mention any Western involvement in his crimes."

"Once Bandar admitted to involvement in the 9/11 attacks, you should've changed mission and held on to him."

"I considered it, but the problem was I had no backup. It would've been easy to get him across the border, but after I did, where was I going to take him? Plus, I was worried about implicating the Emiratis."

"Forcing you to work alone guaranteed that outcome. The decision not to assist you came after a big fight. I was strongly in favor, as was just about everyone within the Agency. The decision was made at the political level."

I lay back on the couch and let my dizziness dissipate for a minute. "So, what now?"

"Within the CIA, the number of people who've been read in on your activities as they relate to Rasheed, Meshal, and Bandar is limited. I'll go back and put everyone through a mole hunt protocol and find the leak. Until we know the players and links, we can't do anything. We need to be very cautious. I need to talk to the senior people I trust before I do anything."

"What should I do?"

"Take a vacation, get some rest, restore your health. Stay out of trouble, and don't take any risks. The situation in the UAE should be safe for you now. If they believed you knew or heard something from Bandar beyond what was on the video you made, they would've killed you to keep you quiet."

"Would it help to identify the guys who were on my boat last night?"

"Of course. If we could get a line on them, we could pull on that thread and see where it takes us."

"I would've thought of this earlier if I weren't starving and my head wasn't pounding. The marina has security cameras that have a view of my boat. The Fish Market restaurant was still open and lit up when this happened. We should see what was captured on the security tape. Let's get lunch and then talk to security at the Intercontinental."

"Will they help?"

"I know the management. I'm fairly sure they will."

"Let's check the tape first and then have lunch," said Mike.

Two hours later, after getting approval from the hotel general manager, Mike and I were behind the console in the Intercontinental security room, reviewing the marina parking lot security camera footage. Only two cameras had a view of the *Houston*, and since we had a good idea of the time frame, we got to the relevant footage quickly.

One camera was mounted on the Fish Market restaurant and aimed toward the line of boats, including mine. We watched two men enter the boat and then saw the intermittent flashlight arcs. Twenty minutes later, the footage showed me enter the boat, and not long after that, a third intruder came into view. He looked like the guy I punched. Because of the tinted windows, we didn't see the attack, but soon after the third intruder entered, all three departed. The camera captured face shots of all three people. I was able to get a USB drive of the entire scene from the helpful security supervisor.

It was almost five when we finished with security, and we moved to the coffee shop in the Intercontinental lobby. I had a turkey panini sandwich and an American coffee. I could feel my vitality returning. The images of the three intruders were high-quality enough to perform face recognition. The UAE, like most countries, conducts a biometric face scan at passport control, and hotels require passport scans at check-in that are entered into a central computer. In the UAE, it's easy for the government to track visitors. The three intruders had the look of American operators. They were white guys in their thirties, all fit and heavily muscled, all sporting the obligatory Special Operations beard.

"The UAE won't be too impressed that someone is conducting operations in their country. I should take that USB to my friends at the Special Operations Command and ask for help tracking those guys down," I said.

Mike considered the idea. "Let's keep it low-key. I'll send the images back to Langley, and they'll ID them and follow up on the lead. Those guys are probably just grunts, so don't expect much to come of it. I know you want to go into Godzilla mode with these guys, but we need to be cautious. The possibility that Bandar had American support is an explosive idea. Let's find out what we're up against before you start shooting people."

"I'll be on my best behavior. I have a lot of work to do this week with Trident and Falcon, and then I'm going to take a vacation. I'll be in the United States and the Bahamas during the Christmas holidays."

"A vacation's a great idea, Pat. You've had a stressful few months. We may be on to something bigger, but it could also turn out to be nothing. Don't jump to any conclusions. The Trident operation remains important. Keep that going, and try not to make too much money."

Chapter 24

600 miles west of Azores, Atlantic Ocean

An Atlantic crossing in the *Houston* had always been in my plans. I'd never really done any blue water yachting and with the trauma of the past few months behind, it was time to untether.

The first leg was a clockwise circumnavigation of the Arabian Peninsula from Abu Dhabi, UAE, through the Gulf of Aden into the Red Sea. I refueled at Sharm el Sheikh, Egypt. The second leg took me through the Gulf of Suez and into the Suez Canal. At Port Said, Egypt, I refueled again and begun the third leg of the trip through the Mediterranean and the Straits of Gibraltar to the Portuguese Azores Island of Ponta Delgada, located three hundred miles west of the Portuguese mainland. The leg I'm on now is the main event, I'm in the middle of the Atlantic between Portugal and Canada.

I pulled the purple Furman College watch cap lower over my ears. Nothing was exposed to the December chill, even though I was in the open air behind the wheel on the top deck helm station. To protect my face, I had a decent salt-and-pepper beard going and my eyes were covered with black climbing sunglasses. A Thermos cup of hot coffee was in my gloved hand. The autopilot was steering the yacht. My only role was to monitor the situation.

Three days in, I was averaging four hours of sleep each day. There was a storm coming, and I'd been mentally debating what course of action to take. I could turn around and head back to the Azores. *Sam Houston* had the speed to outrun the storm, but I'd lose six days in the process, and there was no guarantee I wouldn't hit another storm on the restart. Diverting south to avoid the storm was an option, but even with the extra fuel bladders, that would force a mid-ocean refueling and depending on the seas that carried another kind of risk. The final option is to sail straight into the storm and deal with it. The yacht dealer had trumped the Azimut 64's seaworthiness when I bought the *Houston* and I did my own research as well on the toughness of the composite hull, hatches and windows. In the end, I decided to trust *Sam Houston's* builders and power through.

The sky was gray and the ocean was made up of dark rolling swells that were ten feet high. The heading was straight into the westerly wind. Which thanks to the protection of the helm windshield, made my perch comfortable. Looking at the weather radar on my iPad, I think I have a few hours until the snow will drive me below deck to the wheelhouse.

Being outside in the elements was invigorating and I knew it was going to be the last fresh air I was going to get for a while. I'd done a walk-through earlier and made sure everything was properly stowed and tied down. The tender was secured on the hydraulic platform on the stern; on top of it, I strapped an inflatable emergency raft, along with an immersion suit, rations, water, and locator beacon. If the yacht went over, I could inflate the raft and survive easily enough.

I got up and staggered over to the gas grill behind me and flipped the steak I'd been cooking. For the past three weeks, I'd been subsisting on one meal a day. I'd already lost ten pounds and felt pretty good about it.

The snow began to fall and the wind picked up an hour after I finished lunch. Winds were gusting to fifty miles per hour and seas grew violent. That was my cue to get inside. By four, it was eerily dark, and waves were breaking over the main deck. The wind sensor was topping out at 80 mph. Visibility was down to two hundred yards ahead using the yacht's FLIR system.

Climbing, diving, surfing, skiing and skydiving are lifelong passions. What all of those activities have in common is that at some point, I've always managed to get myself into a spot that made me wish I never took it up, which is exactly where I was with yachting.

The waves were up to three times the height of the *Houston*. The trick is to find the big ones, steer into it them bow-first and then accelerate on the way up and throttle back on the way down. That is a technique that works well when pushing a big board through the surf, and just made sense that the same laws of physics applied to boats. The gyrostabilizers were doing a miraculous job limiting the roll, and while the sixty-four-foot *Houston* was taking a beating, at least it wasn't taking in any water.

It was a crazy stressful night, but by ten the next morning, I could see the first glimmer of daylight. The seas were down to a mere ten feet, and the wind was no longer whistling as it passed through the flydeck. It was calm enough to leave the controls and make a cup of coffee and a tuna fish sandwich.

It eventually calmed enough to do a walk-around of the yacht. I started below deck with the engine room and the sleeping cabins and finished up on the flydeck. There was a lot of snow and ice buildup on the deck, but nothing that warranted concern. Exhausted, I checked the navigation and set the radar to twenty-five miles, grabbed a blanket, and fell asleep in the wheelhouse chair.

Three days later, I was sailing into Halifax Harbor on my way to the Nova Scotia Royal Squadron Yacht Club for fuel and rest. The weather was a frigid eight degrees Fahrenheit on the flydeck. The water was smooth as glass with patches of ice. There were still remnants of the morning fog as I navigated between McNabs Island and Ferguson Cove on the final mile of my first Atlantic crossing.

The Canadian attendant at the Squadron Marina guided me into a slip and even helped me tie down. I put up the Q flag and the attendant contacted the border security authority. The *Houston* was fully refueled and cleaned by the time customs cleared us. I gave the helpful attendant five American Benjamins and told him "Merry Christmas" before going down to my cabin and taking a long overdue shower.

In mid-December, the days in Halifax are short. The sun was already setting at four thirty when a hired car arrived to take me and my two suitcases of dirty laundry to the Marriott Harbourfront Hotel.

I needed two days on dry land before the next and final leg of the trip, which was a seven-day voyage straight south to the Bahamas. The Marriott was a nice break from the boat. It was a weekend, and I was alive and to celebrate the occasion, I decided to hit the town. After a stinging hot shower, I donned my ski parka, gloves, and toque, as the Canadians refer to a watch cap, and headed out for a walk.

Halifax is a very pretty city, especially when it's lit up with Christmas lights and covered in a fresh blanket of snow. The vast selection of pubs and restaurants on the waterfront gave purpose to my wandering. It felt great to stretch my legs and walk on level ground. I caught my reflection in a store window and my first thought was that my face looked like the caveman in the Geico commercial. The beard could use a trim and my face was thinner than I remembered with a hollowness in the eyes. The trip was taxing; I hadn't slept much, but I was filled with energy.

Heading south on Water Street past the piers and the maritime museum with the cold air on my face reminded me of being at sea. Sailing alone halfway across the world was cathartic. The slime fell away with each passing nautical mile. I knew Mike Guthrie would drag me back into the mess. That's what he did after Afghanistan and it's what he'd do again. In the meantime, I intended to forget about the toxic sludge that was the Middle East for a while.

After forty minutes of wandering, I turned around and walked back toward the hotel on Water Street. Music was coming from a bar next to the Marriott and I took that as an omen. I walked past a sign that read "Lower Deck" and made my way inside to a restaurant named the Beer House. The smells wafting out from the kitchen made me salivate. I ordered an Alexander Keith India pale ale, which seems to be far too many words for a simple beer. When the waitress delivered my tall draft, I ordered the grilled seafood platter.

The interior of the pub was nautical-themed, with light oak planking, fishing nets, and neon beer signs. A deejay held a set of headphones to his ear while a band was setting up on a small stage adjacent to the dance floor. The crowd was mostly young people from the neighboring colleges. People from the Maritimes are a unique subset of Canadian. The economy's been depressed for decades which has spread them throughout Canada. I've always thought of them as joyful journeymen. Newfies follow the work to the factories of Ontario, the oil fields of northern Alberta and wherever else they can find it. Tonight's crowd looked to be an excellent example of a people with a reputation for knowing how to have a good time. When the band kicked off with a strong if not ironic rendition of "Summer of 69," I decided to stick around for a couple of sets.

By the second set, I was on my fourth beer. The lights in the bar were turned down low, and the band was blasting Top 40 pop music. It was crowded and a young guy and two girls signaled for permission to sit at the unoccupied chairs at my table, I waved them in. The band was loud, and the dance floor overflowed with the young and a sprinkling of not so young.

When the band took a break and it was quiet enough to talk, the young guy introduced himself as Owen and his two friends as Bria and Olivia. The kids were drinking pitchers of Labatt's Blue, which can only be described as one of the horrors of poverty. I was enjoying himself. Three weeks in solitary can make a person appreciate humanity, and it was nice to see good-natured kids hanging out.

Bria was a socializer, and we began to make small talk. When she learned I was an American, she asked me what brought me to Halifax and what I did for a living. For a split second, I considered telling her the truth—that I was an international arms dealer and a CIA assassin—but instead I told her I worked in logistics. She went silent after that; nothing can kill a curious person's interest faster than logistics and supply chain management.

I was tempted to ask what the kids were studying, but somehow the notion of asking a college student in a bar what her major was at my age seemed a bit depraved. I stayed for a third set and made sure to pay the kids' tab and order them a proper beverage before leaving.

The next day, I rented a car at the Marriott and went food shopping on my way to the Squadron Yacht Club. I spent the day restocking the galley and prepping the boat. When I was done, I felt like everything was ready for the final run to the Bahamas.

For a small city, the food and entertainment options in Halifax are exceptional. That night, I walked three blocks in the freezing cold to the Press Gang Restaurant and Oyster Bar. Unlike last night's venue, this was not a place for impoverished twenty-year-old college kids. The Press Gang is one of the finest restaurants in the city and has a well-stocked bar with live entertainment on weekends. It's in one of the oldest buildings in Halifax, going back to the early nineteenth century. The architectural style is classical, with stone walls, exposed wooden beams, rustic lighting, and a bar with a world-class whiskey selection.

After a flawless dinner of mushroom risotto and an Alberta tenderloin, I retired to the bar to listen to the band. The Press Gang lived up to its reputation. The food was amazing. The restaurant was very expensive by Halifax standards, and on a Saturday night the guests were the well-heeled and those celebrating special occasions. The atmosphere is warm, and I even enjoyed a couple of exotic scotches, including a 1971 Macallan and a 1961 Glen Grant, while listening to the band and crowd watching.

The next morning, I was underway by nine. Not knowing the harbor, I needed to wait for the sun to rise before setting out. It was a cold morning, minus one Fahrenheit with enough of a breeze to put a chop in the water. It was roughly fifteen hundred miles to the Bahamas, and I planned on covering five hundred miles per day by running twenty-four hours at twenty-two knots. The *Houston* had the range to make it all the way without refueling and the weather was forecasted to be clear. I was ready to get back into the warmer climes; every exterior surface of the *Houston* was covered in ice.

After an uneventful leg of the journey, I docked at Runway Cove Marina in Governor's Harbor. Runway Cove is on the protected western side of the island. It's a tiny marina with only twenty slips and a very narrow entrance with a shallow ten-foot draft clearance. The big advantages are that it's within walking distance to my place, and has power and water hookups.

The customs process was a bit of a lark. I called and agreed to go to the airport the next day and get in-processed by customs. I called Jonah and asked him to pick me up. The tiny marina only has one employee, a rail-thin elderly black man with a gray beard and a taciturn personality. Michael lives and works in the marina's lone building. I've been told he's a master mechanic who keeps the aging fishing fleet running.

Arriving at home, I was greeted by Maria and Father Tellez. Jonah took my luggage upstairs, and Father Tellez and I sat at the dining room table. Father Tellez loves spicy food, and Maria had prepared a Creole jambalaya that smelled fantastic.

Sipping one of his super-sweet guava juice concoctions that can give a person diabetes just from looking at them, Father Tellez looked me over appraisingly and declared, "You look much better than the last time I saw you, Pat, really."

"Thanks, Father, I feel great."

"Are you going to keep the beard?"

"No, I don't think so. This was just for the voyage. I'll be clean-shaven tomorrow."

"You're thinner, but also more relaxed," observed the priest.

"I did a lot of thinking on the trip, and I think it's time for me to stay here and retire."

"You're more at peace. Whatever you were involved in, I hope you'll stay away from it in the future."

"That's my plan, padre. I don't look for trouble. It just seems to sort of follow me wherever I go."

"You have a great family, Pat. You should go back to Raleigh."

"Next week the family will be here."

"I'm looking forward to seeing everyone. It will be a marvelous time."

Maria served dinner, and we ate. It was burning hot and absolutely terrific. Over coffee, Father Tellez brought up the situation with the foundation. As usual, he had more projects than he had funds. I told him that I'd take care of it although the concept didn't fit well with my retirement aspirations.

After coffee, the father took a large bowl of jambalaya to his apartment for his sister. Maria had already cleaned up, but instead of leaving, she asked me to sit on the recliner in the adjacent living room. Maria left the room and returned with a towel, a bowl of hot water, scissors, and a razor.

"I take it you're not a big fan of the beard."

Maria just smiled. She hardly speaks, but she hears everything. For the next thirty minutes, she worked with a surgeon's precision and removed my beard. Despite the strong Colombian coffee after dinner, I was exhausted and fell asleep during the shave. Maria had to wake me up and send me to bed.

The next morning, I was on the water at half past six. The water and ocean temperature were both about the same: seventy degrees. I wore a thin wet suit and felt very comfortable. The recent weight loss had me down to 204 pounds, which at six five, gave me a ripped definition I hadn't seen in a decade. The swells were between 1.2 and 1.6 meters, with clean breaks. The conditions would make for an enjoyable morning.

Sitting on my board beyond the break, I saw another surfer walk across the beach and enter the water. I'd been surfing for two hours and had planned to make this next wave my last. A distant silhouette of the lone surfer gave promise that it might be Diane from Tippy's. I stuck around, wanting to say hi if that was the case. Sure enough, as the surfer in the red wet suit reached me, I was greeted with a big smile from my favorite waitress, Diane.

"Where's Finley?" I said.

"Out on the pro tour."

We chatted for a bit. Instead of quitting, I hung around for another hour. It's always nice to have company, especially someone you can learn from. Finally, I confessed to exhaustion and left the surfing star for my last run of the morning.

After a shower, I had coffee on the deck and caught up with my email on an iPad. I saw Father Tellez leaving his chapel and waved him over. The Colombian priest was in his usual joyful mood when he arrived on the deck. Maria magically appeared with a steaming cup of coffee, which is the holy man's only vice.

Between the palms, I could see the dusty pink of the sand and beyond the turquoise water with slow curling waves breaking against the shoreline. The morning sun shimmered off the water, and the only sounds were the birds and the crashing waves. After five or six minutes of beach zen, Father Tellez broke the silence. "Pat, you can't go back to the Middle East."

"I heard you last night."

"Whatever you're doing is destroying you. I could see it when you came home last time. You're involved in something evil, and the weight of it is crushing you."

"I'm not so sure about that, Father, I'm pretty sure I'm the one doing the crushing."

"You don't believe that. You forget I was once a soldier myself," Father Tellez said while leaning forward in his chair.

"There's nothing like a monthlong sail halfway across the world to give a man some perspective."

"And what insights have you gained?"

"In the big picture, I'm just a piece of driftwood tossed around and moved by the tides and currents," I said.

"What do you mean by that?"

"I'm not in control. There are bigger forces at play. Whether I go back or not is probably not even going to be up to me," I said.

"You have more power and control than you think."

"I used to believe that, but I've come to recognize my insignificance. You know, I drove that boat through a North Atlantic storm with waves twice the size of this house in the middle of the night. Mother Nature's power was on full display. That's something I can deal with. It's tangible. It's physical.

"But, when the top guys in the Department of Defense started butting heads in a political war, that's something I can't deal with. I had no idea what was going on until I was tossed out as collateral damage. When the masters of the universe failed to consider the risk of trillions of dollars in toxic mortgages, the government bailed out the banks and left me for dead. Once again, the big boys were playing a game that I not only didn't understand the rules of, but I didn't even know there was a game going on.

"This latest mess I just came out of was more of the same. Although I came out of it all right, I don't feel good about any of it, and I left with the feeling of wondering what the heck is really going on," I said.

"When I saw you last, you didn't appear to feel that what you were doing was right."

"I was definitely doing the right thing. I was comfortable with the what, it was the how that was a bit unsettling."

"I hope it's over, really."

"Same here," I said. "Same here."

THE END

Chapter 1

Brussels, Belgium

Ahmed Eleiwi zipped his leather jacket against the wind as he exited the Bruxelles Central Train Station and entered downtown Brussels. It was a Saturday afternoon and the station was crowded with visitors on their way to enjoy a sunny spring afternoon shopping and sightseeing in the Grand Place Square. As he passed through the main doors of the station, he drew a second look from one of the soldiers positioned in the entryway. Belgium's response to the reoccurring terrorist incidents over the past year had been to station hundreds of military personnel throughout the city. In the congested downtown Brussels area, it was becoming increasingly difficult for a man Middle Eastern in appearance to travel unmolested. Ahmed was purposely carrying no bags to avoid arousing too much suspicion. Despite his efforts, the soldier signaled for him to come over and gave him a quick pat-down from top to bottom. Ahmed reminded himself that it was just a random search and forced himself to remain calm.

Despite his heart kicking into high gear, Ahmed slowly walked away from the guard and continued at a leisurely pace past the Hilton Grand Place Hotel and through the arch passageway, taking him into the square proper. As he entered the Grand Place, Ahmed stopped to get his bearings. Along one side of the rectangular cobblestone square, a rock band was playing on a stage set up against a building wall, midway along one of the sides. It was early afternoon, and the UNESCO World Heritage site was crowded with a festival atmosphere. Tourist guides hustled to corral their charges across the expanse to the many historical and architectural items of interest. It was Earth Day, and several hundred protestors, still wearing green shirts and carrying signs from the morning march, congregated near the stage. The protestors were drinking beer, dancing to the music and having a great time in the unseasonably cool weather.

The small square was bordered by four- and five-story gothic buildings made of grey stone and adorned with gold accents, archways and magnificent spires. He searched for the City Hall, with its distinctive nighty-six-meter tower holding the Archangel Michael. Having found his bearings, he confirmed he was in the northeast corner.

Ahmed looked west and found the Hard Rock Café sign only fifty meters from his location. He checked his cell phone and found a text: "3rd Floor, window." Ahmed stepped inside the narrow restaurant entryway and walked through the souvenir shop to the hostess. Before she could offer to help him, Ahmed interrupted and volunteered that his wife was on the third floor, waiting for him. The hostess pointed him to the stairs. Slightly winded from the climb up the steep spiral staircase, Ahmed emerged from the stairs and surveyed the crowded third-floor dining room for Raghad. He spotted his Iraqi contact in the last table along the windows. He walked directly to her, gave her a peck on the cheek and slid into the seat across the table. Raghad acknowledged Ahmed and turned her attention back to the baby she was feeding in the high chair to her left.

Forcing a smile, Ahmed reached across the table and placed an affectionate hand on the baby's head in greeting. The waiter came over, and although Ahmed had no appetite, he ordered a hamburger and a liter of Leffe Blonde Beer. The window seat had an excellent view of the entire square. Ahmed estimated the crowd at over six hundred in the confined twenty thousand square feet of space. His pulse was racing, and he began to sweat. His beer arrived, and he gulped it down and ordered a second potent Belgian Beer. When his glass was empty, he nodded to Raghad and reached down under the table to retrieve a heavy diaper bag. He struggled sliding the heavy bag across the wooden floor.

Leaving it concealed under the table, Ahmed opened the bag. His practiced hands found the safe to arm switch by feel, and he moved it forward into the arm position. Pulling the bag out from under the table, he slid out of the booth and walked away from Raghad and her baby with the heavy diaper bag on his shoulder.

Ahmed could feel Raghad's eyes bearing down on him as he emerged from the restaurant and navigated his way through the heavy crowd toward the stage. He expected Raghad would wait until he was near the stage, where the densest cluster of people could be found, before triggering the explosive device. He could tell from people's reactions that they were starting to notice the growing panic that was reflected on his face. No longer able to feign calm, Ahmed began to hurry, crashing into people as he scurried toward the stage.

With her baby in her arms and a remote control designed to look like a baby toy in her hand, Raghad watched Ahmed through a window. Seeing Ahmed's panic, she ducked behind a nearby support pillar and triggered the device. Twenty meters from the stage, all six daisy-chained claymore mines, arrayed in a horseshoe inside the diaper bag, exploded. Each claymore, containing one and a half pounds of C4 explosive, launched seven hundred steel balls into the crowd with lethal force. In seconds, every person in the tiny square went from vertical to horizontal. The concussive force trapped inside the square shattered the windows of the Hard Rock Café and all of the surrounding buildings.

Raghad reappeared from the protection of the pillar to witness the devastation. The flying glass had lacerated the exposed and thinly covered skin of the people sitting closest to the windows. Screams and cries for help filled the restaurant.

Worst hit were the Earth Day protestors who had been gathered around the stage moments before. The activists inadvertently served as human shields as they absorbed the brunt of the lethal projectiles before they could reach the larger crowd. A Chinese tourist group was killed in its entirety when the focused spray from a single claymore hit them head-on while they were lining up for a picture.

The damage done by the blast was grotesque. In the first fifty meters fanning out from the stage, few of the bodies remained intact. It was a macabre sight of blood and dismembered bodies. When the last fatality was recorded nine days after the attack, the death toll would reach 174, with another 269 wounded.

Chapter 2

New York City

Michael Genovese felt the familiar burning in his lungs as he once again ratcheted up the pace. His target was less than a hundred yards in front of him, running with a steady, even gait that was deceptively fast.

Michael ran the same six-mile Central Park loop every day. At thirty-eight, he kept himself at the same peak level of fitness he had enjoyed while playing point guard on the basketball team at Harvard. The man he was chasing had passed him two miles back, and now his only goal in life was to retake the lead before his route ended.

His narrowing vision registered the Strawberry Fields marker off to his left, meaning he had less than a mile left to make his move. Michael took great pride in never having allowed anyone to beat him on his daily run. The pain intensified as he nudged the pace. With only a quarter mile to the finish point, he pushed it even harder. His legs were on fire, and there was a searing pain in his lungs. He could feel his vision narrow further as he forced his breathing and pumped his oxygen-deprived legs.

When he closed to within twenty yards of the interloper, he noticed it was a younger man in his twenties. The runner was oblivious to Michael as he effortlessly glided along the course, listening to music through his earbuds. Michael's breath grew even more ragged, and he was saturated in sweat as he transitioned into a full sprint for the last hundred meters to the imaginary finish line.

Barely passing the runner in the last few feet before reaching the end of the course, Michael slowed to a walk and ducked off the trail before falling to his knees. It was a full ten minutes before he was recovered enough to stand and make his way back to his apartment. Tired, but euphoric from his victory, a triumphant Michael gingerly walked across the street and made his way into the private elevator that delivered him to his penthouse apartment.

The elevator opened into a large open foyer. When the doors slid open, the first thing that met his eye was Katrina, sitting on a bench along the side of the entryway. Her bottom lip was swollen and red, and she had a large purple welt on her left cheek. Surprised to see Michael, the skittish Ukrainian withdrew from the foyer and moved behind a couch in the living room. Michael ignored the willowy young blonde and stepped around her two suitcases on his way through the living room to the hallway that led to his bedroom. He made a mental note to contact his personal assistant and request a replacement.

Despite his money and good looks, Michael's penchant for rough play with the ladies had earned him a certain notoriety within his social circles. An unfortunate dating incident with a fiercely resistant actress who happened to maintain an enormous social media network had made him radioactive to the local ladies. That event had spurred him to get creative and discover a website that advertised itself as matching "sugar babies" with "sugar daddies." Michael found that for a nominal fee, he could import some of the most beautiful and willing creatures in the world directly to his doorstep.

When he'd started to find the constant internet searching and endless chatting and messaging needed to ensnare the prospective sugar babies to be time consuming and tedious, he'd pioneered a way to outsource the work. He'd expanded on the information age mail-order concept by hiring a virtual personal assistant from India.

Shahab's daily responsibilities included uploading and managing Michael's profile on several relevant websites. His virtual PA also had the use of a shared WhatsApp messaging account and a shared email account to line up girls for delivery on demand. Michael considered his unique outsourcing method of acquiring mail-order girls to be a textbook case study in optimizing efficiencies through offshoring. Once he'd gotten his system going, he found he had created a pipeline of beautiful girls who not only bolstered his image at social events, but also accommodated his carnal needs. It was pure genius.

On his way to the shower, Michael caught his reflection in the mirror array inside the master bathroom and had to stop. He removed his clothes and posed in different positions as he flexed his well-defined muscles. With the classic Italian good looks of a young Tony Bennett, Michael never tired of studying his reflection. His rigid diet and exercise regimen were rewarded with a single-digit body fat percentage. His six-pack abdominals were his pride and joy and the focus of his gaze. As he flexed with his hands clasped in front of him in what bodybuilders referred to as the crab pose, he thought back to last night with Katrina and he swelled with pride.

After showering, Michael drove to Long Island to have lunch with his brothers. The family home was a twenty-two-thousand-square-foot estate that had been built by his father in 1969. His grandfather, Vito Genovese, had been the Don of the Genovese Crime Family until his arrest in 1957. With roots tracing back to Lucky Luciano in the 1930s, the Genovese family was sometimes referred to as the Ivy League Mafia.

After Benny "Squint" Lombardo had taken the reins following Michael's grandfather's death in prison, Michael's father, Salvatore, had used his sizable inheritance to concentrate on enterprises other than the family staples of loan sharking, drugs, gambling, prostitution and protection. At the beginning of the Vietnam War, a prescient Salvatore Genovese had invested in defense companies. He'd sent his three sons, Gino, Michael and Louis, to the best prep schools and the best colleges. Gino had attended Fordham, Michael, the scholar-athlete, had studied at Harvard, and Louis had gone to Columbia. After graduating from college, the three sons had worked with their dad and, by the mid-1990s they had assembled a strong portfolio of minority positions within the defense industry.

After Salvatore had succumbed to cancer in 1999, the three brothers had worked to secure majority shareholding positions and to unify their defense portfolio under a single management team. G3 Defense had been founded in 1999, and by 2017, the company had revenues exceeding seventeen billion dollars, twenty-seven thousand employees, and sixteen fully owned subsidiaries. In only eighteen years, G3 had become one of the largest defense firms in the United States.

Despite being the middle son, Michael was the chairman and CEO. Gino served as CFO, and Louis was the COO. The board of directors included the three brothers plus the external financiers, which included two private equity firms and Nicky Terranova, the second cousin of Barney Bellomo, the current head of the Genovese mob.

The family estate was Gino's birthright as the oldest son. He and his wife graciously hosted the extended family gathering every Sunday. Gino and Louis were both married and had five young children between them. Michael, the bachelor was a favorite uncle and despite his birth order a patriarchal figure within the family.

Michael parked his Mercedes behind Louis's Range Rover in the driveway. He was barely out of the car before being swarmed by three of his nephews, Louis, Joey, and Danny. The boys moved as a pack, attempting to submit their uncle, imitating moves learned from televised wrestling and UFC MMA. After fifteen minutes of roughhousing, he declared a draw and the joyful boys allowed a disheveled and grass-stained Michael to continue on his way to the main house.

He was met at the door by Gino's wife, Stephanie, who greeted him with a hug.

"Why do you encourage them, Michael? They ruined your good shirt."

"I don't care about the shirt. It's how boys play, Steph," said Michael.

"One of these days, they're going to hurt you."

"I think I have a few years left when I can handle them," said Michael as Stephanie led him into the kitchen by the arm.

After dinner, the three brothers retired to the home theater to watch the Yankees play the Orioles. The brothers were seated in leather recliners, drinking beer in front of an eighty-inch plasma TV and waiting for the start of the game.

"Have you been following the news about what's going on in Belgium?" Michael asked.

"Yes, that was terrible. Those Europeans need to get serious about those immigrants," said Gino.

"I bet we see a spike in our Security and Detection revenues. Nobody sells body scanners better than those jihadis," Louis said.

"That's not the only good that'll come of it. That guy from Abu Dhabi isn't going to be a problem anymore," Michael said.

"What guy in Abu Dhabi? What are you talking about, Michael?" said Gino.

"Nothing… just that I heard a rumor about that guy who was digging into our business a while back. Seems he might have some bigger things to worry about," Michael said. Gino and Louis looked at each other with puzzled expressions and then switched the subject back to the NBA Playoffs.

210

Chapter 3

Eleuthera, Bahamas

Pat straddled his surfboard and positioned himself so that he could watch the incoming swells over his right shoulder and see the beach over his left shoulder. It was a sunny spring day. The rolling waves were turquoise until they broke into a white foam and raced onto the blushing pink strip of sand.

Beyond the beach, Pat could see the top floors of his beach house peeking above the gently swaying palms. He shifted his gaze downward and surveyed the surf line, looking for Diane. He spotted her in a sea of white, working her way out through the surf. Every seven seconds she would vanish under an incoming wave and then reappear without missing a stroke. She moved fast, with the grace and power of an elite athlete. Diane smiled as she reached Pat. It was a dazzling smile accompanied by emerald-green eyes set in a stunningly beautiful face.

"Are you a tourist or a surfer?" asked Diane.

"I'm enjoying the view while I wait for the perfect wave."

"The tide's starting to go out, and it's only going to get worse. You better take what you can get."

"Yeah, you're right. One last wave, then it's time for lunch."

Pat and Diane carried their surfboards under opposite arms as they walked to the house. Between the beach and the house was a narrow trail encroached by lush ground vegetation. The two threaded their way through the narrow trail, past the guesthouse and the pool house until they reached the main house, a three-story peach-colored stone mansion with eight bedrooms.

Pat had been staying at the beach house for almost five months, and the daily surfing and regular workout routine had him in better shape than he had been in a long time. The beach house was his retirement dream home, everything in it built to his specifications. The second-floor deck was his favorite spot, offering a view of the Atlantic Ocean to the east and the Caribbean to the west.

Diane was a surfer girl from Florida. The two had met a year ago when she was waitressing at Tippy's, the neighboring beachfront restaurant where he was a regular customer. Over a period of months, the relationship had progressed from customer and waitress to surf student and surfing guru, and then to soulmates. Pat was head over heels in love with Diane, and for the past three months, the two had lived a honeymoon existence at the beach house.

Pat was just stepping out of the shower when he received a call from Jessica, his office manager. The Trident headquarters were located three miles up island in Governor's Harbour. Trident was a CIA subcontractor that had a single contract with the US government to supply military goods to US allied forces in Syria and Iraq.

Pat answered the call, and before he could even say hello, a panicked Jessica interrupted.

"We have a serious problem."

"What's going on?"

"All of our bank accounts have been frozen, and our export license requests, purchase orders and payments have been put on hold by the government contract office," said Jessica.

"Any idea why?"

"They didn't even give me notice. I was trying to transfer money from the CITI account online and it rejected every transaction. I tried the same with the accounts in the Bahamas and got the same thing. Then I received a notice from DCMA that our contract is suspended, still with no explanation."

"Give me a few minutes to make some calls, and I'll get back to you," said Pat.

Using the secure app on his CIA-issued smartphone, Pat called Mike Guthrie, a friend from his days as a junior officer in the Second Ranger Battalion. The two had gone their separate ways after Delta selection and had been reunited seventeen years later in Afghanistan, when Mike was a CIA agent and Pat was a down-on-his-luck defense contractor working as a military advisor to the Afghan National Army. Mike had recruited Pat as an asset, and the two had been working together professionally for last five years. Mike was currently assigned to Langley in the Clandestine Operations Directorate, while Pat's company, Trident, was part of a black operation that was managed by the Department of Defense. Trident was the conduit for military supplies to the Peshmerga and other forces fighting against ISIS in Syria and Iraq.

When, after ten rings, Mike did not pick up, Pat terminated the call. He looked across the table to Dianne. "I don't have time to explain this. Just pack a bag. We need to be out of here in five minutes."

Pat stood from his chair at the kitchen table and sprinted up the stairs toward his office on the third floor. He quickly opened his safe and removed two packages. One held passports for both him and Diane, and the second contained cash and cell phone SIM cards. Next, he went into a storage closet and withdrew a duffle bag. With the bag filled, he ran downstairs and entered the garage through the kitchen entrance, throwing the heavy black nylon duffel bag into the back of the Tahoe. Diane entered the garage a few seconds later, and they both jumped into the Tahoe and sped off.

Less than a mile away, on the Caribbean side of the island, was a small marina that was home to a small local fishing fleet. The sole recreational vehicle in the marina was Pat's sixty-four-foot motor yacht. The Azimut 64 Flybridge had been his home for three years when he'd lived in Abu Dhabi, United Arab Emirates. Since his relocation to the Bahamas, beyond the occasional fishing trip or quick day trip to Nassau, the boat had largely been ignored.

Pat detached the external power connection and untied the boat from the slip while Diane went to the wheelhouse and started the twin Caterpillar 1150-horsepower engines. Runway Cove Marina had a very narrow access point designed for the smaller fishing vessels. Navigating the narrow passage and the sharp dogleg turn was a tricky maneuver that would have been impossible without the bow thrusters. Once through the gap and into the Caribbean, Pat gradually increased the speed to twenty-eight knots and set a heading for Nassau, fifty miles to the west.

Diane approached Pat while he was sitting at the helm station on the flybridge.

"What's going on?" asked Diane.

"Honestly, honey, I have no idea. All I know is that the US government has suspended my IDIQ contract, and all of my business and personal bank accounts have been frozen," said Pat.

"Are you in trouble with the IRS or something?" said Diane.

"You've seen the scars on my body, and you have a general idea of what I used to do for a living. The government contracts Trident supports are so sensitive I'm not even allowed to discuss them, but they're essential to US policy, and they aren't something that can be casually suspended without serious cause," said Pat.

"So, what does that mean?" said Diane.

"It means anything big enough to cause the government to shut down my business operations is serious enough to make me want to disappear until I can get ahold of the people I work for and figure out what the hell is going on," said Pat.

"Are we in danger?"

"I don't think so. When the US government freezes your bank accounts and cuts off a contract that's strategically important, it must mean an arrest is soon to follow. The only reason I didn't leave you at the house is that I don't know who's after me."

"Why would the US government arrest you?" said Diane.

"I haven't done anything wrong that I know of, but having my money and my business contracts frozen and my contact in the CIA unavailable has me spooked," said Pat.

"Now I'm scared."

"Throw your phone overboard. We need to remain unfindable until I can figure this thing out," said Pat.

It took almost two hours to sail to Nassau Harbor. Diane was clingy for most of the trip, and while Pat would have preferred to spend the time planning, instead he'd found himself responding to an endless stream of questions and concerns from Diane. During the few respites from her desire to be assured, he'd quietly debated whether it would be safer to drop Diane off in Nassau. Ultimately, he'd decided to keep her with him. Partly out of selfishness, since he couldn't stand to be away from her, and partly because he knew it would cause her just as much pain for her to be away from him. It was poor operational reasoning, and he hoped he wouldn't regret it.

Pat docked at a transient slip in the Palm Cay Marina. Unlike his tiny fishing marina in Governor's Harbour, the Palm Cay was built for luxury tourism, and with one hundred and ninety-five mostly occupied slips, his yacht blended in perfectly. Pat booked for two days and paid the docking fee of two dollars per foot per day to the harbormaster. Once they had the power and water connected, they locked up the boat and walked to the car rental office located inside the marina clubhouse.

"What's next?" asked Diane.

"We need to provision the boat with food for a three-week journey. There's a Fresh Market a few miles from here that should have everything we need. We also need lunch, and I need to find Wi-Fi so I can contact my people. Once we load up and prep the boat, we'll fill the external fuel tanks. That'll give us a range of close to three thousand miles and then we'll be ready to depart tomorrow morning," said Pat.

"Depart for where?"

"At this point, it's more about getting off the grid. I really don't have any particular destination in mind."

"That doesn't sound like much of a plan," Diane said with a smile. Pat put his arm around Diane and kissed the top of her head.

"It's not, but if it turns out I have to be on the run, we might as well make a holiday of it."

The first stop was lunch. Still unwilling to put a cell phone in operation, Pat used the navigation system on the rental car and settled on a nearby restaurant called Luciano of Chicago. It was almost three in the afternoon, and the restaurant was nearly empty. While he was waiting for his shrimp and scallop ceviche appetizer, Pat turned on his laptop and connected to the restaurant's free Wi-Fi. Using a TOR app, he was able to mask his IP address and location and encrypt his communications. He went on Google Messenger and sent a message to Mike Guthrie.

"The contract has been suspended and all my personal and business accounts are frozen. What gives?" he wrote.

After devouring a magnificent seven-ounce filet mignon with asparagus and mashed potatoes, he received a reply from Mike.

"Explosives used in Brussels bombing originated from Trident. JTTF has identified you as a subject of the investigation, and an arrest order has been issued," Mike replied.

"Does the JTTF know what I do and who I work for?" wrote Pat.

"No. The director wants to avoid a scandal. The case against you is strong and getting stronger. Disappear and give me some time to find out who's pulling the strings on this," Mike replied.

"Done, will check back with you daily on this channel."

"Any updates you want to share?" Diane asked. Pat sipped his double espresso while looking across the table at Diane's concerned expression.

"The good news is that there's no physical danger. The bad news is as I suspected. I need to disappear while the people I work for clear this problem up."

"What do you mean by disappear?"

"It means we spend a few weeks on the Atlantic, looking for the perfect wave," Pat said.

Diane smiled. "Being on the run with you sounds like fun."